World Odyssey

(Book One in The World Duology)

Lance & James
MORCAN

WORLD ODYSSEY

Published by:

Sterling Gate Books
78 Pacific View Rd,
Papamoa 3118,
Bay of Plenty,
New Zealand
sterlinggatebooks@gmail.com

Cover Painting: *The Ninth Wave,* c.1850
Artist: Ivan Aivazovsky (1817–1900)

National Library of New Zealand publication data:

Morcan, Lance 1948-
Morcan, James 1978-
Title: World Odyssey
Edition: First ed.
Format: Paperback
Publisher: Sterling Gate Books
ISBN: 978-0-473-36373-4

*"Little do ye know your own blessedness;
for to travel hopefully is a better thing than to arrive,
and the true success is to labour."*

~ **Robert Louis Stevenson, 1850–1894**

PROLOGUE

Summer, 1832

ALONE IN HIS FATHER'S STUDY, young Philadelphian Nathan Johnson surveyed the lavishly furnished but slightly musty room. His keen eyes rested momentarily on the titles of some of the hundreds of books lining the shelves behind his father's desk. Many had a nautical theme, alluding to the occupation of the absent Captain Benjamin Johnson.

The boy never tired of being in his father's study and often ventured into it even though Johnson Senior had made it clear the study was out of bounds whenever he was away.

Although physically absent for the moment, his father was present in a sense: a recent portrait painting of the forty-year-old captain hung on the far wall. Dark, curly, shoulder-length hair framed his unsmiling but still youthful face. The ruggedly handsome Johnson Senior had the appearance of someone who didn't suffer fools. His startlingly blue eyes seemed to bore into Nathan's as the boy studied the painting.

Nathan couldn't know it, but he was looking at a mirror image of himself in later years. Even at the tender age of ten he was already a chip off the old block. Tall for his age, he was more mature than his schoolmates, and more serious, too.

Sounds of children's laughter drifted in through an open window. His two older sisters and their friends were making

1

the most of a sunny day after several days of constant rain. From the kitchen downstairs, the clink of crockery could be heard as the maid cleared away the breakfast dishes.

Nathan switched his attention to a faded world map hanging alongside the painting. A dotted line connecting North America's west coast and the coast of mainland China showed where his father had journeyed on his latest expedition. Johnson Senior was a successful trader whose latest enterprise had involved trading goods to the Native Americans for their prized sea otter furs. He had transported those same furs to China where they fetched huge prices.

The thought of sailing to some exotic destination thrilled Nathan to the core. He lived for the day he was old enough to go to sea. Meanwhile, he contented himself studying the world map and dreaming of far-off places.

So engrossed was he, he didn't hear his father arrive home from town. It wasn't until the study door burst open and Johnson Senior strode in that Nathan realized he was in trouble.

When Johnson Senior saw Nathan, he turned livid. He grabbed his son by the hair and began cuffing him hard about the head.

Johnson Senior's mood wasn't helped by the fact he'd been drinking and gambling since the previous night, and had lost a considerable amount of money. As a man of means, it was money he could afford to lose, but that hadn't helped dampen his already foul temper.

Nathan could tell his father had been drinking. He could smell the whisky fumes on his breath, and Johnson Senior was unsteady on his feet and slurring his words as he cursed and beat the son he wished he'd never had.

Determined to remain staunch, Nathan bit his lip to stop from crying out. This further infuriated his father who removed his belt and began flailing the boy with all his considerable strength. The belt's buckle cut into Nathan's bare arm and drew blood.

As Nathan covered up as best he could to protect himself, he fixed his gaze on a portrait painting of his mother hanging on the near wall. It gave him strength. The painting was the work of one of Philadelphia's leading artists and it captured pretty Charlotte Johnson as she was in her early twenties. There was a quiet determination in her sparkling brown eyes.

Charlotte was the mother Nathan had never known for she had died giving birth to him ten years earlier.

The beating ended as quickly as it had begun when Johnson Senior pushed the boy from the study and slammed the door shut after him.

Now alone at the top of the first floor landing, Nathan swore he'd run away from home as soon as he was old enough.

———◦◦◦———

AT THAT VERY moment, across the Atlantic in England, little Susannah Drake was playing with dolls and other girlie things while watching two white swans that had taken up residency in the lily pond behind her Methodist clergyman father's rectory in the affluent west London district of Kensington.

The cute, red-headed, six-year-old closed her eyes to protect them from the bright sunlight reflecting off the pond's surface. When she reopened them, one of the swans had paddled to within an arm's length of her at the pond's edge, causing her to jump back in surprise. Swan and child stared at each other for a second or two before the majestic bird paddled off to rejoin his mate.

On the lawn behind Susannah, her father Reverend Brian Drake was chatting to visiting members of his congregation while her mother, Jeanette, served Devonshire tea. It was a very English scene.

Jeanette, a pretty but frail woman, called out to Susannah who promptly skipped over to join her parents. Jumping up onto her father's knee, she licked the strawberry jam off one of her mother's famous scones as Drake Senior talked to the other adults.

Susannah amused herself as the conversation turned to the missionary work the Methodist Church was engaged in, in far-off places. Drake Senior expressed a desire to become a missionary one day. Jeanette didn't seem to share her husband's enthusiasm for missionary work and quickly changed the subject.

Finding the adult conversation boring, Susannah jumped off her father's knee and ran back down to the lily pond. She laughed delightedly when the two swans paddled to the pond's edge to greet her. Her laughter turned to screams as one of the swans waddled up onto the lawn and proceeded to chase after her, hissing. It seemed the swan was intent on securing the remains of the scone Susannah was still holding.

Chuckling at his daughter's predicament, Drake Senior advised Susannah to give the swan what it wanted. Although frightened, Susannah refused to back down. She rammed the remains of the scone into her mouth and shooed her tormentor away. Beaten, the swan gave up and waddled back to the pond.

The adults laughed and commented how cute Susannah was. Drake Senior and Jeanette observed their daughter with pride. Not for the first time, she had demonstrated that, despite her angelic appearance, she was not easily intimidated.

SEVERAL MILES AWAY, in southeast London, sixteen-year-old Jack Halliday was traipsing from door to door looking for work in the capital's busy dockyards. The Cockney's spirits were uncharacteristically low. Since his mother had kicked him out of the family home two weeks earlier, he'd been job-hunting without success.

Back in the East End, Jack had a reputation for being a lovable larrikin. Shorter than average and not especially good looking, the curly-haired lad nevertheless had a mischievous face and engaging personality which generally endeared him to others. Generally because his cheeky manner ensured he had his share of enemies too. Any who underestimated him did so at their own risk. He never took a backward step and he compensated for his lack of height by fighting with all the fury of a pitbull.

The shadows were lengthening when Jack arrived at Sullivan's Foundry, a large establishment next to the River Thames. Having experienced around twenty rejections from prospective employers that day, he had to force himself to adopt his normally cheerful disposition as he entered the noisy foundry. The fact he hadn't eaten in two days gave him extra motivation. He desperately needed to earn some money. If he didn't land a job soon, he knew he'd have to find money via other means.

Approaching the front office, Jack was suddenly confronted by a big, bad-tempered man who demanded to know what he wanted. The young Cockney guessed, correctly, the man was the foundry owner, Henry Sullivan. When Jack explained he wanted a job, Sullivan advised him he wasn't in the habit of employing runts and ordered him off the property.

Jack stood his ground, his perceptive green eyes flashing with anger. The look wasn't missed by Sullivan who decided to put him to the test. He'd recently laid off an apprentice blacksmith who hadn't measured up, so Jack's interest in a job was timely. Pointing to a thirty-foot long steel shaft resting on the floor nearby, Sullivan challenged the young Cockney to lift it up onto a shelf that was just above Jack's head.

Without hesitating, Jack bent down to lift the shaft. He suddenly realized every eye in the foundry was on him. Taking a deep breath, he managed to straighten up while holding the shaft, but when he tried to lift it up onto the shelf it fell to the floor with a mighty clang. Several onlookers chuckled at his misfortune.

Unimpressed, Sullivan turned his back on Jack and returned to his office.

To the surprise of those still watching, Jack prepared to make another attempt. This time, he put everything into it and, to the resounding cheers of the assembled, managed to hoist the steel shaft up onto the shelf just as Sullivan re-emerged from his office. Suitably impressed, the proprietor immediately hired Jack as an apprentice.

Mindful of the hunger pangs that were now causing frequent tummy rumbles, Jack tried to negotiate his first week's pay in advance. Tightwad Sullivan agreed to pay him two days in advance on condition that he put in some extra hours unpaid. Jack reluctantly agreed. At least now he could afford a square meal.

———◦◦◦———

JACK HALLIDAY, SUSANNAH Drake and Nathan Johnson had no way of knowing their paths would cross one day; their destinies were integrally linked. Fate and the unfathomable twists and turns of life would eventually throw them together on the far side of the world in a place some called *the Cannibal Isles.*

CHAPTER 1

West Coast, North America, 1838

Sixteen-year-old Nathan Johnson was standing at the bow of *Intrepid,* staring down at the sea's foaming surface as the three-masted ship plowed through the chilly waters off the coast of Oregon Country, the remote Northwest American territory that would one day be known as Washington State.

True to his word, the young Philadelphian had run away from home and from his violent father as soon as he was old enough. Strictly speaking he didn't exactly flee his home. Johnson Senior had sent him away to boarding school when he turned twelve. After just three weeks, Nathan had dropped out of school and secured a job as a cabin boy on one of the ships that plied its trade delivering supplies to new settlements up and down America's east coast, and he'd been at sea ever since. He'd never contacted his father and he never intended to.

Nathan's breath was visible in the cool autumn air, prompting him to button up the fur-lined jacket he wore. He looked up hoping to sight the shoreline he knew was only a few miles to starboard, but fog limited visibility to less than one hundred yards. Not even his keen blue eyes could pierce the blanket of gray that surrounded the vessel.

The young man stifled a yawn. He'd just finished working a double shift and knew he should be catching up on sleep, but he didn't want to miss out on his first glimpse of Oregon Country.

"This fog will clear soon," a gruff voice announced. The voice belonged to *Intrepid's* master, Captain Herbert Dawson, who also happened to be Nathan's uncle.

Nathan spun around. He hadn't realized he had company. "Yes Captain . . . ah . . . Uncle."

The young man's hesitation amused Dawson. Nathan was never quite sure how to address his late mother's older brother. The rule was it was *Captain* in front of the crewmen and *Uncle* in private. "You've completed your duties I take it?" Dawson asked.

"Yes sir."

"Good man." Dawson had a sudden coughing fit. He was battling a bout of influenza, as were a number of others on board. The coughing passed—for the moment at least—and the two stood in companionable silence staring out into the mist.

Nathan didn't know it, but his uncle looked on him as the son he'd never had. He reminded Dawson of his sister Charlotte—not physically so much as he'd inherited Johnson Senior's rugged good looks—but certainly in temperament. The boy was calm and unflappable, taking whatever life threw at him in his stride. Studying him now, he couldn't help thinking Charlotte would be proud of her son. Nathan was growing into a fine young man and possessed an assurance that reminded Dawson of himself at that age.

Uncle and nephew had been together aboard *Intrepid* since they'd literally bumped into each other in San Francisco two years earlier. Dawson had been recruiting crewmembers for a trading expedition to southern Africa, and Nathan had pleaded with him to sign him on. The captain had agreed, but only on condition that he combined scholastic studies with his on-board duties to make up for his lost schooling. Nathan had readily agreed to that and, true to his word, continued his studies while carrying out his duties on board.

In the past two years, Nathan had learned the basics of sail-making, rigging, steering and, most recently, navigating. In the process, he'd earned the respect of his uncle and his crewmates alike. There were no two ways about it: he was shaping up to be a fine seaman.

Another coughing fit saw Dawson excuse himself, leaving Nathan alone once more.

No sooner had Dawson retired below deck than an excited shout came from the crow's nest atop the forward mast. "Land to starboard!" the lookout shouted.

Nathan looked to starboard again. The fog was parting and the snow-flecked mountains of Oregon Country could be seen in the distance. Along the tree-lined shore, the colorful autumn leaves of alder and oak trees contrasted with the evergreen fir trees so prevalent in this region, providing a spectacular display of yellows, reds and greens of all shades.

The young Philadelphian felt a surge of excitement. This was only his second voyage to the Northwest and his first to Oregon Country. His first experience of the Northwest had come a year earlier when *Intrepid* visited Nootka Sound, on Vancouver Island. There, they'd traded with the Mowachahts, a warlike native tribe with a history of conflict with visiting whites. On his uncle's orders, Nathan hadn't gone ashore at Nootka Sound. Just as well maybe as a crewmember had been killed and another badly wounded during a trade that went wrong. It was only later Nathan learned the violence had been prompted by the rape of an Indian maiden by one of the visiting sailors — a not uncommon occurrence.

This time, *Intrepid's* crew were here to trade muskets with another tribe, the Makah, for their valuable sea otter fur. Nathan knew from his studies the Makah were every bit as warlike as their Mowachaht cousins on nearby Vancouver Island, but fortunately their violence was usually reserved for other tribes, not for visiting whites.

LATER, AS *INTREPID* entered the dark waters of the Strait of Juan de Fuca, Nathan was joined by other crewmen on deck. For many, it was their first visit to Oregon Country, too, and they studied the mist-shrouded cliffs of Cape Flattery with interest. The cliffs rose straight up out of the sea, reminding Nathan of granite sentinels. And although he couldn't see it through the mist, he knew Vancouver Island was only fifteen miles to the north.

The view was clearer to the east where some of Oregon Country's unexplored interior was faintly visible. A vast region of mountain ranges and lush rainforests, it would later be known as Olympic National Park. Mountain peaks and forest-clad hills stretched toward an eastern horizon hidden behind rain clouds.

As the ship rounded the cape, Nathan noticed signs of life on shore. Two native fishermen were spearing fish from rocks beneath the cliffs. They looked up when they noticed *Intrepid*. Nathan waved at them, but his wave wasn't returned. The fishermen returned to their task. Every so often, smoke rose from a hidden village or encampment, and the occasional totem pole poked up through the canopy of fir trees.

Steady rain began falling as the ship entered Neah Bay, *Intrepid's* immediate destination. Through the rain, totem poles and timber lodges of the Makah tribe's village came into view at the southern end of the bay. Nathan thought the timber lodges reminiscent of those he'd once seen on Vancouver Island. He learned later they were the remnants of dwellings erected by Spanish traders who had come and gone over the previous half-century.

The Makah villagers paid scant attention to *Intrepid* or her crew as they went about their everyday activities. They were well used to the sight of sailing ships in their waters.

Every villager seemed to have something to do: the men fished, carved or mended weapons while the women collected sea shells and firewood or washed clothes in a nearby stream. Frolicking children seemed not to have a care in the world, while on a sandy beach in front of the village teenage boys played their version of tag. The game involved a high degree of athleticism and a lot of bodily contact. Some of the participants ended up bruised and bloodied, but no-one seemed to mind. It was all good fun.

Nathan noted the villagers wore traditional coverings, including colorful blankets and dog or sealskin capes. Nobles, or those related to the chief, and headmen wore finer garments. The Makah braves wore their long hair piled up in a bun on top of their head; most wore white eagle down, or feathers, in their hair and all appeared to be armed. Some carried tomahawks and clubs, others bows and arrows or spears; a select few were armed with muskets.

The young Philadelphian knew the white man's weapons were sought after in these parts, but they came at a high price. His uncle had told him the Makah and the other tribes of Oregon Country weren't as well off as those of their Vancouver Island neighbors. The valuable sea otter was more plentiful to the north.

Asked why *Intrepid* wasn't returning to Vancouver Island, Captain Dawson had informed Nathan the Mowachahts and other neighboring tribes were currently causing too many problems for traders. The Makah, on the other hand, were more receptive.

Nathan spotted dozens of bald-headed eagles hovering above something at the far end of the beach. Closer inspection revealed the object of their interest was a whale carcass. The birds of prey were rapidly stripping the carcass of what little blubber remained. Nathan knew the Northwest Indians were accomplished whalers. They'd undoubtedly feasted well on this unfortunate creature before letting the eagles dine on the leftovers.

As *Intrepid* dropped anchor, Nathan saw a young Makah

11

brave staring straight at him. He guessed the lad was around his age, a fraction older maybe. As tall as him, he had a noble countenance. Nathan thought he may be related to the chief or to one of the headmen at least. In fact, the youth, Tatoosh, was the chief's oldest son. Nathan returned the other's stare. *Have you claimed your first scalp yet?* Nathan wondered. Then he recalled these people didn't scalp their enemies. Unlike their east coast and inland cousins, they beheaded their enemies and displayed the heads atop their totem poles.

At that moment Elswa, the Makahs' chief, emerged from the largest of the lodges. Resplendent in a fine sea-otter cloak, he also wore two white feathers in his hair. Elswa issued an order and a dozen braves immediately launched one of the canoes that were lined up side by side on the beach.

A loud sneeze alerted Nathan and the others that Captain Dawson had rejoined them on deck. Addressing the first mate, Dawson said, "Ensure the reception party is armed and ready, Mister Bates. And no more than four savages on board at any time."

"Aye, sir!" Bates snapped back. The first mate immediately ordered a dozen crewmen to arm themselves and assemble at the portside rail.

The crewmen concerned disappeared below deck and emerged armed with muskets or pistols in less than a minute. Observing them, Nathan marveled at how disciplined the men aboard *Intrepid* were under his uncle's leadership. As always, he felt proud to be related to Herbert Dawson. And as occasionally happened, his thoughts turned to his father. How he wished Johnson Senior was more like his Uncle Herbert.

Within minutes the Makah canoe was alongside *Intrepid*. Looking down over the rail, Nathan noticed Elswa, the chief, sitting in the canoe's bow. His son, Tatoosh, sat directly behind him.

Elswa stood up and looked at Dawson. He seemed to sense the captain was in charge. "I am Elswa, chief of the Makah," he announced in passable English. "Welcome to the Makah Nation!"

"I am Captain Herbert Dawson," the captain responded. "You are welcome to board my vessel."

A sailor threw a rope ladder over the ship's side and the Makah prepared to board.

"Four men only," first mate Bates shouted.

Elswa looked up enquiringly.

"Four only," Bates repeated, holding up four fingers. "And no weapons."

Elswa grunted and issued orders to his braves before scaling the rope ladder. He was followed by Tatoosh and two other braves. All had left their weapons in the canoe as ordered.

On board, the visitors were greeted personally by Dawson who afforded them the respect with which he always treated Native Americans—especially those he hoped to trade with. Despite his habit of referring to them as *savages,* he had a grudging respect for them, their resourcefulness and their culture. Elswa seemed to sense this and nodded to the captain.

"Welcome aboard Intrepid," Dawson said.

Elswa got straight down to business. "You trade musket?" he asked, eyeing the weapons the armed crewmembers were holding at the ready.

"Maybe . . . tomorrow," Dawson answered cautiously. He knew all Native Americans lusted after muskets. He also knew when entering into trade negotiations it didn't pay to look too keen. "You have something to trade?"

Elswa grunted. He knew full well by *something to trade* the captain referred to sea otter furs.

Nathan, who was observing proceedings with interest, took the chief's grunt to mean he did indeed have the prized furs to trade for muskets. It was then he caught the eye of Tatoosh, Elswa's son. A fine-looking boy who carried himself with pride, Tatoosh nodded to Nathan in the fashion of the Makah. The young Philadelphian nodded back.

Trading terms were soon negotiated. It was agreed Dawson would send a trading party ashore with muskets at first light.

CHAPTER 2

Kensington, England, 1838

SUSANNAH DRAKE SAT ALONE WITH her thoughts on the lawn behind her father's rectory in Kensington. Lost in her own world for the moment, the pretty twelve-year-old was aware of the drama that was unfolding inside the family home even if she didn't fully comprehend it.

Around the other side of the house, a procession of grim adults filed in and out of the front door. They were visiting Susannah's mother, Jeanette, who was dying of an illness the local doctors had been unable to identify.

Susannah's father, Reverend Brian Drake, had done his best to shield his daughter from the severity of his dear wife's illness, but despite this, Susannah was aware something wasn't right. The deterioration in Jeanette's condition in recent weeks had been alarming and that was something that couldn't be hidden from Susannah. However, it wasn't in Susannah's nature to expect the worst, so she was hopeful whatever it was that had reduced her mother to a virtual skeleton would soon pass.

A red-eyed Drake Senior suddenly appeared at the back door. "Susannah!" he called.

Susannah dropped the doll she was holding onto the grass and ran to her father. Drake Senior looked at her sadly. Looking down into her bright, hazel eyes, he reached out affectionately and stroked her red hair.

"What is it, papa?" Susannah asked innocently.

Unable to answer her, Drake Senior took Susannah by the hand and led her up the stairs.

The sound of women crying alerted Susannah that something terrible had happened. It was coming from her parents' bedroom on the first landing. She held tight to her father's hand as he led her into the room. There, she found her grandparents and other relatives crowded around her parents' large double bed. The adults immediately made room for Drake Senior and his daughter.

Susannah stepped forward, wide-eyed, and looked at her mother who seemed to be sleeping. "Mother," she whispered.

Grandma Pegden, Susannah's sweet-natured, maternal grandmother, pulled Susannah to her and held her to her bosom. Crying, she murmured, "Mummy has gone to be with the angels, sweetheart."

Susannah felt numb. She tried to make sense of her grandmother's words. *Mummy can't be with the angels,* she told herself. *She's only sleeping.* Susannah studied her mother's lifeless, skeletal features. Slowly, it dawned on her, her mother really was dead. Tears welled up in her eyes.

Intervening, Susannah's stern, paternal grandmother, Grandma Drake, took Susannah firmly by the hand and led her toward the door. "It's not good for her to see Jeanette like this," she announced in a tone that told everyone present she would brook no argument.

Susannah dutifully allowed her least favorite grandmother to lead her back downstairs to the privacy of a small chapel in the rectory at the rear of the house. There, they sat down on a pew, facing each other.

Teary-eyed Susannah tried her best not to cry. She knew Grandma Drake disapproved of children who cried. *Their way of seeking attention,* she always said.

Susannah noticed her grandmother seemed to be studying her critically. The youngster braced herself. She recalled numerous hellfire and brimstone-style lectures she'd received from Grandma Drake, including a lengthy one only the day before. Phrases like *Growing up to be a God-fearing woman* and *Treading a righteous path* as well as *The world being full of sin and evil* always slid off the zealous old woman's tongue with effortless ease. Expecting yet another sermon, Susannah hesitantly turned to face her grandmother.

For once Grandma Drake seemed lost for words. Her glasses kept misting up, prompting her to remove them and polish their lenses with a handkerchief every few minutes. Finally, she said, "Have faith in the knowledge that your mother was a God-fearing woman, my child. Know in your heart that your beautiful mother will be in heaven now with our Heavenly Father and the angels."

Surprised, Susannah looked at her grandmother as if seeing her for the first time. For once, Grandma Drake seemed human. Gone was the rigid woman of the Church she'd come to know. Susannah even noticed tears forming in the old woman's eyes.

"It is impossible to say why God chooses to take some souls from their loved ones," Grandma Drake continued. "This world is often one of pain and misery, and the various forms of suffering we all endure scar us forever."

Susannah's surprise grew as her grandmother kissed her forehead then embraced her warmly.

"Your mother's passing will also scar you, my dear," Grandma Drake said, "but you must have faith in the Lord's grand design of life, death and the afterlife. He *always* has a purpose. Even if we mortals are unable to see the wisdom of His ways."

Susannah hugged her grandmother tightly. As she did, she looked up at a statue of Christ's crucifixion that rested on a shelf on the rectory's near wall. Studying the anguished expression on Christ's face, she began to cry on her grandmother's shoulder. Nothing, it seemed, could stem the flow of tears. To Susannah, who still studied the statue, it felt as though her tears flowed like a river of Christ's blood.

"Let it all out, my child," Grandma Drake whispered as she held her granddaughter as tight as she could without hurting her.

When Susannah's sobbing finally subsided, Grandma Drake grabbed her grand-daughter's hand and squeezed it firmly. "You must to be strong now Susannah, for your father's sake. And for yours. After all, you only have each other now."

———

As THAT AWFUL day drew to a close, Susannah had no tears left. She'd cried an ocean of tears and now just felt empty. The youngster suddenly wanted to be alone. She also felt she needed to be close to nature. Exactly why, she wasn't sure.

Quietly slipping out the back door of the family home, Susannah headed for the lily pond in the yard behind her father's rectory. Fittingly, it was a gloomy day outside as well as inside. Susannah reached out with both hands and touched the leaves and branches of the mature oak and elm trees as she followed the familiar narrow, leafy path to the pond. Their touch was comforting to her.

On reaching the pond, Susannah sat down on a wooden deckchair near the pond's edge and stared at the reflections in the water. The white swans for whom the pond was home paddled over to her, hoping she'd feed them the breadcrumbs she usually brought with her, but on this occasion they were out of luck. They paddled off.

Susannah hadn't even consciously noticed the swans. She was thinking about her mother, or her mother's soul, and hoping to receive a sign. But nothing materialized.

For the first time in her life, Susannah questioned her own faith. *Is there really a God or an afterlife?* She hoped the answer would somehow miraculously come to her. None did. Again she felt a terrible void inside.

A squawking bird flying overhead distracted her. Susannah looked up, but couldn't see the bird, only fluffy white clouds. They covered Kensington like a dome of cotton wool. As the youngster studied them, the tears she thought she'd finished shedding began to flow once more. They stopped almost as soon as they'd started when the late afternoon sun pierced a tiny gap in the clouds. The sun's brilliant rays bathed Susannah and the nearby pond in light. Their effect was mesmerizing.

In that moment, Susannah sensed her mother's presence. It was strong and undeniable; it was as though Susannah was an infant again; it felt like her mother was holding her — and she could feel her unconditional love. *Mother, you really are in heaven now with our Father and the angels!* A calmness descended on her as her faith in God was instantly restored.

Susannah thought she heard her father calling from the house, but she couldn't be sure. She continued looking skyward as the last of the sun's rays disappeared and dusk descended.

Some time later — she hadn't a clue how long for she'd lost track of time — Drake Senior appeared beside her, his hand outstretched. "Dinner is about to be served, my child," he said. "Will you come and join us?"

"Yes, Papa," Susannah nodded. As she stood and put her hand in his, she noticed the grief etched on his face. She'd lost her mother, but he'd lost his wife and one true love, and was obviously a broken man.

Hand in hand, father and daughter walked slowly back to the house. They walked in silence. The clergyman went to say something, but changed his mind.

Susannah looked skyward again. The clouds had all but disappeared and in the darkening sky, the faint twinkle of stars could now be seen. The youngster took this as a further sign her mother was communicating with her. She stopped walking and tugged on her father's hand. "Papa," she whispered.

"Yes my dear?"

Susannah looked up at her father. "I felt mother's presence just now." She hesitated as she pondered how to best describe what she'd experienced. "It was like mother, or God, or maybe both, communicated with me through nature."

Drake Senior stroked his daughter's cheek tenderly. He smiled, but Susannah sensed he didn't draw the same comfort from her experience as she did. They resumed walking.

CHAPTER 3

Southeast London, England, 1837

WHILE LONDON MAY HAVE BEEN the center of the civilized world, for twenty-one-year old Jack Halliday and untold thousands of other working class citizens, it was a place of never-ending hardship and poverty. Not even the approaching coronation of Queen Victoria was enough to lift the black mood that prevailed over the vast majority of the populace.

Of course, poverty was relative. At least Jack had a job. The young Cockney eked out a living as a blacksmith in Sullivan's Foundry down in the dockyards by the Thames. Although he worked six days a week, the wage he made barely enabled him to survive even though he'd served his apprenticeship and was a qualified smithy.

Henry Sullivan, the foundry's hard, mean-spirited proprietor, had a reputation for paying low wages. That he retained his hardworking staff was a reflection of the scarcity of jobs in London. Unemployment was at an all-time high; anyone lucky enough to have a job, did what they had to, to keep it. This opened them up to abuse from unscrupulous employers like Sullivan.

Thankfully, this particular working day was nearly over. For Jack and the others, the day had gone like any other day at Sullivan's. The work was hard, monotonous and sometimes dangerous; the foundry was noisy, smelly and always busy.

From dawn to dusk, the workshop reverberated to the sounds of loud hammering and the clang of steel against steel. As they toiled, the smithies were constantly aware of the hulking figure of Sullivan who, it seemed, was always looking over their shoulders, critically eyeing their work and productivity.

The proprietor stopped to inspect Jack's handiwork as the young smithy skillfully shaped a molten horse-shoe with a hammer. Sullivan asked, "Will Mister Featherstone's order be ready by tonight, Halliday?"

Jack pointed behind his employer to a pile of railings stacked against the wall. "Already done," he said. He continued hammering while Sullivan inspected the railings.

The proprietor seemed impressed. He nodded with satisfaction before walking off.

Jack ceased hammering for a moment to fasten his perceptive green eyes on Sullivan's retreating back. *If me work's that good, how about a raise, or a pat on the back at least?* Anyone observing Jack would have seen the contempt he felt for Sullivan written all over his face.

When the foundry siren sounded, heralding the end of the working day, Jack and the other smithies downed tools. Before leaving, Jack approached the proprietor. He asked, "Mister Sullivan, how about paying me the overtime I'm owed?"

"I thought I told you, I'd pay you when I could?" Sullivan snarled.

"That was two months ago, sir."

Sullivan became belligerent. He leaned forward so his brutish, granite-hewn face was close to Jack's. "Look Halliday, if you don't like it here there's plenty more men who'd like your job."

Jack's right hand closed to form a fist. He was tempted to punch Sullivan then thought better of it. *Not now Jack. Get the old git's quid first.* The young smithy turned on his heel and strode out of the foundry. Although his cheeky face didn't show it, he was inwardly fuming.

Outside, it was already dark as Jack joined a steady stream of workers and others — most of whom were making their way home. The streets were teeming with people. A mixed bunch, they included merchants, laborers, stonemasons, professional men, beggars, pickpockets and drunks.

Jack decided against going straight home. Instead, he lingered outside a working men's bar directly opposite the foundry. Unsure exactly what he was planning to do, he waited.

A SHORT TIME later, Jack pulled back out of view when the foundry lights went out and Sullivan emerged from the front door. The proprietor locked the door and walked off into the night.

Jack hurried across the street and ran to the rear of the vacated foundry. He'd had time to think and now had a definite plan. *If Sullivan ain't gonna pay me, I'll help me self.* Checking no-one was around, he expertly picked the back door's lock, opened the door and disappeared inside.

A short distance away, Sullivan suddenly stopped walking and checked his coat pockets. "Damn!" he cursed. Realizing he'd left his favorite pipe behind, he turned and strode back toward the foundry.

By now Jack had entered the foundry's front office and was rifling through desk drawers looking for valuables. In his haste, he knocked over a heavy bookend. It landed on the wooden floor with a loud thud. He wasn't to know that his employer was just outside the foundry's front door at that very moment.

Jack's search proved unsuccessful. He was about to leave when, at the bottom of a cupboard, a large quantity of hemp caught his eye. He grabbed the precious commodity, stuffed it in his pockets and retraced his steps to the back door. As he opened the door, he was shocked to see Sullivan waiting for him, pistol in hand.

"Well, well, what have we here?" Sullivan asked. "Doing some overtime, are we?" He waved his pistol threateningly under Jack's nose.

The young smithy slammed the door in his employer's face, locked it from the inside then ran through the foundry. *There goes me raise!* Behind him, he could hear Sullivan shouting. Jack flung open a front window, scrambled through the narrow opening and landed heavily on the cobbled street outside.

Sullivan's shouting had attracted the attention of patrons in the bar opposite. They were filing out onto the footpath to investigate, and were greeted by the sight of Sullivan aiming his pistol at Jack who was sprinting down the street as if his life depended on it, which it did. The big man fired a hurried shot that missed its target.

Turning to the bar patrons, Sullivan shouted, "Two shillings to the man who catches that thieving bastard!"

Among the patrons, two burly men immediately joined Sullivan and chased after Jack who by now had disappeared down a dark, side-alley that led to a residential section of the dockside suburb.

Half-way down the alley, Jack hid in a doorway of someone's home to take stock of his situation. Peeping around the corner of the doorway, he tensed when he saw one of the burly bar patrons enter the alley. The young Cockney held his breath as the shadowy figure ran toward him. When the man reached his hiding place, Jack stuck out his foot and tripped him, sending him sprawling. The Cockney was onto him in a flash, knocking him out cold with one punch. Like most smithies, he could usually end a fight with one punch if it landed flush as this one had. He looked behind him just as the other bar patron entered the alley.

Jack ran off, but pulled up when Sullivan appeared at the far end of the same alley. Sullivan raised his pistol toward him. Trapped, Jack looked around desperately. With no time to think, he barged through the front door of the nearest house and found himself in a modest dining room where members of a typical working class family had just sat down for their evening meal.

The young couple and their four children looked astonished as Jack strode through the room. Jack touched his curly forelock and smiled disarmingly. "Sorry to trouble you."

The man of the house started to get to his feet. A steelworker who looked as hard as nails, he prepared to defend his family. "What in God's name do you think you . . ."

Jack motioned to him to remain seated and hurried toward the rear of the house.

"Hey!" the man of the house shouted after him.

Jack opened a door, hoping it would lead outside. He discovered it was a bedroom, and it was currently occupied by lodgers—a middle-aged couple—who were making love on a single bed. The woman was naked except for a pair of dress shoes which, at that moment, were pointing toward the ceiling; her portly male lover's fleshy buttocks were pumping away like pistons and the woman was whimpering like a distressed seal.

Jack couldn't believe his eyes. *Holy mackerel!* He momentarily forgot about the danger he was in. So engrossed were the pair that neither noticed Jack until he was half-way out the near window. A second later, he was gone.

The couple looked at each other and wondered if they'd imagined that a stranger had just passed through.

"Who was that?" the woman asked breathlessly. Her partner shrugged and they resumed their lovemaking.

Back in the dining room, before the family members had recovered from their surprise at Jack's sudden intrusion, Sullivan and his burly companion burst in. At the sight of the pistol in Sullivan's hand, the lady of the house screamed.

"Be quiet, madam!" Sullivan snapped. Addressing the man

of the house, he asked, "Which way did he go?"

Dumbfounded, the man pointed toward the rear of the house. The uninvited pair hurried after Jack, leaving the startled family members looking at each other in disbelief.

Grumbling to himself, the man of the house complained, "This place is getting like a circus!" He then consoled his wife and children who by now were all crying.

The two intruders entered the same room Jack had passed through moments earlier. They arrived just as the portly, middle-aged man was climaxing. The man had the presence of mind to point toward the open window before finishing his business and collapsing into a sweaty heap beside his equally sweaty lover.

Sullivan exited the bedroom to find a rear door while his burly companion climbed out the open window.

"And who in Christ's name were they?" the woman asked her partner as soon as the latest intruders had left. Again, her lover just shrugged. He was spent and beyond caring.

Outside, Jack was sprinting down a lane leading away from the house. As he rounded the corner of a neighboring house, he pulled up when he found he was confronted by a high wall. It was a dead-end. Cursing, he turned back just as Sullivan and the burly man appeared.

Finding they had Jack trapped, Sullivan smiled sadistically. He turned to his burly companion. "I think you should teach Master Halliday the error of his ways."

The burly man, who looked older but no less intimidating than the patron Jack had knocked out earlier, cracked his knuckles expectantly.

Sullivan added, "There's an extra two shillings in it for you."

With that, the man advanced on Jack, keen to earn the extra cash. Jack raised his fists and went forward to meet him. The two went toe to toe. Jack copped a couple of blows to the face and was forced to back-peddle. Another blow to the side of his head dropped him to his knees. *Okay Jack. Time to get serious.* As the man shaped up to kick him, Jack suddenly exploded. He brought his fist up hard into the burly man's testicles. Gasping in pain, the man fell to the ground.

Remembering Sullivan, Jack turned around too late to avoid a swinging blow. The steel butt of his employer's pistol caught him above the eye, knocking him senseless.

CHAPTER 4

Makah Nation, West Coast, North America, 1838

NATHAN WAS BRIMMING WITH EXCITEMENT as he prepared to board *Intrepid's* longboat with other members of the twenty-strong trading party. While his companions were armed to the teeth with muskets, pistols and cutlasses, he was unarmed. That was the way his uncle wanted it. The captain had decreed Nathan would not carry arms until his seventeenth birthday.

Captain Dawson was not going ashore on this occasion. He was still down with the flu, and Doc Masters, the ship's surgeon, had ordered him to remain in his cabin until the illness had passed.

As Nathan was about to climb down the rope ladder into the longboat, Doc Masters appeared from below deck. "Master Johnson!" he called.

Nathan's heart sank. He was afraid the surgeon had come to tell him his uncle had changed his mind about allowing him ashore.

"The captain has asked to see you," the surgeon advised.

"Thanks, doc." Nathan hurried below deck to the captain's quarters. There, he found his sniffling, runny-nosed uncle half-buried beneath blankets on his bunk. "Uncle . . . ah, sir. You wanted to see me?"

"Yes," Dawson smiled. "Close the door."

Nathan closed the cabin door and approached the bunk. Dawson had another coughing fit. He was clearly under the weather. Nathan waited until the coughing subsided.

"I've ordered Mister Bates to keep an eye on you while ashore," Dawson rasped. "And I want you to stay by his side at all times."

Relieved, Nathan grinned. His uncle wasn't going to stop him going ashore. "Yes Uncle. I'll stay close to him."

"Good man." Dawson sneezed then blew his nose. "I'd come with you, but Doc insists I rest up and regain my strength for the journey ahead."

"I understand, sir. Will that be all?"

"Yes."

Nathan went to open the door.

"Nathan."

The young man turned back to face his uncle.

Dawson smiled. "Never mind. I'll talk to you later."

Nathan flashed a quick grin and departed.

Dawson watched as his nephew closed the door behind him. He'd been about to tell Nathan how proud he was of him, but decided that could wait.

Back on deck, Nathan found the first mate, Bates, waiting for him at the ship's rail. He hurried to the rail and clambered down the ladder into the waiting longboat. Bates followed close behind.

"Let's go!" Bates ordered as soon as he was on board.

The oarsmen pushed away from the side of *Intrepid* and began rowing for shore. It was still semi-dark. Even so, it was evident to all it was going to be a rare fine day in Neah Bay.

Although the sun's rays had yet to pierce the eastern sky, already there was a reception party awaiting the visitors on the sandy beach in front of the Makah village.

As the longboat closed with the shore, Nathan looked behind to see they were being followed by a smaller rowing boat which was tethered to the longboat's stern. The unmanned craft was low in the water, weighed down by the weight of three coffin-sized caskets. Nathan knew the caskets contained muskets for the forthcoming trade.

Nearing the shore, the young Philadelphian identified Elswa among the braves assembled on the beach. The chief made an imposing figure standing at the water's edge with arms folded and legs astride. Tatoosh, his oldest son, was at his side.

"Remember captain's orders," Bates reminded his men. "Be vigilant at all times and don't trust these savages."

Those who weren't rowing grasped their weapons tight. Stories of the savagery of the Northwest natives were fresh in the minds of each even though few had experienced, or even witnessed, that savagery firsthand.

Several Makah braves waded out to greet the longboat and pull it up onto the sand. Others waded out to retrieve the smaller rowing boat, but were warned off by the crewmen. *Intrepid's* men were under orders to guard the muskets with their lives.

As soon as the rowing boat was up on the sand, crewmen lifted the caskets out and began carrying them up into the village. They were escorted by Elswa and his braves to a longhouse, which served as the tribe's meeting house.

Following close behind Bates, Nathan took in his surroundings. He was impressed by the level of activity within the village at such an early hour. Women were already attending to their chores, collecting firewood and tending cooking fires, and men were readying nets in preparation for a day's fishing. Beyond the village, a ten-strong hunting party was setting off on foot into the interior. Nathan watched the fleet-footed hunters until they disappeared into the forest.

In the Makahs' longhouse, Nathan looked on as slaves served up whale blubber, raw fish and other so-called local delicacies to the visitors. The *Intrepid* crewmen ate sitting cross-legged in front of the now-open caskets of muskets they'd brought with them.

Facing them were Chief Elswa and thirty or so Makah elders, braves and headmen. They looked on, amused, as their white guests chewed unenthusiastically on the blubber and other food offerings.

Women came and went, attending to their menfolk's every need. It seemed to Nathan the men had it pretty good in this part of the world. Behind the Makah, sea otter furs lay piled up on the floor.

Communication was left to Elswa who appeared to be the only one among the Makah who spoke English. The chief's hawk-like eyes took in everything while his five wives fussed around him, ensuring he wanted for nothing. Elswa's gaze kept straying to the muskets. He looked at them longingly.

Tatoosh sat to his father's right. He seemed intrigued by Nathan and kept staring at him.

As soon as everyone had eaten their fill, Elswa motioned for a peace pipe to be lit. The chief puffed it first then handed it to the headman on his left.

Nathan studied his hosts while the pipe was being shared around. Strong and noble-looking, they carried themselves with pride. One off-putting thing about them, he decided, was they smelled like the whale blubber they were eating. Nathan's companions noticed it, too, and it took all their self-control not to rush outside and gulp in some fresh air. Only later would Nathan learn that, as well as eating blubber, the Makah regularly rubbed it and whale oil over their bodies as insulation against the cold.

Finally, Elswa indicated trading should begin. The visitors and their hosts immediately stood and began bartering.

In the negotiating that followed, the traders eventually

agreed on the exchange of ninety sea otter furs for thirty muskets. It was Nathan's assessment that Elswa had driven a hard bargain.

As trading concluded, a Makah headman objected to the way one of the visitors was ogling his wife. The visitor concerned was Marty Williams, a rigger who misguidedly fancied himself as a ladies' man. Williams and the aggrieved headman began pushing each other.

"That's enough, Mister Williams!" Bates ordered.

Ignoring the order, Williams drew his pistol and pointed it between the headman's eyes. The offended headman drew his tomahawk and raised it threateningly above his head. The two stood toe-to-toe, staring at each other, each daring the other to make the first move.

Watching the action unfold, Nathan noticed for the first time that Williams was drunk. *The captain's gonna have your guts for garters, Williams.* The rigger's eyes were glazed and he was unsteady on his feet. The young Philadelphian looked at Elswa and noted he was watching Williams impassively. Nathan wondered what was going on behind the chief's inscrutable gaze.

Finally, to everyone's relief, Williams lowered his pistol. The headman, in turn, lowered his tomahawk. Then, for no apparent reason, Williams lashed out and struck the headman, knocking him to the floor.

Pandemonium broke out. Women screamed and ran for cover while the Makah braves drew their weapons. One angry brave threw his tomahawk at Williams, splitting his skull in two and killing him instantly.

Quick-thinking Bates drew his pistol and lunged at Elswa, grabbing the shocked chief in a headlock. Holding his pistol to Elswa's head, the first mate said, "Tell your braves to hold off!"

"He-ho!" Elswa shouted.

As one, the Makah braves looked at their chief. Elswa didn't need to say more. It was clear his life was in the balance at that moment.

Bates knew his future, and his men's, depended on what he did next. Determined to keep what slender advantage he'd gained, he glanced at his men. "Form a circle around me!" he barked.

The crewmen jumped to and formed a tight ring around Bates and Elswa, their weapons pointing outwards to keep the incensed braves at bay. Bates held the chief tight to him as if his life depended on it, which it did of course.

Without a weapon, Nathan was feeling naked and very vulnerable. How he wished he was holding a musket or even a pistol at that moment.

Looking at the Makah, Nathan and his crewmates were in no doubt their lives hung by a thread. Although the traders were the ones holding firearms primed and ready to fire, they were hugely outnumbered. Inside the longhouse they were outnumbered almost two to one while outside some fifteen hundred villagers awaited them.

In the middle of the human ring, Elswa squirmed in the headlock Bates had him in. The first mate began dragging the chief toward the near door. "Back to the boat now!" he shouted. "And slowly does it."

Nathan and the others needed no encouragement to leave. Keeping their tight formation around the first mate and his hostage, they began shuffling out of the longhouse, all the while keeping their weapons raised and ready. The Makah braves followed, weapons raised and howling for blood.

Outside, they were greeted by the villagers who had been drawn to the longhouse by the sounds of conflict. The menfolk and some of the women brandished weapons, and appeared ready to use them. War cries rang out.

Recognizing the danger, Tatoosh warned the villagers off, pointing out their chief was being held hostage and explaining that any retaliation would result in his death.

For Nathan and the others, the journey from the longhouse to the longboat that awaited them on the beach seemed to take forever. The Makah braves followed them every inch of the way, baying like crazed animals, frustrated that the whites had their chief and they could do nothing about it despite their superior numbers.

Once in the longboat, the strongest crewmen manned the oars and began rowing themselves and their precious human cargo toward their waiting ship. As they rowed, villagers waded out into the bay, waving their weapons and hurling abuse until the water reached their chests and they could go no further. One or two threw spears, which landed harmlessly short. Others raced along the beach to launch the canoes that rested there.

On board *Intrepid,* Captain Dawson was on deck, having been alerted minutes earlier by the commotion ashore. His heart sank at the sight of armed warriors launching canoes in pursuit of his crewmen in the longboat. Dawson's thoughts immediately went to Nathan. He felt momentary elation when he spotted his nephew's head amongst the longboat's passengers.

Recognizing the danger to his men and ship, Dawson shouted, "Weigh anchor!"

The crewmen aboard *Intrepid* raced to their respective posts and readied the vessel for a rapid departure from Neah Bay. Sails were unfurled and the anchor raised in double-quick time. The crewmen were well rehearsed for such departures. Dawson had made sure of that.

As the longboat closed with *Intrepid,* Bates and another sailor hoisted their Makah hostage overboard. Elswa sank beneath the surface of the water and for a moment the crewmen feared the chief may not be able to swim. Seconds later, Elswa's head broke the surface. He gulped in a lungful of air then began swimming for all he was worth away from his captors.

By the time Elswa had been rescued by his braves in one of the pursuing canoes, Nathan and the others had safely scrambled aboard *Intrepid* and the longboat had been hoisted aboard. Moments later, the ship was sailing north out of Neah Bay.

Only now did the survivors celebrate. They expressed their relief by slapping each other on the back and shaking hands. Many sought out the first mate to personally thank. They knew Bates' quick thinking had saved their lives.

Nathan wandered away from the others. He stood at the ship's stern, looking back at the Makah braves who had now ceased their pursuit. Those who had muskets shot at *Intrepid* even though she was out of range. Ignoring the musket-fire, Nathan looked straight at Tatoosh.

The chief's son stood in the bow of the nearest canoe and looked back at Nathan.

As the two young men stared at each other, feelings of regret flooded through Nathan. He knew the Makah had been wronged that day, and he sensed the actions of his fellow crewmen had made enemies for life. In better circumstances, he sensed he and Tatoosh could be friends.

CHAPTER 5

Kensington, England, 1841

SUSANNAH HAD BLOSSOMED INTO A beautiful fifteen-year-old, so it was somewhat inevitable—to her clergyman father's everlasting consternation—that there was a steady stream of suitors arriving at the Drake family home in Kensington vying for her attention.

Drake Senior had to admit his daughter was stunning. Certainly there was none more beautiful in the district, and perhaps not even in greater London. Susannah's wavy, red hair shone like gold in the sunlight and framed a determined yet still-angelic face, and not even the modest dresses she wore could hide her shapely figure or her toned, slender legs. But it was her hazel eyes that set her apart: alert, intelligent and full of the eternal hope of youth, they were flecked and sparkled like diamonds. Those eyes had the ability to reduce a normally confident, even arrogant, suitor to something akin to a quivering lump of jelly.

The number of suitors had grown so alarmingly of late, several parishioners had been prompted to comment on the fact to Reverend Drake. One had even been so moved to say the rectory was in danger of becoming better known as a meeting place for Susannah and her admirers than as a place of God.

Drake Senior had often tried to broach the subject with

37

Susannah, but she'd always laughed it off before he could get anywhere. Not for the first time, he wished his dear Jeanette were still alive to take their willful daughter in hand and dispense some motherly advice.

One handsome young suitor proved more determined than the others. Blake Dugan was an apprentice chimneysweep and would-be poet who supplemented his meager earnings by hiring himself out as a poet-for-hire at weddings and other such functions around the district. His life's dream was to become a full-time poet, reciting his own poetry to whoever was prepared to pay for the privilege.

Blake and Susannah met one evening during a stage play in the local theatre. They were seated near each other in the audience. The young man saw her and couldn't take his eyes off her. He stared at her throughout the play's first act. By the start of the second act, Susannah was aware of the young man's interest, but pretended not to notice.

So taken was Blake with Susannah that, there and then, he produced a pad and pencil and penned a poem about her.

⸺◦◦◦⸺

WALKING HOME ALONE after the play, Susannah became aware she was being followed. She turned to see it was the same fellow who had been staring at her throughout the play. Judging him on his bohemian attire, she considered him untrustworthy and so quickened her pace.

Blake ran up beside her, startling her. "Please don't be frightened, Miss," he said. "My name is Blake Dugan. I mean you no harm."

Sensing he spoke the truth, Susannah relaxed and slowed her pace.

Blake continued, "I have been watching you, Miss."

Susannah feigned surprise. "Me?"

"Yes. I wrote a poem for you."

Blake pulled a piece of paper from his pocket and prepared

to read his poem aloud. He positioned himself beneath the arc of a street lamp so that he could see the words. So taken was Susannah that she stopped to listen.

The young poet began reciting:

Dear English princess
unconscious and unaware
of your angelic beauty.

Are there no mirrors where you live?
Didn't your mother ever tell you,
you've been born with a face,
that men would fight wars over,
just to be able to touch?

So forgive me if I stumble
and stammer to find the words
to ask you for,
a slow dance at midnight.

As Blake recited his poem, Susannah found herself falling under his spell. She was taken by his good looks and bohemian charm, but most of all by his spontaneity. When he finished reciting, Blake looked at her expectantly, as if for approval.

Susannah immediately applauded. "Bravo, kind sir. You have a way with words."

Visibly relieved, Blake folded the sheet of paper he held and handed it to her. "Please keep this . . . in memory of tonight." Susannah took the note from him. Blake then surprised her by asking, "Will you do me the honor of this dance?"

Susannah looked around, confused. "What dance?"

Smiling, Blake took her hand in his, placed his arm around her slender waist and led off in a slow waltz. Embarrassed but intrigued, she complied.

Susannah soon noticed their display was attracting bemused smiles and a few strange stares from other theatre-goers making their way home. Giggling, she whispered, "Tis a pity we have no music to dance to."

"Ah, but we do." Blake immediately began humming a classical tune.

Susannah giggled again. Encouraged, Blake held her tighter. She snuggled into him and allowed him to press his cheek to hers.

As they danced, Susannah snuck furtive glances at the young man in whose arms she found herself. Although they'd only just met, she felt totally at ease in his presence. It was as if she'd known him all her life.

IN THE DAYS and weeks that followed their first meeting, chimneysweep and would-be poet Blake Dugan called on Susannah at every opportunity. Both of them lived for the moments they could spend together—much to the annoyance of Susannah's father.

Ever-critical Drake Senior was strongly opposed to Blake Dugan's interest in his daughter. He referred to him as an apology-for-a-poet, sparking several rows with Susannah. His opposition to Blake only served to increase Susannah's ardor for the young man.

A serious romance developed and it wasn't long before the two were very much in love. He was Susannah's first love and she had never been happier.

Out of the blue, on a crisp Autumn day, Blake proposed to Susannah. Crying tears of happiness, she accepted his proposal, but suggested he seek her father's blessing for their union. She warned him that would be no easy feat.

The couple spent the next few hours devising a plan of attack.

⚬

LATER THAT DAY, in the confines of the Drake Senior's study in the old rectory, a nervous Blake approached Susannah's father. "Reverend Drake," Blake stammered.

"Yes, what is it?" Drake Senior snapped. The young man had interrupted his preparations for his next sermon. The chosen topic was a difficult one and Drake Senior was annoyed his train of thought had been broken.

"I . . . I would like to ask for your daughter's hand in marriage, sir," Blake ventured.

Drake Senior suddenly forgot all about the sermon he'd been sweating over. He eyeballed the young man critically. *Don't shout at the little toad,* he instructed himself. *You're a man of the cloth after all.* Taking a deep breath, he asked, "And what can you offer my daughter, Master Dugan?"

"Offer? Your daughter?"

"Yes. What security can you offer? How do you make your living? Can you support her in the manner to which she has become accustomed?"

With each question, Blake became more depressed. He realized, as an apprentice chimneysweep and struggling poet with little money coming in and no property or assets, nothing he said would satisfy the clergyman who was looking at him as if he were the least suitable husband for his daughter in the entire world. Nevertheless, he knew he had to try. "I love her, sir," he said simply.

"Oh, so you love her," Drake Senior said sarcastically. "And love is going to feed and clothe her, is it? And feed and clothe the children you no doubt hope to sire? And—"

"And she loves me," Blake added hurriedly.

Now, Drake Senior lost his temper. Jumping angrily to his feet, he growled, "Don't be silly, you young fool! My daughter

41

doesn't know the meaning of love. She's far too young for that nonsense."

"She's nearly sixteen, sir."

"I've heard enough!" Drake Senior shouted. Pointing at the door, he said, "Find your own way out, Master Dugan. And don't let me catch you here again."

Blake departed, defeated.

Minutes later, Susannah stormed into the rectory. Her father had been expecting her, so hadn't even bothered returning to his planned sermon. Instead, he'd sat motionless, staring at the door through which he'd known his strong-willed daughter would burst through any minute.

Flushed and looking ready for a fight, Susannah confronted her father. "Why do you oppose my happiness?" she asked bluntly.

"Where do you want me to start?" Drake Senior responded defensively. "He has no money, no career—"

"He is a poet . . . and a good one."

"Ha! He's a good-for-nothing chimneysweep with no family that I know of, no permanent abode and no prospects. In short, my dear, he is not good enough for you."

Susannah was not prepared to back down. She planted her hands firmly on her hips and said, "I love Blake and I'm going to marry him, with or without your blessing." She turned and stormed out.

As she departed, her father's last words were ringing in her ears. *Over my dead body will you marry him!*

DESPITE DRAKE SENIOR'S opposition, the young lovers continued their courtship, albeit clandestinely. Blake called into the rectory when Drake Senior was away visiting parishioners, and Susannah snuck out to see her beau when her father was closeted in his study preparing for his next sermon.

Predictably, Blake put pressure on Susannah to give herself to him sexually. Out of respect for her father, and for her mother's memory, she resisted his advances although she was sorely tempted.

Drake Senior's opposition to their courtship only served to strengthen their resolve. They made plans to elope.

CHAPTER 6

Central London, England, 1837

A T THE CENTRAL CRIMINAL COURT, it was standing room only as Jack Halliday was led into the courtroom by a bailiff. The young smithy sported a shiner and various cuts and bruises following his run-in with Henry Sullivan, his employer, or more accurately his former employer.

His hands chained together, Jack took the stand and waited to be sentenced. While he waited, he searched the faces of people seated in the public gallery. His eyes rested on his mother, Jessica Halliday, who was sobbing at the sight of her favorite rascal of a son standing in the dock. She managed a strained smile.

Although only fifty-two, Jessica looked all of sixty-two—not unusual for working class mothers of the day. Sitting alongside her were Jack's two brothers and his sister. The young Cockney acknowledged them with a cheeky grin.

Henry Sullivan was sitting immediately behind Jessica. The big man caught Jack's eye and glared at him. Jack glared right back. *I shoulda flattened you when I had the chance, Sullivan.* The Cockney flashed a defiant wink at Sullivan who visibly grimaced at the brashness of his former employee.

A hush fell over the courtroom as the judge entered.

The court bailiff commanded, "All rise for Judge Simpkins."

The assembled stood as the judge sat down behind a large desk at the front of the courtroom.

Looking more like an undertaker than a judge, Judge Simpkins surveyed all through critical, world-weary eyes. He quickly referred to handwritten notes on a pad before peering at Jack over the top of horn-rimmed glasses. "Jack Halliday," the judge intoned, "you have been found guilty of stealing six pounds worth of hemp from your employer. Do you have anything to say?"

"Yes, your Honor," Jack replied. "The hemp was only worth one pound on the black market." He pointed directly at his former employer. "Sullivan owed me wages amounting to three pounds, so he's still two pounds better off than he deserves to be."

Red-faced Sullivan looked ready to explode as laughter and cheers erupted in the public gallery.

Judge Simpkins failed to see the humor. "Order!" he shouted, bringing his gavel down on his desktop with a bang. Once order had returned, the judge looked gravely at the young defendant. "Jack Halliday, you have been found guilty of theft. As this is not your first conviction, I have no option but to sentence you to seven years' hard labor."

Jeers and cries of disbelief came from the public gallery. Sullivan looked smug.

The judge continued, "You will serve your time—"

Jessica Halliday interrupted, crying out, "Dear God, show mercy for my son!"

"You will serve your time beyond the seas in Her Majesty's Colony of New South Wales," Judge Simpkins ordered, bringing his gavel down one last time before striding from the courtroom.

Jessica fainted and pandemonium broke out all around her in the gallery as Jack's friends and relatives vented their feelings against the harsh sentence. Two court officials grabbed Jack and frog-marched him from the courtroom.

Before they reached the door, Jack looked back at his mother. She was being assisted back into her seat. Little did he realize that would be the last time he'd see her or his siblings.

Outside the courthouse, Jack's ankles were shackled in irons and he was pushed up into one of several covered, horse-drawn carts that were being guarded by armed constabulary.

Jack found the cart he'd been assigned to already occupied by half a dozen other newly-convicted felons. They were sitting jammed together on wooden seats. More prisoners were loaded on, singly and in pairs, over the next hour.

While they waited, the felons talked among themselves. Jack quickly realized that, like him, they'd all been sentenced to serve their time in Britain's Colony of New South Wales — some for lesser crimes than his.

"Where is this New South Wales?" the man sitting on Jack's left asked.

Jack shrugged. *Bloody good question.* Like most of his companions, he'd heard of New South Wales, but didn't know where it was.

"It's at the bottom of the world," a toothless man sitting opposite said.

"What's it like there?" someone else asked.

"Buggered if I know," the toothless man said, "but I hear there's plenty o' rum and plenty o' women there."

Everyone except Jack cheered this good news. The young Cockney wondered how accurate the toothless man's information was. He also wondered how far away the bottom of the world was and, equally puzzling, what lay beyond it.

The sudden crack of a whip outside alerted the felons their cart was moving out. They fell silent as their covered cart bounced up and down over cobbled streets. Although they couldn't see outside, it didn't take Jack long to work out they were heading for London's docks.

CHAPTER 7

Makah Nation, West Coast, North America, 1838

AFTER THEIR HURRIED DEPARTURE FROM Neah Bay, Nathan and his crewmates quickly fell back into their everyday routines aboard *Intrepid*. Any sense of relief they had at surviving the wrath of the Makah was soon replaced by the humdrum of life at sea—except for one thing: a mighty storm was brewing.

Captain Dawson had recognized the danger soon after setting sail. Storm clouds had rolled in from the north and a ferocious northerly whipped the sea up into a frenzy. Plans to continue north to nearby Vancouver Island had to be aborted and the captain steered a new course southwest in search of the nearest safe anchorage.

Nathan had experienced many a storm in his years at sea, but nothing like the one that struck that night. In the first hour of darkness, three crewmembers—two riggers and an ordinary seaman—were washed overboard. Before the next hour was up, two more had been lost to the sea along with the aft mast the mighty wind had cracked in half like a toothpick.

In the wheelhouse, Dawson murmured a seaman's prayer as he nursed *Intrepid* southwards in the ever-worsening storm. The wind was approaching hurricane force and the captain was aware his vessel would be condemned to the ocean depths it he didn't find safe anchorage and find it soon.

Intrepid was heading toward an inlet Dawson estimated was about ten miles west of Neah Bay. He inwardly cursed that he hadn't changed course earlier. The rapidly strengthening northerly was a clear sign they'd been sailing into danger. If he'd responded sooner, they'd have reached safe anchorage by now. After he'd changed course, he'd been tempted to re-enter sheltered Neah Bay, but had resisted that temptation as he knew the Makah would have attacked them in force.

Those not required on deck were hunkered down in the crew's quarters below. Nathan was among them. The young Philadelphian was quietly relieved he wasn't among those who had drawn the short straw and ordered to manage the sails and attend to other life-threatening duties above deck. He wasn't alone. All those below deck were happy to be inside at that time.

A mighty cracking sound was the first warning they had that the mainsail mast had split in two. With that, *Intrepid* keeled over. In those terrifying few seconds, Nathan and the others below deck weren't to know that above deck another six crewmates had perished. Three had been killed by flying debris and the other three flung overboard. Those still alive when they hit the water quickly drowned.

Shouts of alarm rang out throughout the ship as the realization set in that *Intrepid* was going down.

Nathan and his crewmates scrambled to save themselves. It was every man for himself as they jostled to be the first to reach the deck and launch the longboat. When they finally emerged from below deck, any thoughts of salvation were dashed when they saw the longboat and the two dinghies had been lost overboard.

On deck, it was mayhem. Torrential rain was blown sideways by the howling wind, thunder rumbled overhead and lightning lit up the sky every few seconds. *Intrepid* lay over at a forty-five degree angle, and Nathan and the others had to hold fast to whatever they could lay their hands on to stop from being swept overboard. Those who couldn't hold fast were promptly consigned to the sea.

A flash of forked lightning lit up the rocky shoreline. To Nathan's eyes the shore seemed only a few yards away. In reality it was a good two hundred yards distant. However, the distance between shore and vessel was diminishing rapidly. Under these dreadful circumstances, *Intrepid* was entirely at the mercy of the wind and the current.

That was the last thing Nathan remembered. A spar from the last remaining mast fell and struck him a glancing blow. He lost his grip on the port-side rail he'd been clinging to and was swept unconscious overboard.

WHEN NATHAN AWOKE, he couldn't remember where he was or what had happened. The storm had passed and a new day had dawned.

The young Philadelphian had been washed up, still unconscious, onto a pebble beach. He'd lain there all night, teetering between unconsciousness and sleep while the storm continued to rage around him.

Now, as he shielded his eyes from the early morning sun, memories of what he'd survived started coming to him. At first they came in snippets; then they flooded back.

Bruised and battered, every joint hurt and he had a bad headache. Dried blood caked his face, a result of the head wound he'd suffered.

Nathan's thoughts went to his crewmates—and to his dear uncle. He tried to sit up. It took two attempts, so weak was he. He looked out to sea, hoping to see *Intrepid* at anchor. *Nothing!* The sea was flat and empty. Then some flotsam caught his eye. Among it were shattered timbers. *They could only be from Intrepid.* Slowly, the realization set in that *Intrepid* had been consigned to the ocean depths and, in all likelihood, he was the only survivor.

The thought of being alone, separated from his uncle and crewmates, suddenly terrified him. He struggled to his feet and shouted. "Hellooooo!" It was a long, plaintiff cry. To his dismay, it went unanswered.

TEN MILES TO the east, at Neah Bay, an elderly Makah fisherman speared fish from the rocks not far from his village. Flotsam in the water nearby caught his eye. He waded out to inspect it. Among the foreign items was *Intrepid's* distinctive bowsprit.

The old man pulled the bowsprit up onto the rocks then hurried back to the village. There he sought out Elswa and described what he'd found. Elswa ordered Tatoosh to inspect the bowsprit and confirm whether it was in fact from *Intrepid*. The chief prayed that it was for he had murder in his heart and yearned to avenge the previous day's actions of the white traders.

It only took Tatoosh a few minutes to reach the bowsprit and confirm to his own satisfaction it had come from *Intrepid*. He sprinted back to the village and relayed this to his father who immediately deduced the vessel had foundered in the storm. Elswa ordered his son to lead a search for survivors.

Tatoosh quickly rounded up twenty armed braves. They split into two groups and headed out of the bay in separate canoes. At the entrance to the open sea, Tatoosh's canoe headed west while the other headed east.

THE MORNING SUN was high in the sky before Nathan had decided what to do. It had taken him an hour to accept that he was the only survivor of the storm; it had taken another hour to decide what he should do. It hadn't been an easy decision.

The young Philadelphian knew he had two choices: to return to Neah Bay and risk torture or death at the hands of the angry villagers or to follow the coast west in the hope of finding a friendly tribe who would give him food and shelter. While the second option was tempting, he realized its success would depend on reaching a village before he succumbed to starvation or exposure, or both. As he had no idea how close the nearest village was to the west, he dismissed that option.

So it was with some trepidation he headed east.

Nathan estimated he'd been walking a couple of hours when he had to rest. He literally stumbled across a small, sandy beach — one of the few on that stretch of coastline — and within minutes had fallen asleep.

The next thing he knew was rough hands were shaking him awake.

Nathan opened his eyes to see half a dozen angry Makah braves standing over him, weapons raised. He recognized one or two of them. Their ranks parted and the chief's son Tatoosh appeared in their midst.

Tatoosh looked down at Nathan. A young brave next to him raised his tomahawk and prepared to deliver a death blow to the captive. Tatoosh grabbed the brave's arm before he could lower the tomahawk. "Let the White-Eye live," he said.

To Nathan's great relief, the young brave reluctantly lowered his tomahawk.

Tatoosh ordered the others to bundle their captive into the canoe. This they did without ceremony, throwing Nathan into the stern of the craft.

As he was paddled back toward Neah Bay, Nathan wondered what fate awaited him.

CHAPTER 8

Kensington, England, 1841

DRAKE SENIOR LEARNED OF SUSANNAH'S plans to elope two weeks after his confrontation with her. The news came courtesy of an observant parishioner who had overheard Susannah and Blake Dugan discussing their plans whilst picnicking at nearby Hyde Park just the previous day.

The clergyman immediately made his way on foot to the Kensington boarding house, which was Blake's last known residence. There, the proprietor informed him the apprentice chimneysweep and would-be poet had moved to another establishment. Conveniently for the young lovers, it was closer to the rectory.

On arriving at the second boarding house, Drake Senior found Blake was indeed in residence there. "Tell the young man I wish to talk to him," the clergyman advised the boarding house proprietor.

"Certainly, Reverend," the proprietor said, respectfully eyeing Drake Senior's telltale clergyman's collar before hurrying upstairs. The proprietor returned almost immediately and ushered Drake Senior upstairs to Blake's first floor room.

The young man did his best to hide his shock at seeing Susannah's father, but failed miserably. Speechless, he stepped aside and allowed his visitor to enter.

Inside a room scarcely big enough to swing a cat, Drake Senior ignored Blake as he studied numerous sheets of paper that lay strewn over the unmade bed and on top of a bedside table. Finished and unfinished poems, and other musings, were scrawled over them.

Drake Senior picked up one of the sheets and read it. "Shakespeare?" he enquired at length without looking up.

"No sir, I wrote that."

The older man concealed his surprise. After a few moments of silence, Drake Senior put his hand into his coat pocket and pulled out an envelope, which he handed to Blake.

"What's this?" Blake asked.

"Open it and see."

Blake tore open the envelope and was surprised to find it contained a bank note. His eyes opened wide as he read the amount.

"You will see it's made out to you," Drake Senior said.

Staring at the bank note, Blake was under no illusions what it was for. It was a trade-off: he was being asked to choose between the bank note and Susannah.

"You can see it is not an inconsiderable sum of money," Drake Senior pointed out. "It's yours if you leave here and never contact my daughter again."

The young man couldn't tear his eyes from the note. The handwritten amount of *Two Hundred & Fifty Pounds Sterling* had a hypnotic effect on him. It represented a small fortune.

As Blake stared at the figure, a myriad of conflicting thoughts collided in his head. He loved Susannah and would die for her, but he had only ever known hard times and yearned to rise above his lowly station. This money would change his life. It would enable him to travel the world and pursue his love of poetry; it would allow him to bring comfort to his dying mother; most of all, it would enable him to escape his poverty-stricken past and make a new life for himself.

Blake's eyes filled with tears as he looked up from the bank note. Without a word, he folded it and placed it inside his shirt pocket.

Drake Senior hid the relief that he felt course through him. He eyeballed his opposite. "I have your word?" he asked.

Blake nodded solemnly. The two shook hands. Drake Senior didn't immediately release the younger man's hand. He applied none-too-gentle pressure until Blake winced.

The clergyman's eyes bore into Blake's. "You understand you must leave immediately and never go near my daughter again?"

Defeated, Blake nodded once more.

Drake Senior slowly released the other's hand. "If you break your word, be aware the wrath of God will be visited upon you." These final words were spoken softly, but the malice behind them was crystal clear to Blake.

Drake Senior departed, leaving the young man alone with his thoughts.

Blake sat down and proceeded to pen the most difficult prose he'd ever attempted to write. It was a goodbye letter to Susannah. He told her he would have left by the time she received it. Blake lied, saying he had never loved her and his departing was for the best. The young man made no mention of his private arrangement with Susannah's father.

LATER, AT A pre-arranged meeting place near the rectory, Blake secretly observed Susannah from behind a hedge. She was pacing up and down, waiting for him.

Blake spied an urchin walking along a nearby lane and hurried to intercept him. "Do you want to earn five pence, son?"

The urchin nodded enthusiastically. Blake opened his closed fist to reveal he was holding five pennies. The boy's eyes widened at the sight of the shiny coins.

"They're yours if you deliver this note to that lady," Blake said, handing the urchin the letter he'd written and pointing toward Susannah who could just be seen through the hedge.

The lad took the letter from him, squeezed through the hedge and ran up to Susannah. Blake watched from his hiding place as Susannah took the letter from the urchin and proceeded to read it. She suddenly began sobbing and had to place her hand on the boy's shoulder to steady herself.

Susannah's distress was like cold steel through Blake's heart. Unable to witness her pain any longer, he ran back to his boarding house where he collected his pre-packed bags and headed into central London.

Blake remained true to his word and never contacted Susannah again. However, fate had as much to do with that as any good intentions on his part.

Despite his newfound fortune, the young man still gave his chimneysweep employer the required fortnight's notice. He was well on the way to completing that notice when he was killed in an accident at a foundry in the East End.

It was by chance that a busybody Kensington parishioner spotted the death notice in *The Times* newspaper a few days later. Aware of the relationship that had existed between Blake and Susannah, the parishioner conveyed the news to Drake Senior.

The clergyman wrestled over whether or not to pass the sad news on to his daughter. In the end, after much prayer and internal debate, he relented and advised Susannah of Blake's passing.

Susannah took the news harder than he'd expected. Coming on top of the passing of her mother, the loss of Blake was a double blow.

ANY THOUGHTS DRAKE Senior may have had that Susannah's first love was more a case of girlish infatuation than true love were dispelled when she plunged into grief mode and didn't come out of it for six months or more.

If the loss of loved-ones had any purpose, it served to teach Susannah how short life could be and how each and every day should be treasured.

Susannah never did learn of the secret agreement reached between Drake Senior and Blake. It was a secret her father would take with him to the grave.

CHAPTER 9

<hr>

North Atlantic Ocean, 1838

JACK AND TWO HUNDRED OTHER convicted men wondered if they'd survive as their floating prison, a brig named *The Journeyman,* pitched violently in heavy seas. Many of them were too ill to care. Some had developed serious health problems; others, like Jack, were just plain seasick.

A month out from England, there was still another three months' sailing ahead before they would reach their destination, the distant Colony of New South Wales at the bottom of the world where they would serve their time doing hard labor.

The convicts had already been incarcerated for three months in the brig's hold when she'd set sail from the London docks. Friends and loved-ones, including Jack's mother and siblings, had been at the docks to wave them off, but they hadn't seen them for the convicts had been permanently confined below deck.

The Journeyman was one of a convoy of seven vessels undertaking the arduous voyage. The vessels had all been converted for the purpose of transporting felons to serve time in the notorious penal institutions of the new colony that would one day be known as Australia.

The need for such institutions in far-off places was seen by some as an indictment on Britain. Crime was now so rampant at home that Britain's jails were overflowing. Petty crime was so prevalent that a gentleman couldn't venture outside after dark without fear of being mugged; and murders, rapes and other serious crimes were increasing by the day.

Hangings had become an everyday occurrence—so much so that the populace was now protesting against the increasing use of the death penalty. People were being hung for offences as minor as stealing half a crown—ostensibly to deter them from committing crimes, but in reality to help ease the problem of overflowing jails.

Afraid of a backlash, the authorities knew they had to come up with another solution. Setting up penal institutions in New South Wales and elsewhere around the world was seen as the best option.

Skeptics questioned the purpose behind the penal institutions of New South Wales. They claimed the real purpose behind them was to help develop the new colony by feeding in a never-ending supply of able-bodied men and women. As a result, those who would normally be hanged for committing often minor offences were now being shipped off to the bottom of the world. In theory, they could return to England after serving out their sentences. In practice, few ever would.

Aboard *The Journeyman*, conditions below deck were so bad some ten felons had died just waiting for the ship to leave dock. Chained together, the prisoners lay shoulder-to-shoulder on wooden bunks. When it rained, the rain poured through the open portholes, drenching the inmates, and in rough seas, seawater also poured in, adding to their misery. It was no surprise that most of the deaths so far had been from pneumonia. Starvation had contributed to the deaths of two others and one man had died after a savage beating at the hands of over-zealous guards.

Sea-sickness and diarrhea were rife. Jack and the others lay on a permanent bed of vomit, urine and shit. In the heavy

Atlantic swells, the vessel pitched violently, causing felons and sailors alike to continuously fear for their safety. All were very aware of the numbers of Her Majesty's vessels that sank or otherwise foundered en route to the various far-flung British colonies around the globe.

As the convoy of convict ships sailed down Africa's west coast, an especially violent storm resulted in the loss of two of the seven vessels. During the storm, *The Journeyman* was separated from the others. She continued to New South Wales alone, her master and crew unaware whether any of the other vessels in the convoy had survived the storm.

HALF-WAY TO New South Wales, conditions below deck had deteriorated to the point where the prisoners' numbers had dropped by nearly a third—to one hundred-and-forty-one. While accustomed to losses on these voyages Down Under, the ship's master knew he'd be blamed if there were too many more deaths. He insisted the ship's designated surgeon lay off the booze and conduct two daily rounds of the prisoners instead of one.

The surgeon, a drunkard who in civilian life also doubled as a barber—and not a very good one by all accounts—reluctantly inspected the felons twice daily. His inspections were perfunctory to say the least. He prescribed extra bread and water rations for those who appeared most likely to die of starvation, and an hour on deck each day for those suffering from dysentery or sea sickness.

Armed marines watched over any felon permitted on deck. They were more concerned about preventing their charges from throwing themselves overboard than causing harm to others. So desperate were some prisoners to escape their hellish situation that several tried to dive overboard. That only one would succeed on this particular voyage would be a tribute to the alertness of the marines guarding them.

Day and night, the bodies of dead prisoners were removed

from the hold, carried above deck and thrown overboard without so much as a word let alone a prayer. The surgeon always checked the bodies first to confirm they were in fact lifeless. Sometimes, the doomed men were ill, not dead. And sometimes they were feigning death. Oftentimes, the surgeon was so drunk, he failed to detect a pulse, and a live prisoner was consigned to a watery grave.

Jack survived by willing himself to overlook the pain and discomfort of life below deck. The twenty-two-year-old Cockney dreamed of his mother and the home-cooked meals she was famous for; he thought of his brothers and sister; most of all, he thought of his many female friends and the intimate moments he'd shared with each of them. Just thinking of his latest love interest — the local butcher's wife — was enough to transport him to another place.

While others around him died or fell ill, Jack remained staunch and more determined than ever to survive.

⚬⚬⚬

THE JOURNEYMAN WAS the last of the convoy's surviving convict ships to arrive at the thriving port settlement of Sydney Town, in New South Wales. Of the seven ships that departed England, only five had made it; of the fourteen hundred prisoners aboard those seven ships, only seven hundred and eleven had survived.

Jack was one of the survivors. Like the other prisoners, he was weak, skinny, unshaven and almost unrecognizable as he filed down the gangplank and onto the wharf at Sydney Town. A sorry-looking lot, the new arrivals were chained together and shackled in leg irons for good measure. Escape, for the moment, was clearly not an option.

The prisoners squinted to protect their eyes from the sudden glare of daylight. Despite the glare, the hot, mid-morning sun was a welcome relief to men who had spent seven months in a ship's hold. Some were unable to walk, so weak were they, and had to be supported by their fellow prisoners.

Jack took in his surroundings. He observed the red-coated British soldiers and armed guards who made up the official reception party on the wharf. They formed a barrier between the new arrivals and a large gathering of curious onlookers for whom the arrival of convict ships was always a source of entertainment and a welcome break from everyday life in the colony.

"Welcome to paradise!" a beefy soldier yelled by way of greeting to the new arrivals.

This caused some mirth among the soldier's comrades.

More like a sunburnt hell-hole, Jack thought as he surveyed the sun-baked land that was now home to him and the others. First impressions were this was an inhospitable land. Jack and his fellow prisoners would soon find out just how inhospitable it could be.

A stone came flying through the air and struck a felon standing two places ahead of Jack in the line. It had been thrown by a young laborer.

"Send the sorry-arses home!" the laborer shouted in a distinctive Liverpudlean accent.

"Aye, send the bastards home!" a sailor shouted in an equally distinctive Welsh accent.

Further abuse was hurled at the convicts. It came from the onlookers whose ranks comprised residents and seamen of various nationalities—many of them already drunk on rum even though it was not yet noon. The prisoners didn't know it, but rum was fast becoming a major currency of the new colony, so sought-after was it. Drunkenness was already a problem in all strata of the colony's white population at least. Later, it would all but decimate the native population.

When the last of *The Journeyman's* prisoners had disembarked, a distinguished-looking Army officer addressed them. "My name is Captain Arthur Shorthall," he announced pompously. "You apologies for men are to be immediately dispatched to various parts of New South Wales where you'll be consigned to certain duties for the duration of your stay." Captain Shorthall then read out a lengthy list of rules. He concluded, "The slightest infringement of any of these rules will result in a flogging or worse."

From within the prisoners' ranks, a rebellious Irishman shouted, "Bugger the English and bugger everyting dey stand fer!"

Captain Shorthall, already red from the sun, was so angered he turned several shades of crimson. "Who was that?" he bellowed.

A sergeant identified the Irishman, unshackled him from his companions and frog-marched him over to the captain. Keen to make an early example of troublemakers, Shorthall ordered that the Irishman receive an immediate flogging as punishment.

Two soldiers promptly tore the shirt off the man and tied him to a whipping post conveniently positioned for such occasions. Another soldier stepped forward holding that most feared of all whips, a cat-o'-nine-tails — feared because each of its nine leather strands contained knots designed to strip away the flesh from a man's back. It was common knowledge that after a hundred lashes, the victim's flesh was usually so shredded that his bones were exposed. Punishments of two to three hundred lashes in the new colony were not uncommon. Being flogged to death wasn't unheard of either.

"Twenty lashes," Captain Shorthall ordered.

The soldier with the whip removed his red jacket, rolled up his sleeves and, at a nod from the captain, proceeded to dispense justice. Each swing of the whip was accompanied by a mighty crack as it struck the Irishman's exposed back.

Even though this was the first time Jack and most of the other prisoners had witnessed a flogging, they were all familiar with the sound. Floggings had been a regular occurrence on board *The Journeyman* for sailors who got out of line, and the sounds had carried to those incarcerated below deck.

After twenty lashes, the Irishman asked, "So when does me punishment begin?"

This prompted laughter from the convicts' ranks.

Captain Shorthall became so angry he looked like he was ready to have a coronary. "Another twenty lashes!" he ordered.

As the additional lashes were delivered, the victim's back became raw and streaked with blood. Jack prayed the Irishman would hold his tongue. Thankfully, he did. After the full punishment had been delivered, the Irishman was untied and frog-marched back to the prisoners' ranks. Jack noted he looked subdued now and was clearly in pain.

"Anyone else want to test my patience?" Captain Shorthall asked. The prisoners remained silent. "Load them up!" the captain ordered.

Soldiers supervised the loading of prisoners onto horse-drawn carts lined up nearby. Jack soon learned that he and some fifty others had been consigned to a penal center at Parramatta, some fifteen miles inland. They were loaded on ten to a cart. As soon as the carts were full, they set off, escorted by armed soldiers on horseback.

As the small caravan of horse-drawn carts followed the well-worn track from Sydney Town to Parramatta, Jack and the others didn't realize it, but many of them would spend the duration of their sentence converting this very track into a road — a hellish task that would cost many lives.

CHAPTER 10

———⊙∘⊙———

Makah Nation, West Coast, North America, 1838

SINCE HIS SURVIVAL OF THE shipwreck and his subsequent capture by the Makah a fortnight earlier, Nathan had been relegated to living as a slave, performing all sorts of mundane chores ranging from collecting shellfish and firewood to repairing his new masters' lodges and anything else that needed fixing.

All but one of his fellow slaves were from neighboring mainland tribes. The odd one out was a bald-headed Mowachaht, appropriately named *Baldy,* from nearby Vancouver Island.

Considered different to the other slaves, Nathan and Baldy formed an unlikely alliance, backing each other up when the others picked on either one as they were prone to doing.

Why his captors had spared him, the young Philadelphian couldn't even begin to guess. *God knows they had every reason to kill me.* What he didn't know was that Tatoosh had made a case to his father for sparing him. He'd argued persuasively that Nathan would be useful teaching them the ways of the White-Eye and acting as interpreter with European traders when the need arose.

Against his better judgment—and contrary to the wishes of

69

the villagers who lusted for revenge—Elswa had relented.

Nathan constantly relived in his mind the events that had brought him here—the ill-fated trading expedition to Neah Bay, the escape that followed and the shipwreck that claimed the lives of his uncle and all his crewmates.

After that fateful day at the village, the head of the drunken rigger who assaulted the Makah headman had been left hanging from one of the village totem poles, serving as a constant reminder of the violence that had occurred. Nathan had thrown up at the grotesque sight—a sight that would be with him for the remainder of his days.

The rigger's head had remained recognizable until the bald-headed eagles and other birds of prey picked it clean of flesh. That had only taken a few days.

Nathan had learned the skull would soon be consigned to a nearby cave that housed the countless skulls of former enemies. He prayed that would happen sooner rather than later as he just wanted to forget the recent ghastly events.

The young Philadelphian lived in hope *Intrepid's* owners, or someone at least, would start searching for the missing vessel as soon as it was realized she was missing. Realistically, that wouldn't be for another month or two, so he was resigned to surviving as best he could until then. *One day at a time, Nate,* he told himself. *One day at a time.*

LIFE AS A slave of the Makah was a trial for the hardiest and most resilient of slaves. For Nathan it was considerably harder. As the only white at Neah Bay, he was looked down on by slaves and villagers alike, and often treated with disdain.

He'd quickly discovered there was a pecking order amongst the slaves. The biggest and toughest—and those with the most allies—had first choice of discarded clothing and food leftovers the villagers sometimes threw their way. And they had first pick of the female slaves if they were so inclined, as most were.

The female slaves, who lived in separate lodgings, were outnumbered three-to-one by the males. Consequently, they were in constant demand, and a major cause of infighting amongst the male slaves.

Nathan's lot changed for the better one fine day. He'd had his eye on a new arrival at the village—a shapely young maiden who had been captured and enslaved following a raid on the inland village that was once her home. She was one of a dozen slaves the Makah had brought back to Neah Bay after that raid.

The young maiden had caught Nathan's eye immediately. He found her very sexy and instantly desired her. So, too, did a number of his fellow slaves.

It came to a head during a work party which saw a number of male and female slaves working together, gathering berries for a potlatch their Makah masters were planning. They were watched over by two bored Makah braves who filled in time by chatting about their latest sexual conquests.

With some clever maneuvering, Nathan found himself working alongside the young maiden. *What a goddess!* He caught her eye and smiled. She returned his smile and he felt his pulse race. "Hello," he stammered in English. He inwardly cursed that he hadn't even learnt how to say *hello* in the native tongue.

The young maiden responded with something unintelligible to Nathan's ear, but she said it with a smile and he imagined she was also saying *hello*.

It was that moment that Sasqua, the self-proclaimed leader of the slaves, chose to interpose himself between the two youngsters. A big, raw-boned bully who stood even taller than Nathan, Sasqua elbowed the white aside and leered all over the young maiden who shrank from him as he gazed at her with undisguised lust.

By now all the slaves were watching. Even the two Makah

braves had stopped chatting to see what happened next.

Sasqua wasn't concerned about the two lookouts. They were only there to ensure the slaves didn't try to escape. Besides, the slave boss looked after them on occasion, supplying them with the prettiest of the female slaves, and they were only too happy to look after him. It was a secret arrangement that suited both parties.

Nathan knew he needed to assert himself if he was ever to gain the respect of his fellow slaves. He'd been looking for the right moment and sensed this was it. *It's now or never.* Looking around, he caught the eye of his ally Baldy, the bald Mowachaht slave. Baldy nodded almost imperceptibly. It seemed the Mowachaht had anticipated what Nathan was planning and was indicating he was ready to back him up.

Sasqua began fondling the young maiden and wasn't expecting what happened next. Nathan caught him with a king hit that landed just below the big man's right ear, felling him. The slave boss looked up, stunned, as the young white rained punches down on him. Somehow, Sasqua managed to roll away and scramble to his feet.

The other slaves immediately crowded around the pair as they went at each other hammer and tongs. Both Makah braves joined the spectators, keen to see the slave boss deal to the White-Eye. To everyone's surprise, Nathan was giving as good as he got.

One of Sasqua's henchmen ran forward to assist his boss, but was tripped up by Baldy who had been waiting for just such an eventuality. Baldy kicked the slave full in the face, almost knocking him out and leaving him minus several front teeth. This served as a warning to the other slaves not to intervene.

Nathan knew he needed to finish Sasqua quickly if he was to prevail. He was keeping the bigger man at bay by firing out jabs like the accomplished boxer he was, but he knew he needed a knockout.

Sasqua, and indeed all those watching, seemed mesmerized by Nathan's demonstration of the pugilistic arts. Boxing was foreign to them. Like all the natives of the Northwest, they resorted to wrestling when fighting unarmed. Fighting with fists apparently hadn't occurred to them.

By now Sasqua had taken so many punches, his face was black and blue. He had two black eyes, a split lip and a nasty cut on his forehead. With every blow, his anger and hatred toward the White-Eye intensified. He threw himself at Nathan, grabbed him in a bear hug and lifted him up off the ground.

Nathan felt as though his ribs were breaking as Sasqua increased the pressure. His vision blurred and he felt himself losing consciousness. *Do something!* He brought his head down hard against the bridge of his opponent's nose, breaking it. Sasqua yelped in agony and released his grip on Nathan long enough for him to wriggle free. Blood now flowed freely from Sasqua's broken nose, which had swollen to twice its normal size.

Breathing hard, the two antagonists began circling each other, each looking for an opening. By now the spectators were urging both fighters on. They seemed divided in their support. Nearly half those watching were supporting Nathan. The gutsy white slave was giving the slave boss a run for his money.

Nathan could feel his energy slipping away. The bear hug had damaged his ribs, his lungs felt as though they were on fire and he feared he couldn't last much longer.

It was now the boxing lessons his father had given him came flooding back. Johnson Senior had been a bare knuckle fighter in his day and had passed on his skills to Nathan. All too often, those skills had been passed on in the course of a beating, but that was irrelevant at this point in time. Nathan could hear his father's voice. *Feint with the left then bring down the hammer.* Johnson Senior always referred to his right hand as *the hammer.* It was something he'd used in anger on Nathan

73

more than once.

Despite the animosity Nathan felt toward his father, he decided it was time to take his advice. *Feint with the left then bring down the hammer.* He fired out two quick jabs. Both landed flush on Sasqua's broken nose, causing the big man to blink back tears of pain.

Sasqua shaped up to throw himself at Nathan. He knew if he could just grab the young white once more, he could crush the life out of him.

Nathan feinted with his left hand. As Sasqua tried to avoid the phantom punch, he didn't see the big right hand that came from nowhere and landed flush on the jaw. The slave boss was out to it before he even hit the ground.

Seconds later, Nathan found himself surrounded by his fellow slaves. They were laughing and jostling as they congratulated him. Even Sasqua's allies joined in. It seemed Nathan had earned the respect of the slaves at least.

The young man looked around for Baldy. He owed him one. Baldy was standing a little to one side. The two stared at each other and nodded. Each had done well that day and they knew it.

Then Nathan looked for the maiden who had caught his eye. Finally, he saw her. They smiled knowingly at each other.

CHAPTER 11

———⊰◦◉◦⊱———

Kensington, England, 1847

SUSANNAH, NOW TWENTY-ONE, SAT talking to her father in his rectory in Kensington. He'd summoned her to discuss something he said had been on his mind for some time.

As they talked, Drake Senior studied his daughter's face. *She's more beautiful than ever,* he decided. The clergyman never tired of Susannah's company. She reminded him so much of his dear departed Jeanette.

Since his wife had passed away nine years earlier, Drake Senior had watched with pride as Susannah developed into womanhood. His parishioners loved her. So, too, did the young children she'd been teaching at Kensington Public School since securing a position there as a teacher a year earlier.

Apart from her dalliance with would-be poet Blake Dugan, Susannah had never given him any cause for concern. She'd been a loving daughter and friend, and her presence had helped fill the void left by his wife's passing.

After Blake's shock death, Susannah had moped about, pining for her lost love. Her school marks suffered and teachers commented she seemed to have lost her old spark. Time rectified that, as Drake Senior hoped it would. A progressive young female teacher—the first woman to teach at Susannah's school—took the clergyman's daughter in hand

and inspired her to apply herself to her studies.

Looking back on that now, Drake Senior realized he had the teacher to thank for inspiring his daughter to stop moping around and to aspire to do something with her life.

Beyond devoting herself to her chosen profession, Susannah helped her father with parish duties, sang in the church choir and enjoyed the companionship of a large number of friends around her own age. *A delightful, well-rounded young lady,* one of Drake Senior's parishioners had recently told him—and he couldn't agree more.

"Anyway," Susannah said, interrupting her father's thoughts, "what was it you wished to speak to me about, papa?"

Clutching his ever-present bible, the clergyman marshaled his thoughts and looked sternly at his daughter. "You know I have been called by God to spread his word?" It was more a statement than a question.

Susannah nodded. "Yes, papa, and I know your parishioners respect the work you are doing here." The young woman sensed her father wasn't referring to the work he was doing in the parish. She was well aware he was a long-time supporter of the London Missionary Society and had long held ambitions to do the Lord's work abroad. However, she wasn't sure she approved and so wasn't going to make it easy for him.

Drake Senior continued, "Well, he has spoken to me and I now know what I must do."

Susannah waited expectantly.

Drake Senior announced, "He has called me to spread his word to the heathens of Fiji."

Susannah was shocked. "But papa, they are cannibals in Fiji."

Drake Senior smiled patiently. "That they are, my dear. However, the missionaries of our church are having some success in converting those same cannibals to Christianity."

The clergyman went on to tell Susannah about the Wesley Methodist Mission at Momi Bay, on Fiji's main island of Viti Levu. He talked with such passion about the missionaries' successes there that Susannah could see his mind was already made up.

As Drake Senior spoke, Susannah slowly came round to the idea of moving to warmer climes—even if that meant living among cannibals. She suddenly liked the prospect of waking up to blue skies and a tropical sun. The gray dome that seemed to permanently cover England for much of the year was beginning to get to her. *I do need a change of scene,* she admitted to herself.

Knowing Drake Senior never changed his mind once he'd decided on a course of action, Susannah interrupted him, saying, "Of course you have my full support, papa."

A relieved Drake Senior smiled.

Susannah added hurriedly, "On one condition."

Her father's smile evaporated.

"That I accompany you to Fiji," Susannah said.

"That's out of the question," Drake Senior responded. "I doubt the London Missionary Society would allow it. Besides, Fiji is no place for a woman."

"Papa, you said yourself the Smiths have been stationed at the Momi Bay mission without incident for the past two years."

Drake Senior couldn't deny that.

Susannah continued, "If the good Lord is watching over me, as I'm sure he is, then I will have nothing to fear going to Fiji."

Over the next five minutes, Susannah proceeded to wear her father down, putting up numerous incontestable reasons why she should accompany him.

"Alright!" Drake Senior said, raising his hands in mock surrender. "I can see you are never going to stop pestering me.

So, young lady, I shall save myself the trouble and relent now."

Susannah laughed delightedly and threw her arms around her father, kissing him on the cheek. "Oh, thank you, daddy!"

Drake Senior smiled. He was secretly thrilled Susannah wanted to accompany him. He'd dreaded the thought of leaving her behind. The proud father privately gave thanks to God for giving him such a fine daughter.

LATER, IN THE privacy of her bedroom, Susannah admitted to herself there was another reason she was keen to accompany her father to Fiji: she wanted to leave England to help her forget her former beau, Blake Dugan. Although six years had elapsed since the young man had been killed, Susannah hadn't forgotten him. She'd had several ardent suitors since, but Blake — or his memory at least — remained the love of her life.

Susannah realized she needed to move on if she was to live a normal life. *Fiji will be an adventure!* She suddenly felt genuinely excited about her forthcoming journey to the South Pacific.

CHAPTER 12

New South Wales, 1838

THE CARAVAN OF HORSES AND horse-drawn carts left trails of dust as it negotiated the fifteen miles between Sydney Town and the penal settlement at Parramatta—and the sun beat down relentlessly on prisoners and soldiers alike. Blue sky disappeared behind bush-covered hills far to the west. In the shimmering heat, a local phenomenon gave the hills a bluish appearance. In between the hills and the caravan, the dry earth was dotted with towering, tinder-dry eucalyptus trees—locally referred to as *gum trees.*

For the soldiers who had acclimatized to life in the colony it was just another day; for the prisoners who had survived the nightmare voyage from Britain it was hell. Several prisoners fainted in the heat and all suffered varying degrees of sunstroke. Their military escorts showed no concern for the plight of their charges.

Taking in his new surroundings, Jack told himself he wouldn't mind a penny for every gum tree he could see. *I'd be a wealthy man indeed.* Kangaroos drinking by a billabong, or freshwater pool, caught his eye. Suddenly disturbed by the appearance of men and horses, the strange animals hopped away. One of the females had a joey, or baby, in her pouch.

Not a hundred paces from the caravan, a lone Aborigine stood as still as a statue. Naked except for a loin cloth, he carried a spear and spear-thrower. The latter instrument was used to help throw the spear further than anyone relying solely on their throwing arm could achieve. The native was covered in the white markings of his tribe. These contrasted with his black skin yet enabled him to blend in with his surroundings. He was almost invisible. Like others of his race, he was lean and sinewy. Jack guessed, rightly, that he could run all day and barely tire. Looking at his fellow prisoners, he noted none had seen the Aborigine.

"Hey!" a sharp-eyed corporal shouted, pointing at the native. "A black fellow!"

Next to him, a young soldier trained his musket on the native. Shooting Aborigines, while not officially sanctioned by the Army, was a favorite past-time of the soldiers. It helped relieve the boredom.

Jack looked on with interest as the Aborigine suddenly ran off and disappeared behind a gum tree before the soldier could fire. This prompted jeers from the other soldiers. Annoyed, the young soldier galloped over to the tree where the Aborigine was last seen. To his astonishment, the native had disappeared. The soldier circled the tree twice to confirm his quarry was not there. He was mystified because the nearest cover was a good fifty paces from the tree. Finally, he gave up and rode back to rejoin the convoy where he received more ribbing from his comrades.

Jack had heard the natives of the colony had mystical qualities. Now, he'd seen it for himself. Looking back, he suddenly saw the Aborigine reappear from behind another tree. How he'd traveled unseen from one tree to the other, Jack couldn't fathom.

THE PRISONERS WERE thirsty and sunburned by the time they reach the penal settlement of Parramatta. There, they found a pleasant surprise waiting: the settlement's convict population included a surprising number of women—a fact that drew lewd comments from a number of Jack's companions. To men who had been deprived of the company of women for so long, even the plainest female convict looked inviting.

Jack took note of one comely lass whose breasts stood out like melons even at a distance. *I think I'll be liking this place.* The young Cockney made a mental note to get to know the voluptuous young woman at the earliest opportunity.

Parramatta resembled a surprisingly normal town. Despite being a penal settlement, there were significant numbers of new settlers in evidence. Their numbers almost rivaled the numbers of convicts and soldiers. Among the settlers were merchants and businessmen who ran the various stores, taverns and brothels that appeared to be in plentiful supply.

Before disembarking from the carts, the new arrivals were issued with tin cups. They quickly assuaged their thirst, dipping the cups into buckets of drinking water which an Aboriginal waterboy carried around. On disembarking, the men received another pleasant surprise when they were addressed by Parramatta's senior Army officer—a man who by all accounts harbored at least a smidgeon of humanity in his heart.

"Gentlemen, I am Captain James Clarke," the officer announced in a middle class English accent. "On my authority, those of you who toe the line can serve your time here unshackled."

The prisoners murmured appreciatively.

Captain Clarke continued, "Leg irons are normally only used when convicts are assigned to duties outside Parramatta—such as working on the new road linking the settlement to Sydney Town." He then ordered soldiers to unshackle the new arrivals.

Looking around, Jack noted there were Army barracks and adjoining stables on the settlement's outskirts. Red Coats were everywhere. They seemed to outnumber the convicts. Commonsense told Jack that, unshackled or not, escape from

Parramatta would be short-lived. A man on foot would soon be chased down by soldiers on horseback — that is if the heat or the natives didn't get him first.

The new arrivals were immediately consigned to wooden barracks. After the ship's hold that had served as their most recent home, these were comparative luxury. Jack and the others enjoyed their first bath and shave in a long time then, after discarding their worn clothes, they donned special-issue prison clothes and lined up for their first square meal in six months. Again, after enduring starvation rations aboard ship, the slops they were served here tasted like food from one of London's finest restaurants.

The holiday was over before it began: although it was late in the day and despite their weak condition, the new arrivals were put to work immediately alongside long-serving convicts laboring on a farm that adjoined the settlement. They were split into three groups. One group cracked rocks using pick-axes while another carried the broken rocks to a nearby mound where the third group used the rocks to construct a stone wall.

Two armed guards watched over them on horseback. They were quick to use their riding whips on any man who lagged behind the others.

So hot was it the waterboy continuously dispensed drinking water to the convicts from a bucket. Each convict gulped down the life-saving fluid to help assuage his thirst.

Jack found himself working in the group constructing the wall. He quickly discovered he was working alongside convicts from all parts of Britain, and a few from elsewhere, too. There was even a black American. Some had been here, or in New South Wales at least, ten years or more. One grizzled, sunburned Scotsman called Scottie boasted he'd been here fifteen years.

"What was your crime?" Jack enquired.

"I stole a half-crown from my landlord, laddie," Scottie said.

"And you got fifteen years for that?"

Scottie chuckled. "No, I got three years for that . . . and another twelve for killing the bugger when he tried to take it back from me."

Scottie's long-serving companions laughed heartily even though they'd heard the same yarn many times before.

As Jack lifted yet another rock into position on the fence, he noticed a group of Aborigines spearing fish in the shallows of the nearby Parramatta River. He noted, too, that they succeeded at almost every attempt, so skilled were they. The pile of fresh fish next to them on the river bank was growing rapidly. Nearby, Aboriginal women stoked a campfire. Some nursed babies while older children played at their feet.

These particular Aborigines were of the Gameraigal tribe whose members were widely admired for their hunting, fishing and tracking skills. As Jack and the others would learn later, it was the latter skill that the British authorities had noted and made good use of: the Army's Aboriginal trackers at Parramatta were primarily Gameraigal.

<hr />

AS DUSK FELL, to the relief of the new arrivals in particular a foreman appeared and advised the convicts they could finish up for the day. The convicts were immediately escorted back to their barracks.

The new arrivals were pleasantly surprised to learn the convicts had the run of the settlement until a ship's bell rang later in the evening. The ringing of the bell, they were advised, would announce the start of a curfew for Parramatta's convict population.

"Any convict found to be still out and about after the bell rings a second time will be flogged," Scottie warned.

Most of the new arrivals were so spent they retired early to their barracks to catch up on much-needed sleep. Jack and a few other hardy fellows took the opportunity to explore the settlement.

While checking out the bars and brothels, Jack spied the comely lass with melon-like breasts who had caught his eye earlier. She was standing on a street corner and seemed to be waiting for someone. Jack wandered up to her and introduced himself. "Evening, Miss. I'm Jack Halliday."

The young woman looked him up and down. "And who da hell is Jack Halliday when he's in town?" she shot back at him. Her lilting accent announced her Irish heritage.

Momentarily taken aback, Jack smiled. "I'm a new guest of Her Majesty's."

The woman suddenly smiled and introduced herself. "I'm Mary O'Brien," she said. "Me friends call me Mary, but," she added with a twinkle in her eye, "ye can call me Miss O'Brien."

The ice broken, Jack said, "What are you doing so far from home, Miss O'Brien?" Try as he may, he couldn't take his eyes off her magnificent breasts.

Mary noted his interest and smiled mischievously. "If ye have a spare shilling, I can show ye what I do."

Jack realized Mary O'Brien was a prostitute. "I . . . I've just arrived," he stammered. "I'm afraid I have nuthin' to offer."

The young Cockney wasn't aware that boat-loads of female convicts had been shipped out to the colony and more would follow. The logic behind this was they were needed for reproduction—to increase the population of the fledgling colony. It was inevitable some, like Mary, would be forced into prostitution. That wasn't necessarily considered a bad thing: the availability of women for sex—even if it had to be paid for—was helping to keep the male convict population under control.

Mary looked him up and down a second time. She liked what she saw. "Tell ye what. The first one's on me." Laughing, she linked her arm with his and led him to a nearby brothel where it transpired she had use of a small room.

The young woman proved to be good at what she did and made Jack a very happy chap. Even if he'd paid her a shilling, he felt he'd have had his money's worth. After they made love, Mary explained how the settlement worked and what he could expect while he served out his time. Jack was especially interested to learn that, despite their lowly status in life, the convicts received a weekly wage. Although meager, it was enough to buy the occasional pint of rum or to buy the likes of Mary's skilled services.

"Next time I see ye, it'll cost ye," she promised him.

Chuckling, Jack said, "Aye and you're worth every penny." As he prepared to ravage her again, a bell rang out. Its chimes echoed throughout the settlement.

Mary literally threw Jack off her. "Ye must be off now," she ordered. "Ye'll be flogged if ye are not back in your barracks soon."

Jack pulled a face. "Not even a kiss goodnight, Miss O'Brien?"

"Get off with ye!" Laughing, Mary pushed him away.

Jack reluctantly retired to his barracks where he fell asleep almost immediately. A second bell announced the start of the curfew. The young Cockney didn't hear it.

THE CONVICTS WERE woken by the ringing of the same bell at dawn. The sun hadn't yet risen, but to Jack and the other new arrivals it seemed the bell had only just finished ringing the previous night — yet here it was already heralding the start of a new working day.

After downing something that resembled porridge in the convicts' mess, Jack found himself being fitted out in leg-irons and loaded onto a horse-drawn cart with nine other convicts. Half a dozen similarly laden carts joined them and they were soon bumping along the same track that had brought them to Parramatta the previous day. Ten armed guards accompanied the small caravan on horseback.

A couple of miles down the track, the carts stopped and the convicts were issued with shovels and pick-axes. The sun rose as they commenced breaking rocks for construction of the road. It was back-breaking labor, but nothing Jack's strong back couldn't take. The former smithy was already looking forward to his first pay day — and to his next liaison with Mary O'Brien.

CHAPTER 13

Makah Nation, West Coast, North America, 1839

AFTER A YEAR AS A slave of the Makah, Nathan's lot hadn't changed. He was still being treated as a worker ant, slaving from dawn until dusk every day, week in, week out for his masters. It was often back-breaking work and always monotonous.

Among the more unsavory tasks he'd been allotted was digging new latrines for the village, and filling them in when they were near to overflowing. Worse was transferring the manure content of those same latrines to the fields where he had to spread it as fertilizer amongst the crops. It was smelly, degrading work that always left him in a foul mood.

While the villagers sometimes went hungry, especially over the cold winter months, the slaves were always hungry. Those who weren't good at scavenging for the little spare food that was available faced the very real prospect of dying. That is if the cold didn't finish them off first. In that first year, five slaves died—three of starvation and two from exposure.

Although Nathan's lot hadn't changed, his appearance had changed out of sight. Now seventeen, he was fast becoming a man: he was another inch or two taller and his shoulders had broadened; his European clothing was now hanging from him in tatters. Fortunately, it was summertime, so it wasn't too cold. Having survived one bitter winter in this godforsaken place, the young white was prepared to put up with the relentless rain that fell over the region provided he didn't have to go through another winter.

Nathan's character had undergone a change too: gone was his previously open and trusting manner. Months of having to stand up for himself to survive the hardships of slavery had hardened him. He now had a look about him that said, *Don't cross me.*

The other slaves had certainly learned not to cross him since he'd dealt to Sasqua, the slave boss. Any further attempts to dominate him had resulted in swift retaliation. Slaves silly enough to test him quickly learnt the White-Eye had power in his fists. It was to Nathan's benefit the Northwest natives had never mastered the pugilistic arts, and he wasn't slow to use that to his advantage when required.

The young Philadelphian still lived in hope *Intrepid's* owners would be searching for their missing vessel and crew. He missed his old life back in Philadelphia. God knows, he even missed his two older sisters though he'd considered them a pain in the neck when he was living with them.

On this particular day, Nathan and half a dozen other slaves collected firewood in driving rain on the outskirts of the village. An armed brave kept watch over them. As always, Nathan carried out his tasks diligently and without fuss. He'd realized very early on his best chance for survival was to stay out of trouble with his Makah masters.

Elswa, the chief, suddenly appeared and motioned to Nathan to join him. "You come with me, Nathan Johnson," he ordered in his native tongue.

"Yes, great chief," Nathan answered in kind. Twelve months living, eating and sleeping with these people had at least given him a rudimentary understanding of the Makah language.

Nathan followed Elswa into a small lodge where he found

Tatoosh, the chief's oldest son, unfolding large sheets of canvass. The young white assumed the canvass had been acquired in the course of trading with the ships that once visited these waters. Those same ships had been conspicuous by their absence since *Intrepid's* visit.

The two youths nodded to each other briefly. Although they'd hardly exchanged a single word to date, there seemed to be a bond developing between them. The chief's son was intrigued by the white slave.

Elswa pointed to the canvass sheets. "You make sails," he ordered Nathan in English this time.

Without hesitating, Nathan took over from Tatoosh, laying out a sheet on the lodge's wooden floor. As he went to work, he wondered how the chief knew his white slave could make sails. Nathan immediately thought of the bald-headed Mowachaht slave. *Baldy!* He had recently confided in him that he'd been an apprentice sail-maker, and the slave had obviously passed that on. Nathan was aware the Mowachahts had a reputation for being gossipers and backstabbers. What he didn't know was that among the Mowachahts, the Makah had a similar reputation.

Elswa and his son looked on as the young white expertly used a needle made from a fine fishbone to fashion a sail that would be fitted to one of the Makah's catamaran-like canoes. The chief nodded to himself. He'd long been satisfied his son's decision to spare Nathan's life was the right one. The slave had proven his worth many times over. He was a willing worker and skilled, too. Elswa and Tatoosh walked off, leaving him alone.

As Nathan worked, he dreamed of his childhood at the Johnson family home in Philadelphia. While there were some bad memories, there were some good ones, too. Like the friends he'd made and the adventures they had. He fondly remembered his father's study and its musty smell, its countless books and the large world map he used to study for hours on end when Johnson Senior was at sea. How he'd love to be transported back there now.

Nathan's daydreaming was shattered by the boom of a musket being discharged outside the lodge. A moment's silence was followed by more musket-fire, screams and shouts of alarm. Fierce war cries sent chills down Nathan's spine. The young man jumped up and went to the open doorway to investigate. He immediately saw the village was under attack from a Mowachaht raiding party.

Some forty Mowachahts had canoed across from Vancouver Island during the night, hidden their canoes and chosen this moment to attack. Although fewer in number, the war-painted Mowachahts had surprise on their side and many bore muskets. They cut down a dozen or more Makah before the unprepared braves could reach their weapons. Women and children unlucky enough to be in the way were shot or clubbed indiscriminately.

A tall Mowachaht warrior noticed Nathan and raised his musket toward him. Nathan saw the danger and retreated inside the lodge. The warrior came after him. Nathan looked around desperately for a weapon. Finding none, he climbed up into the rafters just above the open doorway and waited, heart pounding. When the warrior burst in, Nathan dropped down onto him. The two fell to the dirt floor, wrestling for possession of the musket.

Sensing he was about to be overpowered by the stronger man, Nathan fumbled for the hunting knife the warrior carried in a sheath on his hip. His fingers closed around the knife and he pulled it out. The warrior sensed the danger too late and Nathan plunged the knife's blade into his attacker's chest. The Mowachaht struggled in vain as Nathan pressed home his advantage and worked the blade deeper into the other's chest. *Die, damn you!* Finally, the warrior's eyes clouded over and he ceased his struggles.

Gasping for breath and shaking violently, Nathan

scrambled to his feet. The shock of killing his first man was too much for him and he dry-retched. Then he noticed he was covered in his assailant's blood. That was the final straw. He doubled over again and this time spewed his guts out.

Outside, the sounds of conflict continued. Nathan pulled himself together. He picked up the dead warrior's musket and cautiously poked his head out the door. The Mowachaht invaders seem to be gaining the upper hand. Makah dead and wounded lay strewn in and around the lodges, many of which were now on fire.

Nathan saw Elswa and Tatoosh in deadly hand-to-hand combat outside the chief's lodge. They were desperately trying to prevent five Mowachahts from entering the lodge where Nathan knew Elswa's wives and extended family would be hiding. Without a thought for his own safety, he sprinted to assist the pair. He arrived just as Elswa was clubbed to the ground. As the chief's assailant raised his club to deliver the fatal blow, Nathan shot him dead. Then, using his musket as a club, he helped Tatoosh fight off the other Mowachahts.

The wounded Elswa could only watch as his son and the white slave fought for their lives. Slipping and sliding in the mud, the youths fought with the fury of men possessed. Wielding a tomahawk in each hand, Tatoosh decapitated one Mowachaht then a moment later, with a swing of the other tomahawk, split the skull of another in two.

Nathan clubbed a Mowachaht headman to the ground. He picked up the headman's fallen musket and used it to shoot another attacker who was about to shoot him. Meanwhile, Tatoosh threw one of his tomahawks at a fleeing warrior. Its blade lodged squarely in the warrior's back, felling him.

The youths' actions served to inspire the villagers, and the tide started to turn as the Makah rallied their defenses. Mowachaht casualties mounted. Finally, the attackers were put to flight. Many were shot down by arrow or musket ball as they tried to flee.

As custom dictated, wounded and dead Mowachahts alike were decapitated, their heads thrown into a pile. Later, they'd be displayed at vantage points around the village for all to see.

While the villagers celebrated their victory, Nathan and Tatoosh helped the wounded Elswa to his feet and escorted him into his lodge. Safely inside, the chief was immediately besieged by his wives who fussed around him, tending his wounds. Fortunately, they were only superficial, though Elswa was content to let his wives continue to fuss over him in the belief his wounds were grave—for the moment at least. He enjoyed their attentions.

Neither the chief nor his son acknowledged Nathan's life-saving actions at the time. However, in an emotion-charged ceremony in the village longhouse that night, Nathan was adopted into the chief's extended family in recognition of his bravery. No longer a slave, he would now reside in Elswa's lodge as an honorary member of the family and therefore, by default, an honorary member of the tribe.

After the ceremony, Tatoosh approached Nathan. "You come," he said, indicating the former slave should follow him. The chief's son led Nathan out of the longhouse and into the surrounding forest. They walked in silence for several minutes.

On reaching a grassy clearing, Tatoosh stopped and turned to face his companion. Nathan tensed when he noticed the brave had drawn his hunting knife. Its wicked blade glinted in the moonlight. Ignoring Nathan's hesitation, Tatoosh used the knife to make a deep insertion in the palm of his own hand. He then motioned to Nathan to hold his hand out, palm facing upwards. Nathan complied and Tatoosh performed the same operation on the young white's hand.

After returning his knife to its sheath, Tatoosh clasped Nathan's bloodied hand in his. He looked gravely into his opposite's eyes. "Tatoosh, son of Elswa, and Nathan, son of Johnson, now blood brothers," he murmured in his native tongue. He then looked at Nathan expectantly.

Nathan realized Tatoosh was waiting for him to respond in kind. So he did, repeating the other's words in the language of the Makah.

With that, Tatoosh smiled. It was the first time Nathan had seen him smile, and it transformed his face.

The pair retraced their steps to the village. According to custom, they were destined to be blood brothers and friends for life from that moment on.

CHAPTER 14

North Atlantic, 1848

I T WAS WITH MIXED FEELINGS that Susannah, now twenty-two, viewed the fast-disappearing English coastline as she stood alongside her father at the stern of the brigantine *Minstrel,* the small, two-masted vessel tasked with transporting them from the cradle of the civilized world to the savage south sea islands of Fiji.

Initially, she'd been excited about sailing to the exotic South Pacific and helping her father run the Wesley Methodist Mission at Momi Bay. Now, watching her homeland vanish over the horizon, she was beginning to have serious misgivings about what lay ahead.

Drake Senior had misgivings too. While he'd had a calling to spread the gospel to the heathens of Fiji, he knew the good Lord hadn't called Susannah.

The clergyman-turned missionary had had to do some fast talking to persuade the London Missionary Society's committee members to allow her to accompany him. He'd convinced them Susannah was crucial to his plans. Having taught first-year pupils in a London school for the past few years, she was an experienced and highly regarded teacher — especially for one so young. And, he'd argued, that would prove very useful at the mission station.

After having met Susannah, and been suitably impressed,

the good folk of the London Missionary Society agreed with Drake Senior's assessment of his daughter.

Now that he and Susannah were actually underway, the clergyman just hoped he was doing the right thing.

After deciding to travel to Fiji, Drake Senior had learned of a charter vessel leaving Plymouth for New Zealand, which was just thirteen hundred miles south of Fiji. *Minstrel* had been chartered by one Harry Kemp, a recently-retired British Army colonel who was migrating to New Zealand to take up new business opportunities. The former colonel had advised Drake Senior that in New Zealand he and his daughter could easily secure a berth aboard a trading vessel for the relatively short hop to Fiji.

Despite his misgivings, Drake Senior had immediately booked a stateroom aboard *Minstrel* for Susannah and himself. His misgivings included the fact that *Minstrel's* intended route was a convoluted one, taking her to New Zealand via the Canary Islands, Equatorial Guinea, Cape Colony and Van Diemen's Land to the south of New South Wales. The vessel's master had assured him *Minstrel* was a speedy craft and, all going well, would complete the journey within six months.

Given that *Minstrel* had been departing Plymouth in three weeks and the alternative was to wait three months for a berth aboard a more conventional vessel, Drake Senior had opted for the earlier departure.

Now, as the never-ending sea and sky seemingly threatened to consume the small brigantine, the clergyman wondered whether he should have waited the extra months for a berth aboard a more substantial vessel. He wondered, too, about the suitability of the ship's master, Captain Jeffrey Mathers, for such an arduous voyage. The middle-aged Devonshire seaman was a last-minute replacement for *Minstrel's* usual master who had fallen ill one week before sailing.

Captain Mathers had a reputation for being a fine seaman but a surly and incorrigible drunkard. When Drake Senior got wind of this, he'd complained to the brigantine's owners. They'd sympathized, but explained there were no other takers for the job at such short notice. The clergyman just hoped that decision wouldn't come back to haunt them.

"Penny for your thoughts," Susannah said.

Drake Senior realized she'd been studying him. "Nothing, my dear," he lied. "I was just thinking how lucky I am to have you as a daughter. Your mother would be proud of you."

"Thank you, papa," Susannah smiled.

They both shivered involuntarily as the cold sea breeze whipped their hair about and tugged at their coats. This spring day had a decidedly wintery feel about it.

Drake Senior put a protective arm around his daughter's shoulder and drew her close to him to shield her from the cold. "Best go below deck," he suggested.

"You go, papa. I'll stay here a while." Having just lost sight of Land's End, she wasn't about to admit she was already feeling decidedly queasy. *This doesn't augur well for the rest of the trip,* she told herself. "I'll join you soon."

"Alright, but don't dally long. You'll catch your death." Drake Senior said. He immediately retired below deck.

Alone on deck apart from two riggers who were busy making adjustments to the brigantine's square-rigged foremast, Susannah tried to fight off the feelings of seasickness that threatened to overwhelm her. Although she'd accompanied her parents on voyages to France on three occasions during her childhood, this was the first time she'd ever been out of sight of land and it frightened her.

Suddenly sensing the eyes of the riggers on her, she hurried below deck to rejoin her father.

⸺⟡⸺

THAT EVENING, IN the stateroom she shared with Drake Senior, Susannah sat alone on her bunk. Her father was dining with the other passengers in the ship's dining room.

Still decidedly queasy from the motion of the ship, Susannah had chosen to remain in her quarters. Now, feeling as she did, she wondered if she'd made the right decision. In the confines of the stateroom, the motion of the ship seemed more pronounced than ever. Susannah worried she would be tossed from her bunk if she wasn't careful. She pulled her dressing gown around her, as if for added security.

The young Englishwoman stared at the diary she held. In a small way, it was a historic moment for her: she was about to make her first-ever diary entry. The diary was a gift to her from one of the parishioners they'd left behind.

Dipping her feather quill into an open ink bottle, she began writing.

April 18th, 1848

Dear God, what have I got myself into? This morning, as papa and I boarded Minstrel, I noted how small this vessel is. I cannot believe she can deliver us safely to the far-flung colony of New Zealand. Our Captain Mathers, a disagreeable individual if ever there was, assured us she is a safe and reliable craft. I pray he is right.

Even more of a worry is the company we must keep for the next six months. Of the thirteen crew members, I estimate five at best can be trusted. The remainder look no more trustworthy than the pirates who are known to frequent the waters to the south of here. The other thirty-five passengers are a mixed bunch including married couples, single men and seventeen children, the youngest of whom was born but a week ago.

Some of the men leave much to be desired judging by their penchant for liquor and women. One or two were already intoxicated before we were out of sight of land, and, it seems, all the single men at least lust after anything in a shirt. Not even the married women are safe from their prying eyes. One man in particular, an Irishman by the name of John Donovan, makes my skin crawl. It is rumored he is an escaped felon.

We humans are not the only living creatures on board. So far, I have seen at least six rats scurrying about, one I swear as big as my dear cat, Toby, whom I am missing already. And although I have not yet seen them, I know there are four sheep tethered in the hold for I have heard their plaintive cries. The captain said one will be sacrificed for the dining table on his birthday, which by all accounts is fast approaching.

The stateroom papa has secured is comfortable though cramped. I shall spend as much time as I can outside for the smells below deck are decidedly rank.

A knock on the stateroom door, interrupted Susannah's musings.

"Are you decent?" Drake Senior called out.

"Yes, come in," Susannah replied.

Drake Senior entered and smiled at his daughter. "You missed a fine dinner, lass."

Susannah nodded, hoping her father wouldn't elaborate.

Alas, Drake Senior continued, "I swear the Shepherd's Pie we had was almost as good as your mother made. It was served with roast vegies."

"Papa, please!" Susannah was feeling queasier than ever.

Unaware of Susannah's fragile physical state, Drake Senior continued, "That was followed by as much apple pie and cream as we could eat."

Susannah suddenly climbed out of her bunk and stumbled toward the door.

"Are you alright?" Drake Senior asked.

Susannah didn't even attempt to respond. She flung the door open, raced along the passageway and up the steerage steps. On deck, she ran to the port-side rail and vomited over the ship's side.

A concerned Drake Senior appeared from below deck. "Susannah?" he called to her.

She waved him away. Realizing she didn't want him to see her in such a wretched state, Drake Senior returned below.

Alone in her misery, Susannah vomited once more. Mercifully, after that, she felt considerably better. She breathed in the cool sea air. A movement next to her made her jump. She looked around and saw, by the light of an outside lantern, it was Harry Kemp, the retired colonel who had chartered *Minstrel*.

A big man with a kindly face that was partly hidden behind a bushy moustache, Kemp was concerned for the young woman's welfare. "Sorry, Miss," he mumbled. "Didn't mean to startle you."

"Oh, that's alright, Colonel."

"Please, it's Harry. I'm no longer in the Army, so the rank no longer applies."

Susannah smiled shyly. "I am Susannah Drake," she said, extending her hand.

"Ah, delighted," Kemp said, taking her hand briefly. "I

assume you are the reverend's daughter?"

"Yes. My father tells me it is you we have to thank for this vessel."

Kemp waved one hand dismissively. "Only too happy to have the company," he said. "And the extra passengers helps meet my costs," he added honestly.

Susannah felt very at ease in Kemp's presence. She'd always considered herself a good judge of character. It was her judgement that the former colonel was a true gentleman. "Colonel . . . ah . . . Harry," she asked, "may I enquire as to what business takes you to Equatorial Guinea and other such unusual destinations on this voyage?"

Kemp proceeded to explain why *Minstrel* was deviating from the normal sailing routes. Susannah found his explanation fascinating and promised herself she would note it in her next diary entry.

WHEN SUSANNAH RETURNED to the stateroom, she found her father already asleep behind a curtain he'd drawn. Although she couldn't see him, she could hear him snoring. The curtain effectively cut the stateroom in half and ensured at least a modicum of privacy for the room's two occupants.

Susannah climbed into her bunk, opened her diary and set about completing the entry she'd begun earlier.

Already I feel better about the future having just met the distinguished Mister Kemp, a former British Army officer who is solely responsible for the charter of this brigantine. A finer gentleman I have never met, aside from my own dear papa.

Mister Kemp explained the reasons for the route Minstrel follows. It seems he still has ties with the Army which is part-financing his present venture. Although much of what he is doing is confidential, he confided that he is to deliver certain military documents to Army personnel stationed at various outposts en route. One such outpost is Bata, in Equatorial Guinea. I do hope the natives there behave. First stop however, is Santa Cruz de Tenerife, in the Canary Islands, three weeks sailing time from here. I so look forward to that.

I am missing terra firma already. This sea air is making me tired. Must sleep now. Ship going 6 knots. Course S.W.

CHAPTER 15

Parramatta, New South Wales, 1840

JACK, NOW TWENTY-FOUR, STUDIED the local Gameraigal Aborigines snaring eels in the Parramatta River as he arrived back at the penal settlement. It was the end of yet another hard day working on the new road to Sydney Town.

The horse-drawn cart Jack was on rolled to a halt, and he and the other convicts gratefully clambered off it. A guard unshackled their leg irons and all except Jack walked slowly to their quarters where a cold bath and a meal of sorts awaited them.

Jack lingered by the river, watching the Aborigines snare some of the big freshwater eels that frequented this section of the Parramatta. Even after two years, he never tired of watching the natives fish or hunt.

As Jack prepared to sit down on the riverbank, he saw a movement in the grass. Closer inspection revealed a deadly king brown snake slithering toward him. "Shit!" he jumped back and allowed the snake to slither past. Then he sat down, his heart racing following the close encounter. Like most Europeans, he couldn't get used to the snakes and other creepy crawlies that frequented this untamed land. He had good reason to fear snakes. One convict and a settler had already died, and several others had nearly died as a result of snake bites since his arrival at Parramatta.

By now, the holiday was well and truly over for the young Cockney. After surviving the hellish ocean voyage out from Mother England, Parramatta had seemed like heaven with its brothels, bars and even a weekly wage for its convict residents. It hadn't taken long for Jack to tire of Parramatta's delights. He was ready to quit the place after his first half-dozen floggings—and that was only four months into his stay here. Since then, the daily routine of working on a chain gang from dawn till dusk had gotten to him. Even Mary O'Brien's magnificent, melon-like breasts weren't enough to hold him here now. He had decided he needed a change of scenery.

The recent replacement of Captain James Clarke by a sadistic Englishman appropriately named Henry Gallows had been the last straw for Jack. Under Clarke, life at Parramatta had been plain boring; under Gallows, it was brutal. The man, a failed government official in his former life, had a penchant for flogging convicts, or worse, as punishment for even the most minor offence. Sentences of one to two hundred lashes were now commonplace for so much as talking back to a guard. Striking a guard could mean three hundred lashes, which was often a death sentence, and attempting to escape was now punishable by hanging. As a result, morale, even among the soldiers, was at an all-time low at Parramatta.

Invariably, Jack's thoughts turned to escape. He knew the odds were against him; he'd seen twenty or more convicts try to escape and each attempt had resulted in death or capture. Those who didn't succumb to thirst or hunger in the unforgiving countryside—or *the Outback* as the locals called it—were usually rounded up within a few days by the Gameraigal trackers in the Army's employ. The few hardy souls who managed to elude the trackers were inevitably killed and, according to rumors, sometimes eaten by other Aborigines who came across them.

Until now, Jack had been content to bide his time. Now, he was ready to execute a plan he'd been hatching for some months.

As darkness fell, the Aborigines began smoking their freshly-caught eels over a fire their womenfolk had started. They invited Jack to join them. The Gameraigals had come to know and like the cheeky Cockney who always had a smile and a friendly wave for them. As he had done on several occasions recently, Jack joined them for a meal. The smoked eel they shared with him was delicious, and he indicated as much through a combination of facial expressions, hand signs and the odd Aboriginal word he'd picked up. His frequent misuse of their language prompted smiles among his Gameraigal hosts.

The Gameraigals ate baked grubs with their smoked eel. Their leader, Murrundi, glanced mischievously at Jack then addressed his companions. "You watch when I offer Whitey Jack a grub," he chuckled. "He will accept it rather than risk offending us. Then you watch White Jack's face when he eats it." Assuming a serious expression, Murrundi speared a large grub on the end of a stick, baked it over a flame then handed it to Jack. "You take," he said in pigeon English.

Not wishing to offend his hosts, Jack took the stick from Murrundi and nibbled unenthusiastically at the grub impaled on the end of it. As he finally devoured the last of the grub, Murrundi and the others burst out laughing. Some rolled around on the ground, so great was their mirth. Realizing they'd set him up, Jack smiled good-naturedly.

When the laughter subsided, Jack turned to Murrundi and engaged him in conversation. "What does Murrundi's people think of the Red Coats?" he asked.

Murrundi, a wiry individual whose deep-set eyes gleamed with intelligence, said, "We no like Red Coats."

"If I escape, would your people track me?"

Murrundi gave this some thought then smiled shrewdly. "We track you Whitey Jack, but maybe not find you."

Jack nodded to the Aborigine. "Thank you, my friend."

A short while later, Jack bade his hosts goodnight then

began walking toward the settlement. The darkness soon swallowed him up. As he walked, his mind was racing. Murrundi had basically given him the go-ahead to escape. *Next week,* he promised himself. He suddenly slowed to a halt. *Why not right now?* Jack looked around. Alone in the dark, he realized he couldn't be seen by his Gameraigal friends or indeed by anyone in the nearby settlement.

Feeling a rush of excitement, Jack made up his mind. *Now it is!* He hurried to the nearby riverbank. There, he scouted along the bank until he found a log that had been washed down in some forgotten flood. Without hesitating, he pushed the log out into the river, hung onto it and floated downstream.

As the current carried him away from Parramatta, Jack heard the ship's bell ring out in the settlement, reminding the convict population it would soon be time to retire for the night. Jack smiled to himself at the thought of his fellow convicts turning in. They'd see he was absent and assume he was spending another night with one of his female consorts. *They'll be able to cover for me till morning at least.* By then, he hoped, he'd be well on the way to freedom.

Jack was feeling elated as the current quickly distanced him from his captors. Murrundi had strongly hinted his people would not go out of their way to find him if he escaped from Parramatta, and Jack felt Murrundi's word was his bond. The young Cockney was also confident he had a superior escape plan. Those convicts who had tried and failed to escape had all fled overland. Not one to Jack's knowledge had used the river to try to escape—possibly because most couldn't swim. Jack could. And he was very aware the river meant he'd leave no tracks.

His plan was to float as far as he could downstream—all the way to the river's mouth if he could. Then he'd make his way to Sydney Town and from there stow away on a ship bound for New Zealand or perhaps the Pacific Islands.

SOME TWO HOURS after entering the river, Jack was feeling more confident than ever. The log he used as a raft was doing its job: it was putting distance between him and Parramatta with little effort on his part other than steering it to ensure it didn't run aground in the shallows. *And I'm leaving no tracks!* He chuckled to himself.

Then he saw flickering lights downstream.

As the current carried him toward the lights, the young Cockney saw a party of Aborigines spearing fish by the light of flaming torches. Some of the fishermen were in canoes anchored mid-stream; others were on foot, patroling the shallows along both banks.

Jack identified them as members of the Wiradjuri tribe. Their reputation was less than hospitable toward whites. Realizing there was no way past them, he steered the log to the near bank, climbed out of the river and began heading across country. As he walked, he hoped he was far enough from Parramatta for his tracks to remain undiscovered.

Less than a hundred paces from the river, volleys of musket-fire shattered the silence. Jack instinctively dropped to the ground. When he realized the shooting was not directed at him, he looked back and saw soldiers on horseback shooting the Wiradjuris in the river. The soldiers' red coats stood out even in the dim light of the natives' flaming torches.

The startled Wiradjuris dropped their torches and tried to flee. Most were cut down where they stood. Within seconds, several lay face-down in the shallows, dead. Others managed to reach the riverbank and tried to flee cross-country. The soldiers' horses soon ran them down. The Red Coats laughed as they killed indiscriminately. Jack realized this was sport to them.

One fleet-footed Wiradjuri managed to break through the cordon of soldiers. Jack was alarmed to see he was running straight toward him with two Red Coats on horseback in hot pursuit. *Not this way you bloody idiot!*

Standing in the open, the Cockney realized he'd be discovered if he didn't take evasive action. He started running, trying to distance himself from the Wiradjuri and his pursuers.

As Jack ran through the darkness, his left foot disappeared into a small rabbit hole in the ground. It held fast while his bodyweight was still moving forward at speed, stopping him dead in his tracks. A shooting pain traveled up the length of his leg. "Arghhh!" His agonizing cry attracted the attention of one of the soldiers.

The soldier veered off to investigate, leaving the Wiradjuri to his companion to finish off. A musket-shot brought an end to the native's short-lived freedom.

Jack initially thought he'd broken his ankle. The fact he was able to remain upright convinced him he'd only sprained it. He tried to run, but was reduced to a painful hobble. As he attempted to flee, he heard the thunder of horses' hooves bearing down on him. The Red Coat rode his horse over the top of Jack, flattening him. The force of the impact knocked him out cold.

When he came round, Jack saw he was surrounded by Red Coats. They were laughing and joking, boasting about the number of *black fellows* they'd just killed. The laughter tapered off when they realized Jack was now conscious.

The Red Coats' senior officer dismounted and kneeled down beside the subdued prisoner. "Now what have we here?" he asked in a seemingly affected middle class English accent.

"Do you think he's an Abo, sir?" a soldier asked in jest.

The senior officer grabbed a handful of Jack's hair and tilted the prisoner's face up toward his. "I'm not sure," the senior officer chuckled. "If he is, he's from a tribe I'm not familiar with."

"Perhaps he's from the Convict Tribe, sir," another soldier suggested. This prompted more laughter.

The senior officer tired of the charade. He released Jack's

hair and stood astride him, staring down at him. "What's your name, felon?"

Trying to ignore the pain in his ankle and his thumping headache, Jack looked up at the senior officer. "I'm the Governor of New South Wales and I'm going to have you hung, drawn and quartered for treating me like this," he spat through clenched teeth.

The senior officer saw red and stomped Jack's face with the heel of his boot, knocking the Cockney out for the second time that night.

CHAPTER 16

Makah Nation, West Coast, North America, 1840

WINTER HAD ARRIVED WITH A vengeance in Oregon Country. It was turning out to be even harsher than the first winter Nathan had experienced at Neah Bay, and the Makah village was under a rare blanket of snow.

Now eighteen, the young Philadelphian tossed and turned on the bearskin rug that served as his bed in the lodge of his benefactor, Elswa, the tribe's chief. He'd lived as a member of Elswa's extended family ever since he'd distinguished himself during the Mowachaht raid a year earlier.

After saving the chief's life, and becoming blood brother to Tatoosh, the chief's son, Nathan's fortunes had changed out of sight. He spent his days fishing and hunting with Tatoosh and the other braves, and was able to enjoy the company of the female slaves and village maidens whenever he chose. He'd even been permitted to choose a personal slave for himself, and had selected Baldy, the Mowachaht slave. Nathan treated him well and Baldy reciprocated by ensuring his master was never short of food, clean clothes or the prized wild berries that were so popular in season.

Elswa treated Nathan as a son, and the Makah braves looked on him as one of them. To all intents and purposes—skin color and blue eyes aside—Nathan was one of them. Tall and athletic, he now cut an imposing figure. He'd filled out somewhat and had packed on some muscle. As fit and strong as any Makah brave, he'd already been on several raiding parties against enemy tribes and had a number of kills to his name.

During waking hours he was Makah, but his sleep was filled with dreams of his former life—in particular his childhood years in Philadelphia. Until something had woken him minutes earlier, he'd been dreaming he was playing tag with schoolmates.

Tatoosh appeared out of the darkness. "You awake?" he asked in his native tongue.

"Yes."

"We go now," Tatoosh said.

Nathan, who now spoke fluent Makah, jumped to his feet and began dressing. Although his friend hadn't elaborated, he knew him well enough to know something was up. The sound of men talking in urgent, hushed tones outside the lodge confirmed that.

Tucking his leggings into snow boots, Nathan grabbed the musket and tomahawk he kept by his bed mat and followed Tatoosh outside where, beneath a clear, starry sky, a raiding party of some thirty braves were gathering around their chief. Most carried muskets. A few were armed with bows or tomahawks. They stamped their feet to keep warm and the condensation from their breath hung in the cold night air like mist.

As Nathan joined the others, he was barely distinguishable from them. Outwardly at least he had gone completely native, even down to the hairstyle he wore as a bun atop his head and the two eagle feathers which protruded from it. The one custom he had not adopted was wearing war paint, and so he was the only one among the assembled whose face was not adorned in paint.

Among the braves was a Makah scout who had delivered

some concerning news to Elswa a short time earlier. The scout was still breathing hard after a five-mile run back to Neah Bay.

"A Quileute hunting party is camped up river," Elswa announced. "They trespass in the lands of the Makah Nation."

The assembled braves nodded gravely. Like the Mowachahts, the Quileutes were traditional enemies of their tribe.

Elswa continued, "They will not be expecting to be attacked."

He's right about that, Nathan thought. He knew the Northwest tribes rarely went to war in winter, preferring to wait for the warmer summer months when travel was easier and temperatures were kinder.

As the chief outlined his plan of attack, Nathan glanced around at the Makah braves. They were clearly relishing the thought of action. Their painted faces shone in anticipation of the violence that was coming and they already had the bloodlust in their eyes—none more so than Tatoosh who looked like a hungry dog straining against a leash.

The blood brothers had become close—as close as any two brothers. Consequently, Nathan found he was being included in tribal activities normally off-limits to any Makah not of noble heritage. It was both a privilege and a curse. At times like this, when he was about to go on a raid, he considered it a curse and for perhaps the hundredth time he asked himself, *Why me?* He guessed it was something to do with the fact he was now a crack marksman—the best in the tribe beyond any shadow of a doubt.

Elswa raised his musket above his head. "The heads of our enemies will hang from our totem poles before this day is ended!"

As one, Nathan and the others raised their weapons above their heads and repeated Elswa's promise. It was a promise they made before every raid.

Without another word, Elswa led his braves at a brisk trot

through the snow to the nearby riverbank where they launched several canoes. Nathan joined the chief and his son in the lead canoe.

As they paddled into the darkness, twenty or more women emerged from the lodges to wave their men off. Braving the cold, the women sang a haunting Makah song. The tribe's shaman, an ancient, wizened character, appeared seemingly from nowhere, chanting and offering up prayers to the war spirits.

On the river, the singing and chanting faded as the paddlers put distance between themselves and the village.

Paddling through the night, feeling cold and more than a little fearful, Nathan questioned yet again how he, a white man, had ended up in this predicament. Not for the first time, he wondered if he'd done something wrong in a past life.

DAWN WAS APPROACHING when the raiders reached their destination. Paddling quietly and in unison, they closed with the near bank and tied their canoes to the overhanging branches of trees. Makah scouts quickly determined the exact whereabouts of the Quileutes and reported their enemies were sleeping soundly.

The Makah split into two groups. Elswa led one group along the river bank toward the Quileute encampment while Tatoosh led the other group, whose number included Nathan, in a wide circle that would bring them around behind the encampment. The aim was to attack their enemies from two sides.

Their first task was to locate any Quileute lookouts who may have been posted. Two were located. The first one was asleep, and a Makah scout ensured he stayed that way by smashing his skull with one mighty blow of his tomahawk. The second was located a short distance away. He was busy urinating against a tree. Two braves snuck up behind him. One covered the lookout's mouth with one hand and stabbed him in the back with a hunting knife. As the wounded lookout fell to the ground, the other brave clubbed him, finishing him off.

Tatoosh's braves, and Elswa's, were in place before dawn broke. When it did, it was greeted with chilling war cries. The Makah braves attacked as one.

Nathan quickly found himself in the thick of the action. He shot dead a Quileute warrior on the run. Still running, he reloaded his musket, primed and fired it at another Quileute, killing him, too.

Although surprised and outnumbered, the Quileutes lived up to their reputation as fierce fighters. They managed to kill three Makah and wound several others before succumbing to the invaders' superior numbers and firepower.

Tatoosh was among the Makah wounded. He suffered a nasty head gash when he received a glancing blow from a tomahawk. Nathan half-carried him back to the river while the other braves decapitated their enemies. When the others returned to the river, they unceremoniously tossed the heads of the vanquished into the bottom of the canoes. The valued trophies would be displayed for all to see back at the village.

Nathan looked down at the severed heads and then at the faces of the Makah braves. Their faces still shone with the excitement of battle, and they still had the bloodlust in their eyes. The young white knew from experience their excitement would take time to pass. Like all the natives of the Northwest, they lived for battle, and the tales of this night's deeds would be told around many a cooking fire for many years to come.

For the first time in a while, Nathan remembered he was very different to these people. While he was prepared to kill and do whatever it took to survive, the Makahs' savagery seemed to know no bounds. *This is a game to them.* Looking at the braves around him, he realized he'd never felt more unlike them than he did now.

Nathan became aware Tatoosh was staring at him. The

chief's son, whose head wound still bled profusely, looked at him perceptively. His eyes, which were all-knowing like his father's, seemed to bore into Nathan's soul.

The young white slowly looked away from Tatoosh, and then turned his back on him as well.

Although only a few feet separated the blood brothers physically, in all other respects it might as well have been a hundred miles.

AS WINTER TURNED to spring at Neah Bay and the Makah went about their seasonal tasks of hunting, fishing, growing crops and warring, Nathan's thoughts turned increasingly to his old life. He missed being with his own kind and conversing in English.

Just how much he missed his former life was brought home to him when a sailing ship sailed into the bay. Nathan emerged from Elswa's lodge just as the ship appeared. He couldn't believe his eyes and started running down toward the beach. A shout from Elswa pulled him up. He turned back to face the chief.

"Nathan Johnson stay here . . . out of sight," Elswa ordered. He obviously didn't want it known a white was being kept in village as that could attract unwanted attention.

Nathan reluctantly stayed put. Confined to the village, he could only watch from afar as Elswa and Tatoosh led a trading party out to the ship. He watched, fascinated, when the chief conversed with the white traders. His heart missed a beat when a pretty white woman appeared on deck. She reminded him of his mother. The woman was obviously related to the captain—her husband no doubt. From such a distance, Nathan couldn't tell for sure. The woman returned below deck as trading began on board.

EVENTUALLY, TRADING CONCLUDED and the Makah paddled back to shore while the ship sailed out of the bay. Nathan could only watch her forlornly as she disappeared from sight. He immediately sought out Elswa and confronted him inside his lodge.

"Great chief," Nathan began, summoning up as much respect as possible. "I wish . . ." He hesitated when Tatoosh suddenly entered the lodge. Nathan continued, "I wish to return to my people."

Elswa stiffened as if he'd been insulted. Nathan glanced at Tatoosh. The chief's son appeared more disappointed than affronted.

"Nathan Johnson is now Makah," Elswa said sternly, his gunsight eyes flashing in anger. "Nathan Johnson is a sailmaker, hunter and warrior. Too valuable to release." The chief turned his back on Nathan, indicating the conversation had ended, and began walking away.

"I miss my own kind!" Nathan blurted out.

Elswa pulled up. Furious, he reached beneath his cape, spun around and threw his tomahawk. Its razor-sharp blade lodged deep in the lodge's wall barely six inches from Nathan's right ear.

For several long moments, the chief and the young white stared at each other.

"I have spoken," Elswa said at last.

Shaken, Nathan stomped off. It was now clear the chief would kill him rather than allow him to leave.

Behind him, Elswa and Tatoosh looked at Nathan's retreating back then looked at each other. The White-Eye had given them something to think about.

Chapter 17

Atlantic Ocean, 1848

ONE DAY OUT FROM ENGLAND, *Minstrel* struck a mighty storm which, after one unrelenting week, was showing no signs of waning. All the passengers and most of the crew were continually seasick. Even the captain appeared to be under the weather, although in truth that had more to do with his heavy drinking.

Like many on board, Susannah had hardly eaten since leaving Plymouth. What little food she had forced herself to eat, she'd quickly lost overboard. Drake Senior was faring a little better, although he, too, was decidedly off color.

As the storm continued to rage and *Minstrel* was tossed about like a cork in the mountainous seas, many of the passengers feared for their lives. Drake Senior led the brigantine's God-fearing passengers in prayer, praying for a safe journey. Meanwhile, the roast lamb the captain had promised to celebrate his birthday never eventuated as no-one felt like eating or celebrating.

Fast though *Minstrel* was, she sat low in the sea and took on water whenever a high sea was running. The stench of bilgewater in her hold was evident from the second day and hadn't let up since, adding to the feelings of nausea being experienced by those on board. None of the passengers realized they'd be living with that stench for the next six months.

One day rolled into another. Though Susannah was ill, she still religiously attended to her diary entries. Perched on the edge of her bunk, rolling with the violent motion of the ship to keep her balance, she wrote in her diary.

April 26th, 1848

Yesterday was a day to forget . . . and today is going the same way. The storm seems determined to finish us off. All but the hardiest passengers remain confined to their bunks. Seasickness has spread through Minstrel like some contagious disease. This has not been helped by the ever-present stench of bilgewater.

Our journey thus far has been miserable. It started out in the worst possible fashion with the Jensens losing their week-old baby. The poor little boy contracted pneumonia and received a burial at sea. It was the first such service funeral papa had conducted, and he hopes the last.

To make matters worse, Captain Mathers has been drinking steadily since the 22nd. He claims he's under doctor's orders to partake of a gram of whisky every hour on the hour. I believe he may be telling the truth for, regrettably, the ship's doctor is an alcoholic himself and I have yet to see him sober.

Thank God the first mate, Cornishman Fred Paxton, is a sensible man and a moderate drinker by all accounts. He is constantly at loggerheads with the captain. If we survive this journey, I suspect it will be because of the sensibilities of Mr Paxton.

The one piece of good news is the wind is coming from the north, so we are hastening toward our first stopover. 8 knots. Bad storm. A curse on this seasickness.

Susannah closed her diary just as Drake Senior burst into the stateroom. He was drenched to the bone and looked wild-eyed.

"Papa, what is it?" Susannah asked.

Drake Senior removed his soaked jacket, hung it over a rail and sat down on his bunk, his head in his hands. "We have just lost a crewman overboard," he mumbled, shaking.

"Oh, dear God."

"I saw it happen and I was powerless to help him."

Susannah climbed off her bunk and staggered unsteadily toward her father as the brigantine lurched over the crest of one wave and down into the trough of another. Drake Senior put out his hand to steady his daughter. She sat down next to him.

"Who was it?" she asked.

"It was one of the riggers. He fell from the foremast. The first mate threw a line to him, but he was swept away."

They sat in silence for several long moments, thinking about the dangers the storm posed. Their journey had not started at all well.

"Two deaths and we have only been at sea a week," Susannah said.

Drake Senior looked at her and managed a smile. "It can only get better," he suggested hopefully.

Susannah managed a smile, too. She knew there was some

truth in what her father said. *Things can't get much worse.*

"We should pray," Drake Senior said.

Susannah nodded.

Father and daughter knelt down before Drake Senior's bunk and bowed their heads. The clergyman prayed aloud for the lost rigger's soul and for the safety of everyone on board.

***

ONE WEEK LATER, as Drake Senior had promised, the storm abated; and a week after that, beneath gloriously sunny skies, *Minstrel* approached Santa Cruz de Tenerife, one of the largest towns in the Canary Islands and one of the most strategically important ports in the entire Atlantic Ocean.

The Drakes and all the other passengers crowded onto the brigantine's deck to enjoy the occasion. All were impressed by the island's beauty — in particular the majestic mountain range known as Macizo de Anaga that dominated the north eastern side of Tenerife.

To everyone's surprise, Captain Mathers emerged from below deck in time to take charge of the vessel's arrival in port. Even more surprisingly, he was sober for once. In a quiet moment, the first mate confided that was typical of Mathers. It seemed the captain had a habit of sobering up long enough to impress the authorities at any new port his ship entered before reverting to his old habits.

"We'll be here twenty-four hours," Mathers announced gruffly. "That'll be long enough to take on fresh water and stores. Departure time will be fourteen hundred hours tomorrow. Anyone not here by then will be left behind."

The passengers suspected the captain wasn't joking. The crew, or at least those who had sailed with him before, *knew* he wasn't joking. Only the previous year, he'd left a passenger marooned on an island stopover en route to India — all because the man hadn't reported in on time; the irate passenger had been picked up on the return voyage by an unrepentant

Mathers. The passenger had complained that he'd only been an hour late, but Mathers had remained unmoved.

The Drakes and most of the other passengers went ashore to sample the delights of Santa Cruz de Tenerife. Susannah was intrigued by the exotic markets and the bargains on offer— many of them from the African continent whose western edge, she knew, lay over the eastern horizon. She was moved to comment also on the Spanish architecture that was so prominent.

Drake Senior was most intrigued by the island's prosperity. Over the centuries, its inhabitants had clearly made the most of its location on the sailing route between the Mediterranean and the Americas.

THAT NIGHT, AFTER dining in a Berber restaurant, the Drakes returned to *Minstrel* well satisfied by their time ashore. As they stepped foot onto the brigantine in the company of other returning passengers, they were greeted by a commotion coming from below deck. The sounds of men swearing and shouting reached them.

Drake Senior turned to Susannah. "You stay here, my dear." He walked toward the steerage to go below deck to investigate, but found his way barred by the Swedish second mate, Sven Svenson.

"It would not be wise to go below just now, Reverend," Svenson said.

"What is the trouble?" Drake Senior asked.

"Some of the passengers have been drinking and there has been some fighting," Svenson explained. "The captain and first mate are trying to sort it out now."

"Oh, I see. Unfortunate business."

LATER, IN THEIR stateroom, the Drakes prepared to retire for the night. They were both somewhat shaken after seeing carnage left below deck following the brawl. One passenger had commented it were as though a mighty hurricane had swept through *Minstrel's* interior.

Drake Senior bade Susannah a good night as he pulled the dividing curtain across, effectively splitting the room in half.

"Goodnight, papa," Susannah said. Then, as she'd done every night thus far, she entered the day's main events into her diary.

May 10th, 1848

Today, we enjoyed two major milestones: our first sunny day and our first day ashore in three weeks. The sunshine was a treat after so many cold and stormy days.

The Canary Islands were a sight for sore eyes, and papa and I, and indeed, most of the other passengers enjoyed a delightful time ashore at Santa Cruz de Tenerife.

Unfortunately, the day was spoiled by an incident aboard ship as we returned. Apparently, the suspected felon, John Donovan, had clashed with a fellow Irishman, young Michael Kelleher.

Mr Kelleher is a Dublin journalist and, by all accounts, something of a prankster. They had both had too much alcohol and what started as a scuffle developed into an all out brawl as other passengers and even some crewmembers took sides. The fighting began in the saloon and spilled out into the passageway. It was quite vicious too with bottles and stools being used as weapons. Two men were knocked out and one poor crewman was stabbed in the face with a broken bottle.

I fear the infirmary will be busy for the next few days. I just hope our good doctor can remain sober long enough to treat his latest patients. Fortunately, there were no children around during the brawl. Those children still on board had wisely been confined to their cabins.

We heard the captain, first mate and three other crewmen were trying to restore order, but they were heavily outnumbered. Ultimately, they could do nothing but wait for the fighting to run its course, which it eventually did. When Mr Mathers considered it was safe for those of us waiting up top to proceed below deck, he sent word to us. On making our way to our respective quarters, we were alarmed by the carnage we found below deck. There was blood, broken bottles and upturned tables everywhere.

The main troublemakers, including both Irishmen, were locked in separate parts of the hold to sober up. We learned they will be tried on board when Minstrel sets sail tomorrow. Mr Kemp has threatened to put them ashore if they do not promise to behave for the remainder of our voyage. I hope they are fined heavily at the very least.

Tomorrow we depart for Bata, in Equatorial Guinea. I welcome the prospect of continuing warm temperatures although our captain warns we may be praying for cold weather before long.

CHAPTER 18

Parramatta, New South Wales, 1840

DAWN WAS BREAKING WHEN JACK came round. He found he was draped over the back of a horse being ridden by one of two Red Coats who were escorting him back to Parramatta.

Along the way, they passed groups of convicts heading out for another day's hard work. Those who recognized Jack offered words of encouragement. The would-be escapee was too battered and bruised to respond.

At Parramatta, Jack was frog-marched to the office of Henry Gallows, the settlement's sadistic senior official. Here, while he waited for Gallows to finish breakfast, he was given a dressing down by a senior guard.

"If Mister Gallows spares your life, you'll receive a flogging to remember, I can promise ye that, Halliday," the guard promised.

THE SUN WAS high in the morning sky before Gallows finally appeared. He used a napkin to wipe egg from his chin as he surveyed Jack in silence. Finally, he said, "Mister Halliday, you have given me a dilemma. Do you know what that dilemma is, Mister Halliday?"

Jack shook his head, indicating he didn't.

"I should hang you for trying to escape, but my guards tell

me you have a strong back and can do the work of two men," Gallows continued. "Completing the road to Sydney Town is more important to me than sparing your worthless life, so I shall spare you . . . this time"

Jack didn't react, but inwardly he felt immense relief. He was sure he'd be hung.

"However," Gallows added, "I need to make an example of you, or the others will think I've gone soft." He leaned closer to Jack. "I'm going to have you flogged to within an inch of your life."

AT DUSK, AS another working day ended, the other convicts returned to the settlement. They were ordered to assemble in the central courtyard where they were greeted by the sight of a naked Jack who was tied to a whipping post. He'd been there under the hot sun since early afternoon, and his back and buttocks were badly sunburned. The sunburn couldn't hide the faded marks of previous floggings.

Gallows stood behind Jack. He was flanked by senior Army officers, and behind them, the settlement's official flogger waited with his trusty cat-o'-nine-tails in hand. The flogger was a bare-chested, muscular chap who relished his job and who had long-since lost count of the number of convicts he'd flogged.

The convicts had had their working day curtailed so they could witness Jack's punishment while it was still daylight. As soon as they were assembled, Gallows addressed them.

"This sorry individual," Gallows said glancing at Jack, "tried to escape last night. As you can see, like all before him, he failed." Gallows waited for his words to sink in. "For this transgression, he will receive three hundred lashes."

Gasps came from the convicts. It was common knowledge that three hundred lashes had finished off many a strong man.

On hearing his sentence, Jack didn't outwardly react, but

inwardly he cringed. *Dear God have mercy on my soul.* Twice now he'd received two hundred lashes, and each time he'd taken weeks to fully recover. On both occasions, the flesh had been literally torn from his back, which remained scarred to this day. How he'd survive three hundred lashes he wasn't quite sure.

Gallows nodded to the flogger who stepped forward and, as was his habit, cracked his whip to test it. Satisfied, he proceeded to deliver Jack's punishment.

With each crack of the whip, a young, pasty-faced English soldier counted off the lashes. "One, two, three . . ." The young soldier, a new recruit and recent arrival in the colony, could hardly watch as the flogger went about his work. Having never witnessed a flogging before, he was perilously close to fainting and had to steel himself to remain upright.

As each lash was delivered, Jack flinched involuntarily — such was its impact. Determined to block out the pain, he conjured up a mental picture of past lovers, or those he could recall at least. Then he recounted the different sexual positions he'd enjoyed with them. Finally, he graded each lover from one to ten, giving points for good looks, shapely legs, kissing technique, inventiveness and, last but not least, breast size. The butcher's wife won this little contest, but Mary O'Brien, with her large melons, was a close second.

When the soldier's count reached one hundred, the pain left Jack incapable of rational thought. He let his mind go blank.

<hr>

DUSK WAS FADING to night as the count reached two hundred. Jack was barely conscious. His back was a bloody mess. Even the flogger was splattered in blood. Gallows had stepped back a few paces to avoid being splattered.

Still the count continued, "Two hundred and one, two hundred and two, two hundred and three . . ." the pasty-faced young soldier recited hoarsely. By now he was so close to fainting, he visibly swayed on his feet.

Seeing his plight, a senior officer standing close by dismissed the soldier and took over the count. In the change-over, he missed counting two lashes, thereby condemning Jack to an additional two.

———⬦⬦⬦———

BY THE TIME the count reached three hundred, Jack was unconscious and darkness had fallen. Despite the large gathering of men, the compound was deathly silent. No-one spoke or moved.

It was Gallows who finally broke the silence. "Take him to his quarters," he ordered.

Two soldiers untied Jack and dragged him away. Looking on, the assembled convicts couldn't be sure whether he was alive or dead.

CHAPTER 19

―◦◊◦―

Makah Nation, West Coast, North America, 1841

NATHAN, NOW NINETEEN, JOINED MAKAH braves and headmen as they filed into the chief's lodge. Inside, they were greeted by Tatoosh who had been chief of the tribe since his father, Elswa, died in a hunting accident the previous summer. The young chief saw Nathan and offered a Makah salutation. "You look well today, my brother."

Nathan responded in the Makah tongue. "And you, my brother."

It was evident to all the bond between the two remained as strong as ever.

The men sat down, cross-legged, around an open fire. Tatoosh puffed on a ceremonial pipe then handed it to the respected headman, Klussamit, who took a puff and passed it to the next man. The assembled spoke in hushed tones.

Tatoosh held his hand up for silence. "Makah braves, I greet you."

Conversation ceased immediately and every eye was on the young chief.

Tatoosh announced, "Our neighbors on the long island say the big fish have returned to these waters."

The announcement was greeted with cheers from the

assembled braves. They beat their feet and fists on the lodge's walls and floorboards to express their delight and began talking animatedly among themselves.

Nathan was aware Tatoosh was referring to the whales that passed through the Strait of Juan de Fuca each year. The gray and humpback whales, and the occasional orca, were regular visitors to these waters. He was aware, too, the reason for the braves' excitement was the Makah hadn't had a successful whale hunt for more than two years and that was a major problem for people who relied so heavily on the whale for its blubber and a multitude of other things.

So-Har, a belligerent brave, leaped to his feet. "We must spear the big fish now!"

There were shouts of agreement from the others.

Tatoosh raised his voice to make himself heard. "No! Today we make preparations for the hunt."

There was some dissention, but most saw the wisdom in this. Preparation was the key to a successful hunt, and past failures could be attributed to lack of preparation.

"Tomorrow the Makah will kill some big fish," Tatoosh continued. "Then we will have so much blubber to eat we will be as fat as pregnant women!"

Wild cheering broke out again. So-Har reluctantly joined in. Several braves uttered shrill war cries and brandished their weapons.

Tatoosh raised his hand again for silence. As the din subsided, he looked in Nathan's direction and said, "I put it to the council that Nathan Johnson be permitted to join the hunt."

The drawn-out silence that followed indicated that few, if any, favored the chief's suggestion. It was the Makahs' belief that the spirits of the sea had decreed only those of their blood be permitted to hunt the big fish.

Tatoosh added, "I remind you the White-Eye is my blood

brother."

"He is not Makah!" the belligerent So-har said. Several braves murmured their agreement.

An even longer silence followed. It was a stark reminder to the young white that the Makah did not consider him their equal. While he'd saved the life of Tatoosh's father and had fought alongside the Makah in battle, he remained an outsider in the eyes of most. He'd earned their respect through his deeds and easy manner, and his friendship with their chief counted for much, but an outsider he remained.

"The council has spoken." It was the elderly Klussamit who broke the silence. "Nathan Johnson is not Makah. He cannot hunt the big fish. The sea gods have decreed it."

Again this was greeted by murmurs of assent.

Tatoosh had no choice but to accept the council's decision. Grim-faced, he stood to signal the meeting was over.

As the braves filed from the lodge, Tatoosh took Nathan aside. He said solemnly, "Tatoosh, son of Elswa, cannot go against the wishes of the council, Nathan Johnson."

"I understand, my brother," the young white assured him.

Tatoosh nodded and the two parted.

Nathan suddenly felt the need to be alone. The events of the past few minutes had brought home to him he was a foreigner in a foreign land. *I've been here too long,* he told himself. *I'm becoming one of them yet I'll never be accepted as one of them.* He knew he looked and acted like a native; now he worried he was starting to think like one too.

As always, his thoughts turned to home. The young white remained perplexed as to why no-one had come looking for *Intrepid* and her crew. He'd once been confident the ship's owners would sail into Neah Bay as they conducted an exhaustive search for their missing vessel and crew up and down the west coast. As the years passed, that confidence had evaporated.

Nathan wasn't to know that bloody skirmishes between neighboring tribes and traders meant that trading vessels now bypassed this stretch of coastline. Neah Bay, it seemed, had gained a reputation for being a dangerous port of call—a reputation that was largely undeserved.

Deep in thought, Nathan walked slowly toward the far end of the beach. As he walked, he was unaware that Tatoosh was observing him. The young chief, in his wisdom, suspected the White-Eye was still yearning for his previous life.

What Tatoosh couldn't know was how much Nathan was yearning for his past life.

The novelty of living as a Makah, with the Makah, had long worn thin. Nathan's respect for these people was rapidly being replaced by feelings of resentment toward them. Resentment because they were keeping him from his own kind.

They expect their token white man to embrace their beliefs and customs, and to feel grateful for their hospitality. Truth be known I'm still a slave!

Nathan felt his resentment growing. He suddenly felt superior to the Makah and the other native peoples of the Northwest. Thinking on it further, he realized he viewed their customs and beliefs as Stone-Age, and shared few of their values. How he longed to break free of this place and venture out into the world to see wonderful new sights, and to make his fortune.

EARLY NEXT MORNING, as Tatoosh led a small flotilla of canoes out of the bay on the first whale hunt of the season, Nathan walked alone up into the hills behind the village. He had some serious thinking to do.

With his long stride, the young white covered the miles effortlessly as he walked deeper into the hills. Almost without thinking, he followed a familiar path—a path he'd been using increasingly of late. It led him to the home of Tagaq, a young Makah woman who lived with her family, away from others of their tribe, in a remote valley four miles from Neah Bay. The family had been banished from the village after the man of the house, a proud Makah warrior known as Kenojuak, had slept with a headman's wife. Faced with death or banishment for him and his family, he'd chosen the latter.

Nathan had stumbled across Kenojuak's family on one of his walks two months earlier. He'd struck up an immediate rapport with the banished warrior and had taken a shine to Kenojuak's oldest daughter Tagaq, a sultry beauty only a little younger than Nathan. For the young couple it was lust at first sight, and Nathan had visited the maiden as often as he could to satisfy his desires. Those desires had become more intense of late and Tagaq was the first female he'd met who could totally satisfy him — physically at least.

It was a liaison that suited Nathan. It suited Kenojuak and his family also as the young white always came bearing gifts — as was the case on this occasion. The backpack he carried — crafted from deerskin by his faithful slave Baldy — was bulging with dried saltwater fish and other food items the family didn't normally get to enjoy.

On reaching the top of a bluff overlooking the valley that was home to the family of outcasts, Nathan stopped to admire the view. He smiled to himself when he saw Tagaq. She was picking wild herbs. As always, Nathan felt his pulse quicken at the sight of the young woman. Long, black hair framed a face that was beautiful by any standard, and her slender, athletic limbs and golden skin gave her a goddess-like appearance. But it was her eyes that had ensnared Nathan. They were all-seeing and smoky gray, and they beguiled any man she looked at.

Beyond Tagaq, Nathan had a view of the young woman's home. It was a tiny, dilapidated version of the lodge she and her family had been forced to leave back at Neah Bay. The structure leaned at an alarming angle and Nathan knew from experience it leaked like a sieve in the rain and threatened to collapse in a strong wind. For the family's newest member, a baby boy named Keno, after his father, it was the only home he'd known. For the other family members, Neah Bay was but a memory for to visit it would be punishable by death.

So it was with some enthusiasm that Tagaq and her family looked forward to Nathan's visits.

As he walked down to the tiny lodge, he was greeted by two of Tagaq's younger siblings. They raced up to Nathan and squealed with delight as he drew two small, hand-carved, wooden items from his backpack.

Tagaq was next to greet him. Her greeting was more sedate. In the custom of her people, she walked up to Nathan. "I see you Nathan Johnson," she purred softly.

"And I see you, Tagaq, daughter of Kenojuak," Nathan smiled

Barely a foot apart, the two young lovers avoided touching each other. That was the Makah way. The touching would happen soon enough, and when it did it would be all go. That was also the Makah way—as Nathan had discovered to his great delight during his first year with the tribe. Even when still a slave, he'd had his choice of many of the village maidens who, with few exceptions, had been attracted to the handsome young white.

Kenojuak and his youngest wife, Eu-tintla, emerged from the family lodge. They, too, greeted the visitor with smiles and gratefully accepted the food and other gifts he'd brought.

Custom dictated that Nathan share food with the family before satisfying his desires and making love to Tagaq. As always, the delay only served to increase his desire for the young woman. It was the same for her also, although she always took care to hide her passion for Nathan in front of her family.

Kenojuak and his two wives were under no illusion over what brought their white friend back to their valley so often. The feelings Nathan had for their daughter, and her feelings for him, had been obvious to them from the outset.

So, when Nathan politely suggested he and Tagaq go for a walk, Kenojuak chuckled to himself. The warrior smiled knowingly at his wives as the couple departed.

Outside the lodge, Tagaq led Nathan by the hand into the forest to a cave she'd discovered soon after the family's arrival in the valley. She'd not mentioned its existence to anyone else, so she and Nathan were assured of privacy when they needed to be alone—as they did now.

As they approached the cave's entrance, they walked faster. It had been two weeks since Nathan's last visit and they both needed each other urgently.

Inside the cave, they were greeted by the sight of a rug which Nathan had brought to their second romantic liaison. He'd *borrowed* it from the village and it had served as a warm bed mat for the couple ever since.

Suddenly reserved, Tagaq smiled shyly at Nathan. In the semi-darkness, her eyes flashed and Nathan could see she desired him as much as he did her. He took both her hands in his and kissed her, gently at first.

Before either of them knew it they were tearing at each other's clothes. Now naked, Nathan lay her down on the rug and began caressing her breasts with his lips. Tagaq made it clear she needed him now rather than later when she parted her thighs, grasped his throbbing member and inserted it into her womanhood.

Nathan gasped when Tagaq tightened her grip on him. He was transported to another place as she worked her magic beneath him, rolling her hips in time with his and groaning as he thrust deeper inside her.

Time vanished as their bodies became one.

The delicious sensations reminded Nathan yet again why he now avoided the attention of the eligible females back at the village and sought out Tagaq whenever he could. She was an exquisite lover. Where she'd learned her skills, he couldn't even guess. As far as he knew, the family had had no contact with others since their banishment from the village, and he was pretty certain she was a virgin when he met her.

LATER, AFTER MAKING love for the second time in as many hours, Nathan and Tagaq regretfully said their goodbyes. It was time for Nathan to return to Neah Bay.

For both, parting was the worst part of their liaisons as each knew it could be weeks before they saw each other again.

"I will try to return before the next full moon," Nathan promised.

"I will count the days until then," Tagaq murmured.

Not wanting to make their parting any more difficult than it was, Nathan kissed her then turned and struck off into the forest.

Behind him, he couldn't see the look in Tagaq's eyes. It was a mix of longing and regret. Longing because she loved her white beau more than anything or anyone she'd ever loved; regret because she could sense her love for him was not reciprocated. Tagaq knew in her heart Nathan would one day tire of her and that would be it. He was that sort of man.

As Nathan followed the track back to the village, he walked with a spring in his step. He felt blissfully satiated and, not for the first time, congratulated himself on finding Tagaq. She fully satisfied his desires and would continue to satisfy them. *At least until I get outta this place!*

CHAPTER 20

<hr>

Gulf of Guinea, 1848

TEN DAYS AFTER DEPARTING THE Canary Islands, *Minstrel* found herself becalmed off Ghana, in the Gulf of Guinea, en route to Equatorial Guinea. Conditions on board were so unbearably hot and sticky that the Drakes and their fellow passengers regretted they'd ever left the balmy refuge of Santa Cruz de Tenerife.

The Drakes and most of the other passengers had taken to living and sleeping on deck, so stifling were the conditions below deck. Even outside, the temperature was so hot and the humidity so dense that breathing was an effort and the slightest exertion resulted in torrents of sweat. But at least there, the passengers could escape the stench of bilgewater.

Now, as the mid-day sun beat down, passengers were sheltering beneath whatever shade they could find. Lying on the deck toward the bow, Susannah intermittently dozed and read her bible in the shade of a blanket her father had strung up for her between two lantern poles.

The young Englishwoman had no shortage of reading material for the long voyage. When she wasn't reading the bible, she often studied a textbook of translations of Fijian words in order to gain some understanding of the language before reaching Fiji. Handwritten, it had been lovingly compiled by another English missionary couple, Harold and

Charlotte Simpson, who were traveling to New Zealand aboard *Minstrel*. The couple had previously served as missionaries on one of Fiji's outer islands, and were more than happy to share their first-hand knowledge of the destination with Susannah.

The excited shouts of children alerted Susannah to activity on the far side of the brigantine. She hurried to the starboard rail as fast as her lethargic limbs would allow and saw the object of the children's excitement: schools of flying fish. They were literally flying by.

"Look mama!" a young girl squealed. "The fish are flying!"

Susannah became caught up in the moment and laughed delightedly as several fish ended up on *Minstrel's* deck. Just then she caught the eye of Irishman John Donovan. He'd been giving her the eye ever since the captain had released him from the hold following the recent brawl below deck. Donovan grinned at Susannah lecherously. The young woman studiously ignored him. *Awful man.* He gave her the creeps. She tensed as Donovan sidled up to her.

"I know a quiet place we can escape the heat below deck, Miss Drake," Donovan ventured.

"I'm sure you do . . . Mister?" She knew his name, but wasn't going to give him the satisfaction.

"Donovan," the Irishman grinned. "Me friends call me John."

Susannah noted his face still bore the marks of the recent brawl. "I am sure I have better things to do than go below deck with you, Mister Donovan," she said haughtily.

Donovan's arm suddenly snaked around Susannah's waist. He pulled him to her and forcibly tried to kiss her.

Susannah slapped his face hard and pushed him away. Her feisty response surprised the young Irishman.

Donovan hid his surprise behind a lewd smile. "Me invitation still stands," he smirked.

At that moment, Kemp appeared behind the pair. "Is everything alright, Susannah?" the former colonel enquired.

Donovan executed a mock bow in Susannah's direction and, without acknowledging Kemp, retired below deck. Kemp looked at the young woman enquiringly.

"It was nothing, Mister Kemp . . . ah . . . Harry," Susannah said, making light of the incident. "I was just making Mister Donovan aware I have no intention of socializing with him."

"Very wise, young lady," Kemp suggested. "He's nothing but trouble that one." Kemp was momentarily distracted by another school of flying fish that scudded past the vessel. Smiling, he pointed at the fish. "One of nature's strangest sights."

Kemp's schoolboy enthusiasm for such things further endeared him to Susannah and helped her forget the unpleasantness of a few moments earlier. His enthusiasm contrasted with his military bearing and otherwise serious demeanor.

"How long are we likely to remain becalmed?" Susannah enquired.

"Ships have been known to be delayed weeks on end in this part of the world."

Susannah was horrified at the thought.

Kemp added, "But the first mate advised me he believes we should be underway in the next two or three days."

Susannah didn't know whether to laugh or cry at this prediction. She wasn't sure she could stand even one more day of the stifling heat. However, she managed a smile for Kemp's benefit. "That is good news."

"Ship ahoy!" the cry came from *Minstrel's* lookout.

Susannah and Kemp looked about them, trying to sight the other vessel. Kemp spotted it off to port. It was just a dot on the horizon, approaching from the direction of the Ghanaian coast.

Finally, Susannah saw it, too. "How can it be moving yet Minstrel is stuck fast?" Susannah asked.

Kemp didn't hear her. He was too busy studying the other craft.

The first and second mate suddenly appeared on deck. Concern was written over their faces as they studied the approaching vessel through telescopes.

Kemp wandered over to talk to the pair. He returned moments later and confided to Susannah the first mate had advised him the approaching party could be pirates. "He doesn't wish to alarm the others in case it's a false alarm," Kemp added.

Susannah nodded, suddenly afraid. She studied the other vessel a moment and noticed, as it drew closer, it appeared to be a brigantine—like *Minstrel* but smaller. And like *Minstrel*, her sails were unfurled and hanging limp in the still tropical air. Nevertheless, she was drawing closer. Bemused, Susannah turned back to Kemp.

Anticipating her next question, Kemp said, "She is being rowed. See." He pointed toward the brigantine. "You can just make out the splashing of the oars."

Susannah focused on the approaching craft. Sunlight reflected off the disturbed water around it, just as Kemp had said.

Kemp continued, "The first mate said pirates are the only people likely to be rowing a brigantine in these seas."

By now, a number of crewmen had gathered around first mate Fred Paxton. He fired orders at them and the men began running in all directions. Significantly, there was no sign of Captain Mathers. There were no prizes for guessing where he was: he was dead drunk in his cabin. He'd been there since *Minstrel* had departed Tenerife.

Susannah became aware of just how serious their situation was when she noticed the crewmen were arming themselves. Several were loading muskets and pistols while almost all carried swords or knives.

"It seems Mr Paxton's fears have been confirmed," Kemp said resignedly. "You had best alert your father, Susannah."

Susannah realized she had been so engrossed, she'd forgotten about Drake Senior. "Oh, yes! Excuse me." She hurried away. As she neared the steerage, she met her father who was on his way topside to investigate the commotion he'd heard. He was clutching a large bible, which was well thumbed and rarely left his side.

"What's going on?" he asked as soon as he saw Susannah.

"Another brigantine approaches," Susannah said breathlessly. "The crew fear it could be pirates."

Drake Senior hurried to the port-side rail to see for himself. Susannah caught up to him. The approaching brigantine was closer now. Her oars could clearly be seen, working in well-practiced unison and glinting in the sunlight. The craft was making good time despite the absence of wind in her sails.

The Drakes were joined by Kemp. Susannah noticed he now wore an Army-issue cutlass in a scabbard on his hip and had a pistol tucked into his belt. The two men greeted each other with a nod.

"A serious business, Mr Kemp," Drake Senior mumbled.

"Indeed, Reverend."

Under the directions of Paxton, the crew began taking up defensive positions. Susannah noticed all crewmembers were now on deck—even the cook and the steward, and their assistants. They'd been joined by a dozen or so male passengers. Like the crew, the passengers had been issued with firearms, which had been stored under lock and key below deck for just such an occasion. Missionary Harold Simpson was among them.

Crewmen began ushering women and children below deck.

The Swedish second mate, Sven Svenson, approached the Drakes. "Best get below deck," he said.

Drake Senior immediately turned to Susannah. "You heard Mister Svenson, my dear. Go below now."

"But papa, what about you?"

Drake Senior moved his bible aside to reveal the butt of a pistol protruding from his waistband. "I shall be fine," he promised. He caught Kemp's eye and winked.

Before Susannah could debate the issue, Svenson nodded to *Minstrel's* rotund German cook, Hans Schmidt, who was hovering nearby. "See Miss Drake safely to her quarters, Herr Schmidt."

"Ya," Schmidt responded. He gently but firmly grasped the young woman by her elbow and steered her away.

Below deck, Susannah found the children and other female passengers assembled in the saloon. The women were fearful. They sensed something wasn't right.

"What is happening?" Charlotte Simpson asked.

Schmidt shot Susannah a warning glance. "No sense in causing unnecessary panic," he whispered. "I suggest you barricade yourselves in." The big cook hurried off to join the others up top.

Adopting a forced smile, Susannah announced lightly, "The menfolk are performing a firearm drill."

This seemed to satisfy some of the women, but not all. Several had already heard the whispers about pirates. Some of the children began crying.

"Is it true we are being attacked by pirates?" a heavily pregnant woman asked.

"They are not sure," Susannah replied. "They are only taking precautionary measures. I suggest we barricade ourselves in . . . Just in case."

Above deck, the menfolk had finally been joined by Captain Mathers. The steward's assistant had done a good job making the captain presentable following his latest drinking binge. Having had a bucket of water thrown over him and having been force-fed several mugs of strong, black coffee, Mathers looked almost sober. Even so, he had the good sense to give his first mate the authority to prepare *Minstrel's* defences — for the moment at least.

Paxton had wisely recruited the services of Kemp to help organize their defences. The former colonel had immediately swung into action and ensured those armed with muskets occupied the best vantage points.

By now, the approaching Brigantine was less than one hundred yards to port and showing no signs of slowing. The oars powering her flashed ominously in the sunlight.

CHAPTER 21

Parramatta, New South Wales, 1841

IT HAD BEEN NEARLY A year since Jack's ill-fated escape attempt. His back still bore reminders of the lashes he'd received on that occasion, and of the many others he'd received prior to that. Since then, he'd kept his nose clean and, thankfully, had suffered no more floggings.

Now twenty-five, Jack knew he was lucky to survive that last dreadful whipping. After three hundreds lashes — or three hundred and two to be exact — his flesh had been torn from his back, leaving portions of his spine and ribs temporarily exposed; infection had set in and only the intervention of a conscientious doctor, and the loving care of Mary O'Brien, had kept him alive.

Now, as he wielded his pick-axe, cracking rocks on the road that linked Parramatta with Sydney Town, he marveled at how well he'd recovered. Few thought he'd survive his wounds. Not only had he survived, but he'd never felt stronger.

As his pick-axe rhythmically rose and fell, Jack's thoughts once again turned to escape. In fact, escape was all he'd thought about since that last flogging. He was still intent on stowing away on board a vessel bound for New Zealand or the Pacific Islands. If he could just make his way to Sydney Town, he was confident he'd succeed. The problem was getting to

Sydney Town.

Opportunities to escape were few and far between, and this particular day was shaping up to be like any other. Except, for no apparent reason, the Red Coats guarding the convicts today were more numerous than usual. The ratio of guards to convicts was one to five as opposed to the normal one to nine. As a result, the Red Coats weren't expecting any trouble and were noticeably less vigilant than usual.

And then, as Jack had hoped would happen, an opportunity came out of the blue.

The shadows were lengthening when a guard approached a small group of convicts whose number included Jack and Scottie, the hard-bitten Scottish convict Jack had met on arrival at Parramatta. "You men, lend a hand over there," the guard ordered, pointing to two Sydney workmen who were loading rocks onto a stationary, horse-drawn cart nearby.

The convicts walked over to the help the workmen. As they walked, Scottie said, "These bloody rocks will be needed for that new construction project in Sydney Town, I'll wager."

That got Jack thinking. "You sure about that, Scottie?"

"I'd bet me left testicle on it, laddie."

"I thought ye lost that testicle in a bet last year, Scottie," a big, raw-boned Irish convict commented, prompting laughter amongst the other convicts.

Scottie didn't join in the laughter, however. He glared at the Irishman who glared right back at him. There was clearly no love lost between the two.

As they started loading the rocks onto the cart, Jack maneuvered himself so that he was close to Scottie. "I need you to create a diversion," he whispered.

Scottie stared at Jack for a moment then glanced over at the big Irish convict. Finally, he said, "You're in luck, Cockney. I'm itchin' for a fight."

Jack grinned.

"Just don't do anything silly," the Scotsman warned.

"I can't promise that," Jack said.

Scottie rolled his eyes theatrically. "I was afraid of that." He then walked over to the Irishman who had ribbed him moments earlier and, without warning, punched him on the nose.

The Irishman was momentarily dazed. Shaking his head, he asked, "What da hell was that fer?"

"For being such an ugly son-of-a-bitch and a disgrace to the Celtic race," Scottie advised him.

As expected, the Irishman retaliated. Soon it was all on. Some of the other convicts joined in and an all-in brawl quickly developed. The brawlers were hampered by their leg-irons, but still gave a good account of themselves. The Red Coats didn't intervene. Like their charges, they welcomed anything that relieved the boredom. Soon, guards and convicts alike were shouting encouragement to the various factions involved in the brawl.

Jack noted the two workmen were engrossed in the brawl also. Picking his moment, he crawled beneath the cart he and the others had been loading the rocks onto moments earlier. Climbing up onto its axle, he made himself as comfortable as he could and waited for the brawl to end.

It was then he noticed he wasn't alone: a long, grey-colored snake was curled up around the other end of the axle, not three feet away. Jack froze. *Oh shite!* He debated whether to roll out from beneath the cart. The snake's black eyes bore into Jack's. Scared stiff, he tried to identify it. Whether or not it was a poisonous variety of snake would determine whether he stayed or fled. Jack was unsure if it was a deadly brown or a harmless carpet snake. He gambled on it being the latter.

By the time the brawling convicts ran out of steam, it was home-time. The guards ordered the convicts to board the half-dozen horse-drawn carts waiting to take them back to Parramatta. They willingly obliged.

Hidden from view, Jack prayed the guards would not do a head count. He was reasonably confident they wouldn't for it had been over a year since the last escape attempt from Parramatta and the guards had progressively become less zealous in carrying out their duties. He also prayed his reptilian companion wouldn't bother him. The snake still hadn't taken its eyes off the uninvited guest.

Jack listened nervously as the carts moved out one at a time. There was no head count. The two remaining workmen loaded the last of the rocks onto Jack's cart then jumped aboard. Soon, the cart was lurching down the road toward Sydney Town. As it negotiated the bumpy road, Jack's leg-irons clinked alarmingly. He repositioned his feet to keep the leg-irons taut. That did the trick.

Unfortunately, the movement of Jack's feet alarmed the snake. It hissed at Jack.

"Easy boy," Jack whispered. *And take your beady little eyes off me!*

The snake's eyes continued to bore into Jack's. Without warning, it struck out, sinking its fangs into Jack's nearest leg. Its movement was so quick, Jack didn't even know he'd been bitten until he felt a pain just below his left knee.

At that moment, the cart lurched, dislodging the snake from the axle and nearly dislodging Jack too. The snake fell onto the road. Jack watched, relieved, as it slithered away. Then his thoughts turned to his own mortality. He realized he'd soon find out whether the reptile was a brown snake or a carpet snake. *If it's a brown, I'll be dead inside the hour,* he told himself.

An hour after being bitten, Jack was no worse for wear other than feeling tired, sore and thirsty. The fact that he was still breathing confirmed to him the reptile was a carpet snake, not a deadly brown.

As the cart traveled through the night along the unfinished road to Sydney Town, every muscle in his body ached. Still, he was thankful he was alive and remained undiscovered. To pass the time, he listened to the conversation of his two unwitting companions atop the cart. He'd discovered they were Cockneys like himself. Both were single. The older man had been in the colony five years, the younger man less than a year.

It quickly became evident to Jack that both men missed home. They spoke fondly of English cider, bangers and mash, roast beef, Cornish pasties, and steak and kidney pies, and they named their favorite drinking taverns around London. Jack was familiar with them all. Right now, he was longing for a pint of bitter and a pie.

———⟨⟩———

JUST BEFORE DAWN, the cart rolled to a halt outside a cluster of workingmen's barracks at a construction camp on the outskirts of Sydney Town. The two workmen bade each other goodnight and retired to their quarters.

Jack gratefully dropped to the ground and peered out from beneath the cart. There was no sign of life. He was relieved to find the workmen had left the cart in front of a trough. The thirsty horses were noisily drinking from it. Keen to assuage his thirst, Jack crawled out from beneath the cart, pushed himself slowly to his feet and immersed his whole head into the trough. Ignoring the horses which were now both observing him strangely, he scooped handfuls of water into his mouth until he'd drunk his fill.

Anxious to get into town before daylight, he then hurried off into the darkness. His clinking leg-irons reminded him he must remove them quickly if he was to avoid being captured.

The young convict scurried toward Sydney Town's docks. Besides the occasional drunk and a solitary prostitute, the streets were mercifully deserted.

———⟨⟩———

HOURS PASSED BEFORE Jack found what he was looking for: a blacksmith's shop that was accessible to someone, like himself, who didn't possess a key to its front door. Breaking into it via a rear window, he quickly located the tools he needed to remove his leg irons. The young Cockney wrapped cloth around the leg irons to muffle the sound then attacked them with an axe and a heavy mallet. Three well placed blows with the former and two heavy blows with the latter was all it took.

Free of his leg irons, he then scouted around for a change of clothes. When he couldn't find any he hurried outside and walked along the street until he came to a residential suburb. Rows of modest cottages lined both sides of the narrow, dusty street.

Dawn was breaking and residents were beginning to emerge from their homes. Mainly workers, the residents appeared to be in a hurry to report to their respective work-places. Few took any notice of Jack.

The escapee spotted men's clothing hanging from a makeshift clothesline at the rear of a cottage whose occupants did not appear to have surfaced yet. He hurried to the line, selected a near-new shirt and a pair of trousers, and changed into them before hiding his discarded convict clothing in a rubbish bin. The shirt and trousers were a near-perfect fit.

Jack strode off down the street, confident he could now merge in with the civilian population. He could already taste freedom as he headed for the waterfront. *Don't get ahead of yerself Jackie boy,* he cautioned himself. *You ain't free yet. And if they catch you again, they'll flog ya until there ain't nuthin' left to flog."*

DOWN AT THE docks, Jack surveyed the various vessels in port. There was any number that could meet his needs. On the wharves, seamen mingled with waterside workers while unemployed civilians queued outside the labor office hoping to secure casual work.

Jack made a beeline for the labor office. He pulled up when he noticed Red Coats doing random checks of civilians queuing up for employment.

The Cockney guessed the soldiers were checking for escaped convicts. He just hoped they weren't searching for him. *Unlikely,* he thought. *They'll have only just discovered I'm absent without leave back at Parra.* Logic told him there hadn't been time to get word out about his escape from Parramatta. Even so, he didn't want to take any unnecessary risks. He turned his back on the docks and returned to town.

Storekeepers were displaying their wares and setting up for the day as Jack walked along the main street. His rumbling stomach reminded him he hadn't eaten since the previous day. He spied a tavern nearby and headed for it just as the establishment's proprietor stepped outside, humming a popular Scottish folk song. "Are you the owner?" Jack asked.

"Aye, Joseph McNeish," the proprietor answered in a strong Scottish brogue. "And who wants to know?"

"Billy Kennedy," Jack lied. "I'm lookin' to earn me breakfast. Can you spare a penny or two if I do some sweeping or something?" He flashed a cheeky grin.

"Have ye tried for work down at the docks?" Joseph asked.

"Yeah, but they're full up today. I just missed out."

Joseph looked like he was about to send Jack on his way when he had second thoughts. "Matter of fact, there may be something for ye." He began walking back inside the tavern. "Follow me, Billy Kennedy."

Jack followed the proprietor through to the kitchen where the previous night's unwashed drinking glasses, jugs and dinner dishes lay stacked almost to the ceiling.

Joseph turned back to the Cockney. "Our bottle washer's off sick today." He looked around at the unwashed dishes. "Think ye can wash and dry these without breaking any?"

Jack nodded with as much enthusiasm as he could muster.

"I pay two pence an hour less one penny for every plate ye break. Fair?"

"Fair."

"Well get to it Billy and I'll have cook rustle up some brekky for ye out back."

Jack polished off the dishes without breaking a single plate. He received sixpence for the three hours it took him and he enjoyed a cooked breakfast better than any he could remember. The accommodating proprietor, who had taken a shine to the young man he knew as *Billy Kennedy,* even threw in a bottle of Guinness to help wash the food down.

CHAPTER 22

Makah Nation, West Coast, North America, 1841

TRUE TO HIS WORD, NATHAN set out to see Tagaq before the next full moon. The two weeks since he'd last seen her had seemed like a year. Tagaq's naked body occupied his thoughts from dawn till dusk, and his nights were filled with dreams of their lovemaking. He could feel himself hardening at the thought of her.

Even though he ran the four miles to the valley where Tagaq and her banished family lived, it seemed to take an eternity. He was breathing hard as he reached the top of the bluff that overlooked the valley that was home to the family of outcasts.

Nathan stopped to catch his breath. All seemed quiet in the valley below. There was no sign of Tagaq or any of her siblings. Smoke curled from the hole cut in the roof of the tiny family lodge, indicating someone was home at least.

Avoiding the temptation to run, Nathan walked down the hill toward the lodge. As he neared it, the sound of women wailing greeted him. *Something's wrong!* He started running toward the dwelling.

Before he reached the lodge, Tagaq's father, Kenojuak, emerged. His grim face told Nathan something was definitely wrong.

The old warrior stepped forward and, in the manner of the Makah, clasped Nathan's left shoulder with his right hand. "I see you, Nathan Johnson." He had to speak loudly to be heard above the sound of wailing.

"And I see you, Kenojuak," Nathan replied.

"You have come to be with Tagaq?"

Nathan nodded.

"She awaits you inside." Kenojuak stepped aside and allowed Nathan to enter.

Nathan had to stoop so his head cleared the top of the doorway as he entered the lodge. As his eyes adjusted to its gloomy, smoky interior, he saw Kenojuak's two wives and their younger children. They were sitting in a circle in the middle of the room. The women ceased wailing as soon as they saw their visitor.

At first Nathan didn't see the object lying at the feet of the two women. When he did see it, it took a few seconds for him to work out the object was a lifeless woman. *Tagaq?* She was unrecognizable. The flesh and eyes had been torn from her face.

As his eyes ran down her body, Nathan realized he was looking at Tagaq, or what was left of her. "Tagaq!" he screamed. Nathan fell to his knees alongside her. He stroked her hair as he repeated her name over and over. *Where is your face? What have they done to you?* He couldn't make sense of anything.

The young white suddenly had to get away. He pushed himself to his feet and drunkenly lunged for the doorway, cracking his skull against it as he stumbled out into the fresh air.

Kenojuak had been waiting for him. As soon as he saw Nathan, he came toward him. Nathan didn't even see him; he ran into the surrounding trees and didn't stop running until exhaustion halted him in his tracks.

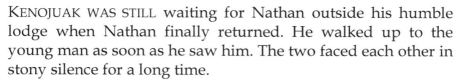

KENOJUAK WAS STILL waiting for Nathan outside his humble lodge when Nathan finally returned. He walked up to the young man as soon as he saw him. The two faced each other in stony silence for a long time.

Since the shock of seeing Tagaq, or what was left of her, had passed, Nathan had had time to think. He realized she must have been attacked by a wild animal. "Was it a puma?" he asked at length.

Kenojuak shook his head. "Black bear."

"When?"

"Yesterday afternoon. She was collecting herbs." The warrior pointed in the direction of the cave that Nathan and his lover had so often frequented. "Up there."

"Where will she be buried?"

Kenojuak shrugged. "I have not yet decided."

"I have a place in mind."

"Show me."

Nathan led Tagaq's father off toward the cave.

LATER THAT DAY, Nathan looked on as Kenojuak and his family laid Tagaq to rest in the cave the two lovers had come to know so well. Wrapped in the rug they'd so often made love on, Tagaq was gently lowered into a shallow grave before Nathan joined the family members in shoveling freshly dug earth over her.

That done, they filed somberly from the cave. Nathan helped Kenojuak roll a large rock over the cave entrance so the gravesite would forever remain undiscovered and animals couldn't disturb the body.

Kenojuak's wives resumed chanting and wailing as they led the young children back to the lodge, leaving the two men standing outside the cave's concealed entrance.

"I must go now," Nathan said. He needed to be alone.

"I know."

"I will not see you again, Kenojuak."

"I know that also, Nathan Johnson." Kenojuak grasped Nathan by the shoulders and looked deeply into his eyes. "Take this blessing with you."

So blessed, Nathan turned and walked away.

"There is something you should know," Kenojuak called out.

Nathan turned back to face the older man.

Kenojuak smiled for the first time that day. "She was going to tell you she would be your woman and would go with you to the distant lands of the White-Eye."

The words hung in the air between them. Nathan's mind raced as he tried to make sense of what he'd just heard.

It slowly dawned on Nathan that Tagaq knew he was going to flee Neah Bay, and she'd loved him so much she wanted to go with him. The realization saddened him. Finally, he said, "Thank you, Kenojuak." With that, Nathan turned and walked away. He never looked back.

CHAPTER 23

⸺◦⊙◦⸺

Gulf of Guinea, 1848

M INSTREL'S CREW KNEW THEY WERE under attack for the approaching brigantine had made no effort to answer the semaphore messages second mate Sven Svenson had been flashing non-stop for some time now. Nor did she bear a visible name on her hull or a flag of origin on her mast—sure signs the vessel's crew had bad intentions.

"Give up, Mr Svenson," first mate Fred Paxton advised him. "They have no intention of responding."

Svenson lowered the flags he'd been waving above his head, picked up the musket he'd left at his feet and took up his allotted firing position alongside Drake Senior atop a bulkhead. The two men studied the fast-approaching brigantine as she closed with *Minstrel*.

"She means business," Drake Senior observed as he nervously checked his pistol.

"Aye, that she does," the second mate agreed. The Swede studied his companion, trying to reconcile the man of God he knew the reverend to be with the gunman lying next to him.

Drake Senior could read his companion's mind. *The good Lord helps those who help themselves.* He smiled to himself.

Further along the deck, beyond Svenson, the clergyman saw Harold Simpson familiarizing himself with the musket

159

someone had handed him. It was very evident by the clumsy way he handled it he'd never even held one before. Drake Senior whispered a silent prayer for the missionary.

The approaching brigantine was now only fifty yards away. She was on a collision course with *Minstrel* and looked set to ram her mid-ships.

"She's gonna ram us!" someone shouted unnecessarily, for it was obvious to all.

Now they could see the crew of the other craft. Around thirty strong, they were a cut-throat bunch armed with a variety of weapons ranging from swords and daggers to axes and lances, but mercifully not a firearm in sight.

"We have superior firepower," Svenson murmured to himself.

Drake Senior could see the pirates appeared to be of indeterminate nationality. Predominantly light-skinned, their features were a mix of African, European and possibly Asian. In fact, they were a mix of all these and more. They were the last remnants of the feared Barbary Coast pirates — the privateers who operated out of North Africa and who, since the Sixteenth Century, had struck fear in the hearts of voyageurs throughout the Mediterranean and down West Africa's Atlantic seaboard and beyond.

"No-one shoots until I give the word," Kemp reminded everyone.

Too late. A very nervous Simpson fired his musket at the enemy craft. The shot went wide.

"I said no-one shoots till I say so!" the former colonel repeated. Kemp was exerting the authority the first mate had given him now that conflict was imminent. This gave Drake Senior and the others some confidence: Kemp was clearly no stranger to conflict.

The men could only watch as the bow of the other vessel rammed into *Minstrel's* side. There was an awful cracking of timbers followed by the sounds of women's screams from below.

"Fire!" Kemp shouted.

A dozen musket shots rang out almost in unison accompanied by small arms fire. Drake Senior saw five pirates fall in the first volley. He was pretty sure he'd shot one of them. Certainly, the pirate he'd aimed at had been struck down. The clergyman didn't realized it, but the pirate he thought he'd shot was the pirates' leader. This would be fortuitous for the men aboard *Minstrel* for, although outnumbered, they were now fighting a leaderless enemy.

The pirates threw grappling irons over *Minstrel's* near rail, to secure the two brigantines together, then began swarming aboard, swinging their cutlasses at anything that moved. Fierce fighters, they found themselves seriously disadvantaged in the face of firearms. Four more were felled by musket and small arms fire. Nevertheless, they had some success. Three of *Minstrel's* defenders including the steward's assistant, a lad of only eighteen, were killed.

"Stay together!" Kemp shouted. Having positioned the men close together so they could cover each other's backs, he was anxious they not become separated.

In the saloon below deck, the women and children huddled together fearfully listening to the sounds of battle raging above. Using tables and chairs, they'd barricaded themselves in, in case the pirates prevailed and came looking for them. Many were crying.

Hiding her own fear, Susannah led the women in prayer. The other women took strength from this. Knowing she was the clergyman's daughter, and a determined young lady to boot, the others automatically turned to her for comfort. Susannah recited the Lord's Prayer with all the confidence she could muster, all the while hoping her father survived the violence on deck.

On the bulkhead above deck, as he furiously reloaded his pistol, Drake Senior noted Captain Mathers was giving a good account of himself despite his hung-over state. Armed with pistol and sword, the captain shot one pirate then dispatched another with a blade through the chest.

The rotund German cook Hans Schmidt was also proving an asset. Schmidt shot one pirate then, wielding a cutlass, despatched two more overboard. They were quickly taken by the sharks that were now circling the two brigantines. More sharks arrived and a feeding frenzy quickly developed.

Much of the gunfire was wayward as many of *Minstrel's* men were using their weapons in anger for the first time. Some however — like Kemp, Mathers and Schmidt — were no strangers to violence and were making their presence felt. For every defender struck down, two or three pirates fell.

Three pirates came at Drake Senior and Svenson. The clergyman shot one between the eyes; the second mate shot the other at point-blank range. The third pirate, a fearsome character with a sword in each hand, advanced on them before either man could reload. With one thrust of the sword in his right hand he ran the blade through Svenson's chest, mortally wounding him, and with his other sword he slashed Drake Senior diagonally across the abdomen. The wound went deep, gravely wounding the clergyman who was catapulted backwards onto the deck. He landed heavily and lay there groaning.

The pirate turned his attention back to the second mate who was raising his musket, club-like, for one final act before departing this world. Before Svenson could bring the musket down, the pirate decapitated him with a single slash of the sword he'd just used against Drake Senior.

Svenson's head rolled along the deck. The sight of it galvanized the surviving defenders into action. Led impressively by Kemp, they fought with a fury most never knew they possessed.

Simpson was one of a number who both distinguished himself and surprised himself at the same time. After priming and firing his musket twice more and failing to find his target even once, the missionary threw the weapon aside, picked up a fallen cutlass and quickly despatched two pirates over the side. He'd collected a minor head wound for his trouble, but so far was otherwise unharmed.

Gradually, the tide turned and the surviving pirates were forced to back-peddle. One by one, they leapt the short distance back to their own brigantine. As soon as the grappling irons had been disengaged, a dozen pirates manned the oars and began rowing away from *Minstrel* as fast as they could.

On board *Minstrel,* Kemp directed musket-fire at the departing craft. He had the satisfaction of seeing two more pirates struck down before they were out of range. One was the fellow who had struck down Drake Senior and Svenson.

Throughout all this Drake Senior lay unmoving where he'd fallen.

Below deck, as the sounds of conflict faded, Susannah and the other women hurriedly removed the makeshift barricade they'd set up. Wives, partners and children were desperate to find our how their menfolk had fared. Through the port holes, they'd seen the pirates' brigantine rowing away and heard the defenders cheering, so realized their menfolk had prevailed.

Not so sure of the outcome was Irishman John Donovan who had concealed himself in the hold at the first sign of trouble. Hidden amongst water barrels, he couldn't be sure the defenders had prevailed so he chose to remain concealed for the moment.

Susannah led the women topside while two of the single women stayed below to look after the children. No-one wanted the young ones to be exposed to the aftermath of the violence that had occurred above deck.

As Susannah emerged into the sunlight, the first sight that greeted her was the still form of her father lying in a pool of blood on the deck. She cried, "Papa!"

CHAPTER 24

Sydney Town, 1841

THE INITIAL EXCITEMENT OF ESCAPING from Parramatta was starting to wear thin for Jack who was facing the prospect of having to overnight in Sydney Town. He'd been observing the docks since early afternoon, hoping an opportunity would present itself for him to stow away aboard one of several ships that were being provisioned alongside the main wharf. Alas, no such luck.

If anything, the number of Red Coats he'd seen earlier had increased. The soldiers were closely monitoring all comings and goings on the wharves, and checking the identities of anyone who looked out of place. *They're looking for me!* He considered it a safe bet his escape from the penal settlement had been reported. *That'd explain all those bloody Red Coats.* Jack decided to give it another five minutes then he'd give up for the day and try again tomorrow.

Five minutes dragged out to ten and then fifteen until a disheartened Jack finally flagged it and wandered back up into Sydney Town. He was resigned to finding lodgings for the night and trying his luck down at the docks again tomorrow. His next problem was money: he didn't have enough for both lodgings and a meal, and the fine breakfast he'd had that morning was already a distant memory. The hunger pangs were beginning to gnaw at him.

First some food then I'll worry about a bed.

Jack entered the first eatery he came to and used the sixpence he'd earned earlier to buy a splendid cooked meal and a jug of stout to wash it down. Fellow patrons included an assortment of local residents, visiting seamen and, to Jack's consternation, several off duty soldiers.

Before he'd finished his main course, Jack found himself in conversation with a group of rowdy laborers who occupied an adjoining table. They insisted he join them and, against his better judgment, he did. It turned out to be a fortuitous development as one of the laborers, a Cornishman, told him of a vacancy for a live-in handyman at a nearby boarding house.

Jack realized that could be the solution to his need for temporary lodgings until he managed to stow away on one of the ships. He bolted down the remainder of his meal, thanked his newfound friends for their company and excused himself. Before his friends allowed him to leave, they made him promise he'd return to the eatery the following evening. He agreed to that and hurried off.

It was dark by the time Jack found the boarding house his Cornish friend had told him about. A crude, hand-painted sign hanging from a first floor balcony read: *Live-in handyman wanted – Pays 1 shilling a week & full board.*

Jack rang the front door bell and was greeted a minute later by the establishment's middle-aged proprietor, Jim Todd, a timid little Welshman who had just downed his third gin of the evening and looked decidedly unsteady on his feet.

"Can I help ye?" Todd asked.

"I'm here about the vacancy," Jack said with a cheery grin.

"Ye'll have to come back in the morn," Todd said. He began to close the door.

Jack stuck his foot in the doorway, preventing the proprietor from closing it.

"Hey!" Todd objected.

"This is a one-day only offer," Jack said cheekily.

"Who is it, Jim?" a woman's voice enquired from inside.

"Just a chap here about the job, dear," Jim replied.

"I'll be right down." The voice, which sounded assertive to Jack's ears, belonged to the proprietor's wife, Joan.

Todd stared at Jack glumly as his wife descended the stairs to talk to the visitor.

Before he'd even met her, Jack decided the proprietor's wife wore the pants in this marriage. That was confirmed seconds later when Joan appeared in the open doorway and shooed her husband back inside as though he was a pet dog.

The not unattractive Welshwoman ran an appraising eye over Jack. She liked what she saw and she made no secret of that. "You're here about the job, young man?"

"Ah . . . I'm Jack . . . ah . . . Billy Kennedy, ma'am," he said, adopting the moniker he'd used earlier that day. "I've come about the job."

"Are ye a handyman, Billy?" Joan asked with a twinkle in her eye.

"That I am, ma'am." Jack wasn't sure if there was a double meaning in Joan's question, but he hoped there was. He found Joan Todd very fetching even if she was older than the women he was usually drawn to.

"Well ye best come in and tell me why I should give ye the job." Joan stepped aside and motioned to the Cockney to enter.

Inside, Jack heard laughter and the hum of male conversation. Through an open doorway at the rear of the establishment he saw a dozen or so men eating dinner in the dining room. He guessed they were the boarders. More laughter. It was a happy establishment, Jack decided.

"Dinner's served at six o'clock sharp," Joan said. She spoke as though Jack already had the job. "Have ye eaten, Billy?"

"Yes, ma'am."

"Then ye won't mind talking to my husband and me while we finish our dinner." She led Jack upstairs to the private quarters she shared with her husband. There was no sign of any children.

They entered a dining room where Todd was in the process of emptying the remains of a gin bottle while pecking at a hot cooked meal. Jack realized he'd interrupted the Todds' dinner. He mumbled an apology, but Joan waved one hand dismissively and motioned to him to join her and her husband at the dining table while they finished eating.

Joan proceeded to demonstrate she had a hearty appetite as she attacked her meal, finishing it even before Jim finished his. She offered her husband no explanation why she'd invited Jack to their dining table, and Jim didn't question her. He seemed content to leave his wife to attend to all business matters.

As soon as Joan finished eating, she began quizzing Jack on his background. Thankfully, he'd had time to concoct a convincing story, advising his prospective employers he'd been traveling around New South Wales hiring out his services as a handyman since arriving in the colony a year earlier.

Joan didn't buy a word of what Jack was telling her, but the young man intrigued her and she decided to humor him for the moment.

What Jack didn't know was the saucy Welshwoman had long since tired of her inadequate husband who was more interested in liquor than in her or anything she had to offer. She'd only tolerated his continued presence at the boarding house because it was his money that financed the business and the reasonably comfortable lifestyle it provided. Otherwise, he'd have been out on his ear long ago.

To compensate, Joan occasionally and discreetly took on a younger lover. Sometimes, the chosen one was a boarder she liked the look of.

Fortuitously for Jack, his arrival at the boarding house coincided with a long period of abstinence on Joan's part. A long period by her standards at least: she hadn't had a man in more than three months and she was like a dog in heat.

While Jack wasn't good looking by any means, there was something about him that attracted her to him. For the life of her, she didn't know what that something was, but she was determined to find out. "De ye still want the job Billy?"

"Yes ma'am," Jack said without hesitation.

Joan quickly outlined the terms of employment, explaining that Jack would be expected to work from five o'clock in the morning to five at night Monday to Saturday. In return he'd receive one shilling a week and full board including meals. Jack had no objection to the terms. Besides, he didn't imagine he'd be here more than a few days at most.

Jim Todd contributed nothing to the conversation and appeared to take no interest in it. He was content to drain the last of the gin from the bottle and was now glassy-eyed and inebriated. Without excusing himself, he stood up and lurched toward the door.

As soon as he'd gone, Joan turned to Jack as if her husband had never been in the room. "Now let me show you to your quarters and you can get settled in." The accommodating Welshwoman stood and led Jack out of the dining room. She paused at the top of the stairs and turned back to her newest employee. "If we are going to be living in the same establishment, ye best tell me your real name, *Billy*."

Jack realized he hadn't fooled her at all. "Ah . . . Jack Marshall," he lied. *Can't hurt letting her know me first name at least.* He looked at her to see if she'd bought it.

Joan smiled knowingly. "Jack Marshall," she whispered. "Don't worry, your secret's safe with me." She reached out and squeezed his shoulder with all the familiarity of old friends.

Jack suddenly felt excited. Right now stowing away with rats and other creatures in the hold of some ship was the last thing on his mind.

CHAPTER 25

Makah Nation, West Coast, North America, 1842

THE SPRING THAW HAD ARRIVED in the Northwest. Oregon Country's rivers were swollen from the melting snows, and the hills were a blaze of color as flowers that had laid dormant over the winter burst into life.

Makah hunting parties took advantage of a rare fine day to venture deep into the interior in search of the elk and black bears that were plentiful at this time of year. Others scoured the coastline in search of the increasingly elusive sea otters. The Makah remained ever hopeful the traders' ships would resume their visits to trade their muskets for the valuable sea otter fur.

Nathan and Tatoosh had gone their own way, hunting elk in the hills that overlooked Neah Bay. The blood brothers studied the ground for tracks and other spoor as they climbed one of the highest hills in the area.

Only days shy of his twentieth birthday, Nathan cut a fine figure in his traditional native garments. Tall and broad-shouldered with rugged good looks and startling blue eyes, the young white was considered a fine catch by the many maidens who desired to share his lodge. As a result, he seldom slept alone at night.

As he followed the young chief up the hill, his mind was on his latest dalliance—a pretty slave girl from a tribe to the south. While not as skillful in the love-arts as Tagaq had been, she'd proven an adventurous lover since Nathan had lured her to his lodge several weeks earlier, and he found he was looking forward to their next liaison.

There had been no shortage of women, whether they were from Neah Bay or from neighboring villages, for the young white. They'd been a pleasant diversion, but he longed to be able to pursue and bed eligible Philadelphian gals, and to converse with them in English.

Tagaq was now but a distant memory. Nathan had soon gotten over her violent death of almost a year earlier. While he'd been fond of her, he quickly realized after her passing that their relationship—for him at least—had been based on lust, not love. He'd replaced her with another willing maiden within a week of her death, and had shared his bed mat with more than a dozen others since then.

Even so, on the rare occasions he thought of Tagaq, he did experience a twinge of guilt. Nathan was aware her loss should have affected him more. If he was honest with himself, it was unlikely he was capable of ever truly loving a woman. Conditioning had taught him to view women as the Makah men viewed them—as companions to warm them at night and as workers to attend to chores by day.

As he reached the summit of the hill they were climbing, Nathan saw he'd fallen some distance behind Tatoosh. His hunting companion had picked up spoor and was now running down the other side of the hill, away from him.

Normally, Nathan would have been overtaken by the thrill of the chase and joined in the pursuit. On this occasion, he stopped to admire the three hundred and sixty-degree view. Behind him, to the south, clouds scudded across snow-capped peaks that stretched all the way to the horizon; ahead of him, to the north, shadows cast by other clouds moved like living beings across the waters of the Strait of Juan de Fuca.

Something caught Nathan's eye. At first he thought it was a low cloud scudding across the strait. Then he realized it was the billowing sail of a ship. His heart jumped and the rare sight made him lose his breath momentarily. The ship, a two-masted schooner, sailed from west to east, or left to right, through the strait.

Tatoosh had seen it, too. He immediately forgot about the hunt and jogged back up the hill to his friend's side. "They have come to trade muskets to our neighbors to the east," he said matter-of-factly.

"How far to the east?" Nathan tried to sound casual.

Tatoosh shrugged. Thanks to the *forest telegraph* that was so efficient in these parts, he knew exactly where the ship was bound, but he had no intention of sharing that with his friend. Nathan had seemed withdrawn in recent times, and Tatoosh suspected he still harbored a desire to return to his former life.

The young chief was right. It had been nearly four years since Nathan had been captured by the Makah, and eight since he'd left his hometown of Philadelphia. Increasingly, his thoughts had been turning to the family and friends he'd left behind. He had long since given up any hope that anyone was looking for him and other survivors of the shipwreck. However, he hadn't given up on escaping Neah Bay. Seeing the schooner got him thinking.

The blood brothers watched the vessel until she disappeared from sight then, without a word, began walking down the hill in the direction of the tracks Tatoosh had been following. As they walked, the young chief observed his companion out of the corner of his eye. He could see Nathan's mind was far, far away.

THAT NIGHT, AS the villagers slept, Nathan lay on his back staring at the wooden rafters of his lodge. For some time now, he'd had his own lodge—a gift from Tatoosh's now deceased father Elswa. Next to him, fast asleep, lay the pretty slave girl whose company he'd been enjoying of late.

Nathan couldn't get the sight of the schooner out of his mind's eye. *That's my way outta here!* A plan was beginning to take shape.

Although Tatoosh hadn't specified where the schooner was bound, Nathan thought it likely she was heading for a sheltered bay that marked the eastern boundary of the Makah nation. Known as Whale Bay, it was home to a Makah sub-tribe. It also had a large colony of sea otters, and traders were well aware of that.

The young white had visited Whale Bay several times on trading ventures with the Makah. They'd traveled by canoe. From memory, the fifty-mile sea journey in canoes laden with trade items had taken almost a full day. *Too long,* he thought. He was under no illusions any attempt to escape from Neah Bay by canoe would be doomed to failure. *They'd catch up with me within a few hours.* One man in a canoe was no match for a canoe manned by seasoned paddlers.

Nathan thought he could reach the bay quicker and more safely on foot. Across country, the distance would be half that by sea. He estimated he could complete the journey in less than half a day. Nathan sat bolt upright, his mind racing. *It's now or never.* If the schooner was even where he hoped it was, he couldn't be sure she'd stay there for any length of time. Every minute was critical.

The young white strained his ears, listening for any foreign sound. Aside from the rhythmic breathing of his sleeping partner, the occasional hoot of a distant owl was the only sound to be heard. Nathan quietly pushed himself to his feet. He poked his head out of the door of his lodge and looked around. The village slept. There was no moon, which suited his purposes nicely. The only signs of life were two lookouts who could be seen conversing quietly on the far side of the village.

Climbing up into the rafters of his lodge, Nathan retrieved a survival kit he'd hidden there for just such an occasion. It contained smoked fish and various preserved foods, a water bottle and other essentials, and was wrapped in a blanket. He descended to the floor and stuffed the kit into his backpack, which he slipped over his shoulders. Taking care not to wake the slave girl, he tucked his hunting knife and a tomahawk into his belt then ventured outside. When he was satisfied no-one else was around, he moved silently between the lodges to the nearby beach. There, he placed his backpack in the bottom of a canoe. After pushing the craft into the water, he climbed aboard and quietly paddled into the darkness.

Freedom here I come!

Nathan still planned to flee across country, but before he did anything he wanted to throw any pursuers off his scent. The tracks he'd left on the beach, and the missing canoe, would serve that purpose nicely — he hoped.

CHAPTER 26

Bata, Equatorial Guinea, 1848

O NE WEEK AFTER THE PIRATE attack on *Minstrel* in the Bay of Guinea, the brigantine and her survivors finally reached the safety of the port city of Bata, in the African nation of Equatorial Guinea. There, Captain Mathers, who had mercifully remained sober since the violent incident, took stock of casualties.

Seven of Minstrel's men had been killed, including three crew and four passengers, and a further eight wounded. All those involved in the violence had cuts and bruises at the very least.

For Captain Mathers, who had already lost a rigger overboard early in the voyage, the further loss of crew would require him to recruit replacement crewmembers from amongst the out-of-work seamen and various riffraff known to frequent Bata. Mathers was in no doubt he'd have his work cut out recruiting suitable replacements. The city had become a magnet for adventure-seekers, treasure and bounty hunters, former slave traders and other equally colorful individuals.

Among *Minstrel's* wounded was Drake Senior who, at this moment, was fighting for his life in the stateroom he shared with Susannah. His chances of survival hadn't been helped by the fact the brigantine had frustratingly remained becalmed for a further two days after the attack, thereby delaying her arrival at Bata.

None aboard *Minstrel* was more frustrated than Susannah. She had been toiling day and night, without rest, caring for her father. She'd been assisted, in her words, *by an angel*. That angel was one Nessie Finch, a middle-aged Englishwoman who was an experienced nurse. Miss Finch's expert attention had kept Drake Senior alive over the long days and nights following the attack.

The clergyman's injuries were severe. His attacker's sword had left a diagonal wound across his abdomen so deep it had pierced his lower intestine. In addition to the trauma caused by the cut, he'd lost a lot of blood. Miss Finch had stemmed the blood loss and stitched the wound, but infection had set in.

As *Minstrel* berthed alongside the main wharf in Bata, Miss Finch turned to Susannah. "We must get him to the hospital immediately," she urged. "I have done all I can for him."

"Yes, Mister Kemp has already sent word," Susannah advised, "and a carriage is standing by to transport papa to the hospital." The hospital she spoke of was a former British infirmary—a remnant of Britain's official presence here up to five years earlier. For fifteen years, Britain had occupied bases in Bata and on an offshore island to combat the slave trade that had thrived in this region.

As soon as *Minstrel* berthed, crewmembers carried Drake Senior above deck and onto the wharf where the waiting carriage transported him the two miles to the hospital. Susannah, Miss Finch and Kemp accompanied the patient.

Susannah was desperately worried. Her father seemed to be in a coma and was burning up with a fever. Miss Finch didn't like the clergyman's chances of survival, but said nothing. Kemp didn't like Drake Senior's chances either. He'd seen similar battle wounds, and he knew the signs to look for when death was approaching, but he, too, said nothing.

The young Englishwoman was too preoccupied watching over her father to observe her new surroundings. She left that to her companions who were intrigued by the colorful mix of nationalities on Bata's streets. While Bantu was the predominant race, other native races were evident—some light-skinned, some dark. There was no sign of the original pygmies who had populated this region, but the results of European unions could be seen on every street corner. Many of these were of Spanish or Portuguese descent, and Spanish was the official language.

An unseasonal downpour drenched everyone not beneath some form of shelter, but no-one seemed to notice it even if the official wet season had ended almost three months earlier. They'd long-since learned to live with the torrential tropical downpours that seemingly arrived out of the blue and went away just as quickly every year. The unseasonal rain added to the humidity, and left streets and buildings steaming in the relentless heat.

Susannah and Miss Kemp were unaware that, despite the country's name, no part of Equatorial Guinea was located on the equator. In fact, it lay north of the equator. Not that they'd have noticed any difference: to these fair English damsels, the heat felt decidedly tropical.

On arrival at the hospital, the visitors were pleasantly surprised to find several English doctors and nurses on the hospital's staff. Kemp was able to pull some strings and secure a private room for Drake Senior.

After the wounded clergyman had been officially admitted, Miss Finch and Kemp bade Susannah farewell and returned to the brigantine. They'd tried to persuade her to return with them, but she'd insisted on remaining at her father's bedside. Before leaving, Kemp assured Susannah that *Minstrel* wouldn't depart Bata until her father was well enough to travel. Susannah was mightily relieved to hear that.

As soon as the pair had departed, Susannah settled into a bedside chair, pulled her trusty diary from her overnight bag and prepared to start writing. She had a lot of writing to do as this was the first free time she'd had since the pirate attack.

May 27th, 1848

Our voyage aboard Minstrel has gone from bad to worse. After being becalmed in the Gulf of Guinea for what seemed like a month, but was in fact one week, we were attacked by pirates. Our brave menfolk fought them off, but we lost seven good souls in the process. Some were married with children. I do feel so for their families.

Poor papa suffered a grave sword wound to his abdomen. My dear friend Miss Finch has worked tirelessly day and night to keep him alive thus far. I call her my angel. Miss Finch has been a great comfort to all the wounded and her nursing experience has been well received by all who have needed care. Helping her has given me at least a basic understanding of nursing and taught me some rudimentary nursing skills, which no doubt will stand me in good stead.

Now that papa is in hospital in Bata, there is nothing more we can do for him. His future is in the doctors' hands, and in God's.

After the attack, there was much conjecture over where the ruffians came from. The first mate thought they may have come from the Barbary Coast, but the captain thought they were too far south to hail from that notorious coastline.

There was conjecture also over the whereabouts of the escaped felon—for I am sure that is what he is—John Donovan during the attack. One of the crew accused him of hiding below deck. The crewman suffered a black eye as a result of that accusation and Mr Donovan was incarcerated in the hold for the second time on this voyage. We shall never know if he did hide, but it is interesting that he is the only man on board who did not suffer so much as a single scratch.

I hope never to witness as much sorrow as I have in the past week. The burial of so many at sea was a mournful thing indeed. It fell upon Harold Simpson, who acquitted himself so well by all accounts during the violence, to officiate at the burials. He did us a great service, bless him. These last few days, Minstrel has been as quiet and as gloomy as a morgue—for that is what she was for a while.

Suddenly the relentless heat and the stench of bilgewater seem such trifling matters when compared to the losses suffered by others. I pray for papa's speedy recovery.

ONE WEEK LATER, Drake Senior made a recovery the doctors described as nothing short of a miracle. His fever had abated within two days of his being admitted to hospital. The infection had disappeared from his system three days later and, though still very weak, his wound was healing nicely. His dramatic recovery meant the brigantine could depart Bata not too far behind schedule. The short delay was actually welcomed by Kemp as it enabled him to comfortably attend to all official business engagements the British Army had arranged for him in the city.

Susannah was delighted and relieved at her father's speedy recovery. Despite what Kemp had promised, she'd had visions of *Minstrel* departing Bata while Drake Senior rotted away in hospital.

Captain Mathers had made good use of the enforced layover in port by recruiting replacements for the four crewmembers he'd lost. More correctly, his first mate Fred Paxton recruited the replacements. Mathers had quickly fallen back into his familiar ways and ensconced himself in his cabin with several bottles of his favourite whisky. He'd rarely been seen outside his cabin in the past four days, and then it was only to grab a breath of fresh air before disappearing inside again.

It was late afternoon when Drake Senior and Susannah arrived by carriage at the wharf. Susannah helped her father gingerly disembark from the carriage then assisted him onto *Minstrel's* deck. Their arrival coincided with the first mate briefing the newly recruited crewmembers on their duties.

Of the four crewmembers Paxton had hired, only three had shown up. One of them, a young, golden-haired English lad who had been taken on as a rigger, caught Susannah's eye. The two exchanged a glance as Susannah escorted Drake Senior slowly along the deck. Susannah couldn't resist a glance back at him as she led her father below deck. The rigger flashed a smile her way and she felt her heart skip a beat.

As father and daughter shuffled slowly toward their stateroom, Susannah lectured him on what he could and could not do. "Now papa, Miss Finch said you must remain in bed, or you could have a relapse."

"Yes, dear," Drake Senior said patiently.

"And Miss Finch said you must keep your fluid intake up. Furthermore, you really must try to eat."

"Let me guess who said that," Drake Senior chuckled. "Miss Finch?"

Susannah smiled despite herself. Though her father made

jokes about Miss Finch, she knew he held her in the highest regard—as he should. After all, she'd saved his life. "Yes, it was Miss Finch as a matter of fact. And she speaks a lot of sense does Miss Finch."

"Yes dear."

THE SHADOWS WERE lengthening when *Minstrel* sailed out of the port. Ahead of her, all going well, was a three-week journey to the next port of call, Cape Town, in Cape Colony. There, *Minstrel's* passengers and crew would enjoy a ten-day stopover in preparation for the dangerous leg that would see them sail through the Roaring Forties to Van Diemen's Land, south of New South Wales, before crossing the Tasman Sea to New Zealand.

AFTER DINNER THAT evening, Susannah ventured out on deck alone. She stood at the port-side rail watching Africa's west coast pass by as *Minstrel* sailed ever south. The rugged coastline slowly became indistinguishable from the sky as darkness fell.

A noise behind her alerted Susannah that she wasn't alone. She turned to see the Irish troublemaker John Donovan leering at her.

"Ah, so you got me message," Donovan said mischievously.

"What message?" Susannah hadn't a clue what he was talking about.

Donovan suddenly grabbed her. "That we meet here in private." Laughing, he tried to kiss her.

Susannah slapped his face. This only served to galvanize the Irishman who forcibly kissed her.

Before Donovan could have his way with Susannah, the golden-haired rigger she'd seen earlier appeared from nowhere. He pulled Donovan off her. "Leave the lady alone!"

he said threateningly.

Donovan threw a punch, which the rigger easily avoided.

The rigger flashed a disarming smile at Donovan. "Are you sure you want to be doing that now?"

The Irishman hesitated, momentarily confused by the handsome young man who had pushed in where he wasn't wanted and had interposed himself between him and the young woman he lusted after.

Susannah could see Donovan desperately wanted to maintain his macho reputation, but he also valued his physical wellbeing. There was something about the rigger that Susannah sensed was dangerous, and her antagonist sensed it too.

"I'll see you later," Donovan promised the pair before slinking off into the night.

Susannah watched him go. She turned back to thank her rescuer, but he'd returned to work and was already half way up the near mast. He stopped climbing when he reached the first cross-spar, and looked down at Susannah.

"Thank you, kind sir!" she called out to him.

The rigger waved at her then resumed climbing. Susannah watched him for as long as she thought proper then retired below deck for the night.

Try as she may, she couldn't get the rigger out of her mind. He was the first man she'd really been attracted to since she'd lost her first love, chimneysweep Blake Dugan, back in Kensington.

THAT NIGHT, SUSANNAH dreamed of the golden-haired rigger who had come to her rescue. She dreamt he took her in his arms and taught her the art of lovemaking. The dream was so vivid that when she finally awoke next morning she would feel as though she'd just lost her virginity.

CHAPTER 27

≈◦◉◦≈

Sydney Town, 1841

JACK'S PLANS TO STOW AWAY aboard a ship bound for New Zealand or the Pacific Islands were about to be put on hold. He didn't know it yet, but he would soon.

After a good night's sleep in his private room at the Todds' boarding house, the accommodating Joan Todd put her new employee to work, replacing aged and faulty door hinges throughout the two-storied establishment. It was light and easy work, and Jack toiled as speedily as he could in order to make a good first impression. In fact, he'd already made a good impression, though not for the reason he thought.

Late morning saw him replacing the hinges on Jim Todd's bedroom door. The room's single bed gave away the fact that he and his wife had separate bedrooms. Jack would learn later the couple had slept apart since arriving in the colony two years earlier.

Considering it was a full house with no vacancies, the establishment seemed unnaturally quiet. Jack realized the boarders must be out, laboring at their respective workplaces. In fact, most were out job hunting, either in town or down at the docks, for employment was harder to find than usual due to a recent influx of new arrivals from the home country.

The silence was broken when arguing erupted from the upstairs kitchen. The Todds were at each other, and not for the

185

first time since Jack's arrival. Joan could be heard telling her husband off for drinking too often and too heavily. Jim countered that he'd only had one drink that morning, but it was obvious to Jack that he'd had more than one: he was already slurring his words.

"Why don't ye go to bed and take your gin bottle with you?" Joan snapped. It was more an order than a question.

Jack heard Jim mumble something. Moments later, the henpecked, drunken husband emerged from the kitchen. Gin bottle in hand, he stormed past Jack and slammed his bedroom door shut, leaving the young Cockney out in the hallway.

Joan emerged from the kitchen. "I'm sorry ye had to hear that," she said.

"No problem," Jack responded as cheerily as he could. "I'll carry on downstairs." He gathered up his tools and headed for the staircase.

"Before ye go," Joan said.

Jack stopped and turned around.

"There's something I need ye to attend to upstairs," she said.

Jack saw the familiar twinkle in her eye and wondered what she had planned for him. "Yes Ma'am." He followed her to her bedroom. As he walked, Jack could feel his excitement rising. He looked down and realized that wasn't all that was rising.

Joan's bedroom was conveniently located on the far side of the establishment, well away from her husband's room. When she opened the door, Jack was pleasantly surprised to see the room accommodated a double bed. And not just any double bed; it was a grand four-poster complete with lace drapes and other feminine decorations.

No sooner had Jack entered the room than Joan closed the door and locked it. If there was ever any doubt about her intentions, that doubt had now vanished. Jack grinned at the saucy Welshwoman and waited for her to make the next move.

"Why don't ye make yourself comfortable on the bed?" she suggested.

Grinning, Jack pulled the lace drapes aside and stretched out on the bed. Across the room, Joan disappeared behind a screen and began undressing. She emerged wearing a revealing nightgown that barely contained her fulsome, mature figure.

Jack forgot all about Mary O'Brien at that moment.

What followed seemed like a dream. Joan glided over to the bed, undressed Jack and then began kissing him all over. He quickly established she was an expert and experienced lover. While he knew a thing or two about the art of lovemaking, he felt like a student as she went to work on him.

Jack didn't know it, but Joan was as excited as her young lover. The months that had passed since she last made love seemed more like years, and she felt she was ready to burst. She mounted Jack and, sitting astride him, began pleasuring herself quite unabashedly.

They were so excited they quickly came together in a frenzied tangle of sweaty arms and legs.

As Jack regained his breath, he realized they'd somehow ended up on the floor. One of the bed's drapes had been torn loose and it now covered them like a sheet. He started chuckling. Joan saw the funny side, too, and soon they were both laughing out loud.

So BEGAN A new chapter in Jack's life. His days, and occasionally his nights, were filled with lovemaking sessions with his sexy employer.

Plans to stow away were shelved, for the moment at least, because he was enjoying himself too much. Joan was proving to be an insatiable lover. She was like a drug to Jack—a drug he couldn't get enough of. All rational thought went out the window.

CHAPTER 28

Makah Nation, West Coast, North America, 1842

NATHAN ESTIMATED HE'D PADDLED ABOUT half a mile from the village when he steered the canoe toward the rocky shoreline on the eastern side of Neah Bay. Stopping alongside a large rock, he threw his backpack onto it then proceeded to attack the bottom of the canoe with his tomahawk. In no time, he'd smashed a gaping hole in its timbers.

The young Philadelphian jumped onto the rock and watched as the sabotaged canoe sank from sight. Satisfied he'd left no trace, he scrambled over the rocks and disappeared into the trees.

Nathan headed east toward Whale Bay and the schooner he hoped was anchored there. Resisting the temptation to run, he walked briskly, taking care not to leave any tracks. For the first three or four hundred yards, he used a shrubby branch to cover any tracks he happened to leave. This slowed his progress, but he figured it would help his chances of remaining undiscovered.

The escapee was in no doubt the missing canoe and his absence from the village would be noticed at dawn, or soon after, and the Makah would come looking for him. He reckoned he had, at best, a four-hour start on them.

When he was satisfied he'd put a safe distance between himself and the spot where he'd clambered ashore, Nathan dropped the branch and began running. Now he made no attempt to cover his tracks. His only concern was reaching his destination in the quickest time possible.

UNFORTUNATELY FOR NATHAN, his disappearance from the village was noticed earlier than he'd hoped. Tatoosh had risen before dawn and had gone to Nathan's lodge to rouse his friend to accompany him on a pre-dawn hunt for bear. When he didn't find Nathan either in the lodge or anywhere in the village, he'd wandered down to the beach and immediately noticed one of the canoes was missing.

Now, after raising the alarm, Tatoosh and eleven of his braves were paddling two canoes toward the open sea. The young chief was in no doubt Nathan was heading for the ship they'd seen the previous day.

As he paddled, Tatoosh could feel his anger growing toward his blood brother. The Makah had spared the White-Eye's life and allowed him to live as one of them yet despite this great honor Nathan had shown no gratitude or loyalty. Worse, he'd double-crossed them.

Tatoosh felt insulted and aggrieved. His heart felt heavy, too, for he knew custom dictated that when they caught the White-Eye, they'd have to kill him.

Nearing the entrance to the open sea, Tatoosh put himself in Nathan's place and considered the options open to him. A thought suddenly occurred. He stopped paddling and held up his hand. His fellow paddlers stopped paddling also. Tatoosh waited for the rear canoe to catch up to his. He then addressed the paddlers in the other canoe. "You keep going on the water," he ordered. "We will go over the land."

Without a word, the paddlers in the other canoe resumed paddling. As soon as they reached the open sea, they turned right and headed east along the Makah nation's northern coastline.

Meanwhile, Tatoosh and his five companions paddled back the way they'd come. This time, they kept close to shore. Tatoosh suspected Nathan may have tried to throw them off the scent by pretending he'd escaped by canoe.

Not far from where the young white had scrambled ashore, the paddlers nosed their canoe in amongst the rocks.

"We look for tracks," Tatoosh said. Holding up his musket, he added, "One shot if you find his tracks."

The braves, who all carried muskets, climbed out of the canoe and ran into the forest. Each followed a different path to the east. In the gray light of dawn they zigzagged as they ran, scanning the forest floor for Nathan's spoor.

THE SUN HAD not long risen when a member of Tatoosh's party saw a man's footprints in a patch of mud half a mile east of Neah Bay. Bending down to inspect the tracks, there was no way of knowing whose they were, but the brave was aware it was very likely they belonged to the White-Eye.

The brave primed his musket and fired a single shot skyward.

Within minutes, Tatoosh and the others had rendezvoused at the site of the brave's discovery. The brave had already established that whoever left the tracks was heading east.

Tatoosh was in no doubt the tracks were Nathan's. Without a word he led his braves eastward at a fast trot.

AS THE SUN rose higher in the sky, Nathan was feeling anxious as he ran ever-eastward. The terrain was steeper and the vegetation more dense than he'd allowed for, and his progress was slower. By mid-day he estimated he wasn't even half way to Whale Bay. Already, his legs felt like leaden weights and his chest heaved as he gasped for air.

Despite his weariness, he forced himself to dig deep and maintain the unrelenting pace he'd set. He'd already discarded his backpack and was tempted to discard his tomahawk to lighten the load. After an internal debate, he kept it.

It was around mid-day when Nathan emerged above the forest's tree-line and found himself on the grassy knoll of a hill. It stood higher than most of the surrounding hills and it afforded his first glimpse of the Strait of Juan de Fuca away to the northeast. His heart sank when he saw how far away it was. By his reckoning it was still a good ten miles away.

Nathan looked behind him, searching for a sighting of any pursuers. He sighted nothing unusual and wondered if his ruse had worked and his pursuers were traveling the long way to Whale Bay — by canoe.

Then he saw something — a faint movement in a forest clearing two miles or so distant. He thought he was seeing things at first. *There it is again!* A tiny figure, no bigger than an ant, ran across the clearing before being swallowed up by the trees. Then another figure. *And another!* Although he couldn't even ascertain at that distance whether the figures he saw were people, his gut told him they were Makah trackers. They were following the exact route he'd taken.

Adrenalin pumped through his veins and Nathan took flight downhill, seeking to at least maintain the present distance between himself and his pursuers. He knew that was an ambitious goal. Fit and fast though he was, he'd learned from experience there were none more fleet-footed than the Northwest natives. They knew the forest like the back of their hand, and they could run all day long and almost as fast as the wind.

CHAPTER 29

South Atlantic, 1848

TEN DAYS AFTER DEPARTING BATA, in Equatorial Guinea, Drake Senior was feeling stronger and some color had returned to his cheeks. Five days earlier, he hadn't been sure he'd made the right decision discharging himself so soon from hospital: his abdominal wound had been causing him pain and he was so weak he couldn't leave his bunk without assistance.

Susannah had been terribly concerned for his welfare. Her concern had deepened when her nursing friend, Miss Finch, advised her she was afraid Drake Senior's wound had become re-infected.

The tireless attention of the two women combined with Drake Senior's naturally hardy constitution saw him make another dramatic recovery over the next five days. His improvement had come as a great relief for Susannah who couldn't bare to think of how she'd cope if she lost her father after having already lost her mother.

Now, sitting by the rail at *Minstrel's* bow, Susannah offered up a prayer of thanks for her father's recovery then prepared to make an entry in her diary. As she opened the diary, she became aware she was being observed by the handsome young English rigger who had caught her eye. He was at his normal work station, high in the rigging of one of the masts, making running repairs to a sail.

Susannah hadn't spoken to the rigger since he'd intervened when Donovan had tried to have his way with her. However, some discreet enquiries had revealed his name was Oscar Archibald and he hailed from Kent. Although she now knew his name, she thought of him as *Goldie* because of his golden locks.

The young Englishwoman had also learned Goldie was only traveling as far as Cape Town aboard *Minstrel*. There, he would be taking up a job he'd arranged before departing England four months earlier—as an assistant to his older brother who had a thriving boat building business in the southern African port settlement.

Susannah didn't like the thought of Goldie parting company with *Minstrel*. For a start, his presence on board had served to discourage Donovan who hadn't bothered her again. The main reason, however, was she found him very pleasing on the eye and a welcome relief from the daily tedium of shipboard life.

On these hot summer days—as was the case today—Goldie had taken to working bare-chested, and Susannah had been quite taken with his chiseled physique. She wasn't the only one: several other women on board had started spending more time above deck than usual so they could catch sight of the young god as he went about his work in the rigging.

Putting Goldie out of her mind for the moment, Susannah dipped her quill into a bottle of ink and began writing a diary entry.

June 13th, 1848

Today is the first day papa has been above deck since we departed Bata. The tireless Miss Finch believes the worst is behind him now. Certainly, he looks more his old self.

Two days out from Bata, we were becalmed once again. The heat was, and remains, as oppressive as ever. Fortunately, the wind soon befriended us and we have been tootling along at a steady 7 knots ever since.

The first mate told us we are presently off the coast of Angola. I will take his word for no coastline is visible to us. Since our experience in the Gulf of Guinea, everyone is nervous the pirates will return. I must say we view every foreign vessel with suspicion these days. Mr Kemp assures us we have nothing to fear.

On Thursday, we crossed the Equator. "Crossing the line" the crew called it. Those of us who hadn't crossed the line before had to subject ourselves to some elaborate rites of passage as part of our initiation into the so-called Ancient Orders of the Deep. A very drunk Captain Mathers officiated and it was all a bit silly really. Any who refused to be initiated, were referred to by the crew as "pollywogs" or "slimy wogs." Papa was exempt from this of course.

So many adventures and we are not yet half way to New Zealand. I dread what the remainder of the voyage will bring.

Cook has rung the dinner gong so I must go now. I am hoping papa can join us for dinner. Praise God, papa is returning to full health and his appetite is returning.

Minstrel is flying now. 8 knots and a strengthening northerly.

A shadow fell across the page as Susannah completed her diary entry. She looked up to see it was Goldie, the rigger. He was looking down at her.

"Hu . . . hello," Susannah smiled.

"Hello, miss."

The pair stared at each other for a couple of drawn out seconds. He seemed as taken with her as she was with him.

Finally, Goldie pointed up at the near mast. "The boys are about to unfurl the mainsail, miss," he mumbled, "so best you move away or you could get hurt."

"Oh, of course." Susannah went to stand when Goldie extended his hand. She took it and he helped her to her feet. "Thank you, Gold . . ." She blushed when she realized she'd nearly used the nickname she'd bestowed upon the rigger in her dreams. "I'm sorry, I don't know your name."

"Oscar," he said. "Oscar Archibald." Goldie met her gaze levelly. Only now did he realize he was still holding her hand. It was hot to his touch and he made no attempt to release it. "And you are the clergyman's daughter?"

"Yes." *He's been asking about me!* "Susannah Drake." Only now did she withdraw her hand from his.

Goldie stooped and picked up Susannah's diary and ink bottle then escorted her further along the deck out of harm's way. "You'll be safe here," he announced.

"Yes I'm sure I will. Thank you." Susannah smiled at him. It was a genuine smile and he responded in kind.

"I best be getting back," he said, turning to go.

"Of course."

Goldie hesitated and turned around. "I'm working a double shift today, so I'll be here after dinner . . . in case you happen to be on deck at that time."

Susannah blushed again. "I may well be."

The rigger hurried off. As Susannah watched him, she found her pulse was racing. She couldn't wait for nightfall.

———◦◦◦———

STRAIGHT AFTER DINNER that night, Drake Senior retired to the stateroom he shared with Susannah. The sea air and the events of the day had caught up with him and he needed an early night. Light from a solitary lantern cast a warm glow over the room.

Before turning in, the clergyman took Susannah's hands in his and looked at her gravely. "My dear Susannah, I haven't thanked you enough for the way you have cared for me these past few weeks."

Susannah tried to protest, but he shushed her.

"I am so proud of you," he continued. "And your mother would be proud of you, too."

"Papa, it is Miss Finch you should really thank," Susannah insisted. "It was she who nursed you back to good health."

Drake Senior shook his head. "I know I will forever owe a debt of gratitude to Miss Finch. She provided the necessary nursing expertise, but you provided a daughter's love and care, and that's what helped me survive. The clergyman kissed his daughter's forehead. "Shall we pray?"

Susannah nodded. Evening prayers with her father had been a daily ritual for as long as she could remember. As they'd done aboard *Minstrel* every evening up until Drake Senior had been wounded, they knelt before his bunk, their hands clasped in prayer.

Drake Senior started praying. "Dear Lord, we thank thee for watching over us and delivering us from the recent troubles that have beset Minstrel . . ."

As her father prayed, Susannah's mind strayed to the young rigger she knew, or hoped, was awaiting her above deck. Try as she may, she couldn't dispel the image of Goldie and his sculpted physique, and for the first time ever she wished

Drake Senior would hurry up and finish praying.

What seemed to Susannah like an age later, the clergyman mercifully concluded, "And finally we ask for forgiveness for our sins, Lord. Banish any impure thoughts and give us the strength to follow the Christian path. Amen."

"Amen," Susannah whispered.

Drake Senior climbed onto his bunk and pulled a sheet up over himself. It was too hot for blankets.

It took all Susannah's control not to rush from the room. "I will get some fresh air on deck before turning in, papa," Susannah said as casually as she could.

"Alright, but be careful," Drake Senior warned. "The Atlantic is a big ocean."

"Night papa," Susannah said as she extinguished the lantern flame and left the stateroom.

Climbing the steps to the deck, she suddenly had second thoughts. Her father's words came back to her. *Banish any impure thoughts and give us the strength to follow the Christian path.* She felt a twinge of guilt and hung back momentarily. Images from her past flashed through her mind: sitting with her mother in church as her father delivered a Sunday sermon; saying grace at the dinner table; attending bible class with her friends.

Susannah debated whether to return to the stateroom. She had been raised as a Christian in a Christian household, and it had been instilled in her during her teenage years she must save herself for her husband, for in the eyes of God only a union between husband and wife would be blessed.

The young Englishwoman was in no doubt what her secret assignation with the young man awaiting her above deck would lead to. She desired him and she was in no doubt he desired her. There could only be one outcome.

Susannah reluctantly turned back and began retracing her steps to the stateroom. Then another image skittered through her mind. This time it was Goldie. In Susannah's imagination, the young rigger was working half-naked up the mast, his taught muscles moving in perfect unison as he climbed out along a spar high above the deck. His sweaty body gleamed under the hot sun. *Forgive me, Lord!* Susannah spun around and ran back up the steps.

CHAPTER 30

Sydney Town, 1841

T HREE WEEKS HAD PASSED SINCE Jack had taken up residence at the Todd's boarding house, and he was no closer to stowing away aboard a ship. He could feel himself slipping into a kind of lethargy. The Cockney realized that every passing day was a day closer to being captured, but he couldn't help himself: his employer and landlady Joan Todd was like a drug, and he remained addicted to her.

The sexy Welshwoman was addicted to him, too. She'd taken to encouraging her husband to drink just so he was out of the way and she was free to indulge herself with her latest lover. Just as she satisfied Jack in every way, he satisfied her. It was a mutually beneficial arrangement that resulted in them going at it like rabbits at every opportunity.

So taken was she with Jack, the normally discreet Joan had thrown discretion to the wind. After the first week, everyone in the boarding house except Jim Todd knew she and Jack were an item; after the second week, even Jim knew. It was an arrangement that suited him: the henpecking had stopped and he was allowed to drink as much and as often as he liked. All he needed to do was turn a blind eye to his wife's shenanigans. He was more than happy to do that. It took the pressure off him.

Joan had suspected her young lover was an escaped convict.

She'd seen the welts left by the flogger's whip on his back, and he'd mentioned things that alluded to his recent past, but she kept her thoughts to herself.

As far as Jack was concerned, his stocks in life had risen. He was being paid well for the little work he did, and he had a job with great perks; he ate like a king and shagged like a horny goat as often as he liked.

He sensed it was too good to last. And as always, his sixth sense was spot on.

It happened on a Sunday—his day off. Jack was drinking with the same laborers who had befriended him when he dined at a local eatery three weeks earlier. Sunday afternoon drinking sessions at the same eatery were fast becoming a regular engagement for the tight group, and it was something Jack looked forward to.

On this particular Sunday, an off duty soldier noticed Jack. There was something about the Cockney that set him apart from his companions. The soldier, who had been stationed in the colony long enough to recognize convicts by the way they looked and carried themselves, suspected Jack was an escapee.

Jack became aware of the other's interest in him before the soldier could act on his instincts. Just as the soldier had developed an instinct about convicts so, too, had Jack about soldiers.

The soldier caught Jack's eye. Their eyes locked and they stared at each other. It was as though time stood still.

Jack was oblivious to the conversation swirling around him even though some of his companions' comments were directed at him. Beneath his casual exterior, he was tense, like a sprinter at the start line, and ready to flee. Jack was watching the soldier's right hand. He knew that was the hand that would reach for the pistol he'd spotted tucked into the soldier's belt.

As soon as the soldier reached for his pistol, Jack sprang to his feet and rushed for the door.

"Stop!" the soldier shouted. He'd already drawn his pistol

and was aiming it at Jack. Unfortunately for him, other patrons were in the firing line. Before he had a clear shot, Jack had disappeared out the door. The soldier gave chase. He was joined by several other off duty soldiers.

In the few seconds that elapsed between the time he knew he was under suspicion to the time he fled, Jack had mapped out an escape route in his mind. The route took him away from the boarding house that had served as his refuge these past few weeks and down narrow alleys that ran between shops and factories in Sydney Town's commercial district.

The circumstances in which he now found himself reminded him of a similar escapade in London four years earlier when Henry Sullivan, his employer at the time, had chased after him with a pistol after he'd stolen some hemp. *That was the start of me troubles,* he reminded himself. The memory of how that escapade turned out lent speed to his feet, which flew across the ground as he sought to distance himself from his pursuers.

Jack's start was too great for the soldiers to catch him, and they soon gave up the chase. Even so, the escapee waited until after dark before returning to the boarding house and to the loving arms of the lady of the house.

Before Jack stepped inside the front door, he paused on the verandah to re-evaluate his current situation. He realized he hadn't given his departure from Sydney Town the priority he should have, and he chastised himself for putting his sexual desires ahead of escape. *That's called thinking with yer cock instead of yer brain you stupid bastard!* There was no denying he'd gotten his priorities wrong. He determined that he'd rectify that.

Joan sensed something was wrong as soon as she saw her young lover. "What's troubling ye?" she asked.

Jack assumed his usual cheerful expression. "Not a thing," he lied. "All's well." He hurried to his room before she had time to further question him. He'd no sooner entered his room and stretched out on his bed than there was a knock at his door.

"It's me," the familiar voice whispered.

Jack hesitated to open the door, but finally relented. He rolled off the bed and opened the door. Joan entered without waiting to be asked and motioned to him to close the door after her. The Cockney obliged, not sure what was coming next. He didn't have to wait long to find out.

Joan was wearing a lightweight house coat she used for when she was on dusting duties. She quickly unbuttoned it to reveal she wore nothing underneath.

Now Jack knew what was coming. What he didn't know was how horny Joan was feeling. It had been two days since she'd had him and she needed him badly.

Jack didn't get a chance to object. Not that he would have.

Joan pushed him back on the bed and ripped his trousers off. She then adopted her favorite position, mounting him and riding him. Jack enjoyed the experience as always. But it was different this time. This time, he knew it would be their last time together. Tomorrow he'd be leaving Sydney Town one way or the other.

JACK WAS DOWN at the docks at dawn next day. He was pleased to see there wasn't a Red Coat in sight. *Too early for them lazy bastards.* His gaze rested on *Besieged,* a two-masted schooner berthed nearby. On the wharf, unemployed men of all ages were lining up, hoping to find work loading or unloading her. Jack wandered over to investigate.

A prospective worker suggested he join the queue. Jack did so and within minutes he and his companion were among the thirty or so men hired for the day by the schooner's first mate. The work was hard compared to what he'd been doing these past three weeks, but nothing after the rigors of Parramatta. Jack's job was to help carry boxes of supplies up the gangplank and load them in *Besieged's* hold. He learned the supplies were needed for the schooner's voyage to Fiji and she was scheduled to depart that night.

On his first visit to the schooner's hold, Jack noticed an open door leading to the storeroom. Peering inside, he saw the unoccupied storeroom offered a myriad of hiding places for a stowaway.

LATER THAT MORNING, after delivering yet another box to the hold, Jack picked his moment and slipped unnoticed into the storeroom. None too soon, he decided, as there were now a few Red Coats arriving at the docks to check workers' identities.

Making his way to the rear of the cavernous storeroom, he spied a row of large tea chests. He pushed against each one until he found one that was almost empty. Forcing open its lid, he climbed into it and pulled the lid down tight above him.

Inside the tea chest, the smell of tea was almost overpowering, but the smell of freedom was even stronger. Jack held his nose and closed his eyes. He was keen to catch up on some sleep. Ahead of him was a two thousand-mile voyage east to Fiji — a three-week journey all going well.

He dozed off like that, still holding his nose, dreaming of tropical climes, swaying palm trees and sensual Fijian women.

That night, on schedule, *Besieged* set sail for Fiji. Her master, a tough Welshman by the name of Harold Jones, didn't realize it but, in addition to his thirty-strong crew, he had a non-paying passenger on board.

CHAPTER 31

Makah Nation, West Coast, North America, 1842

NATHAN HAD ALMOST RUN HIMSELF into the ground when, cresting a rise, he caught a glimpse of Whale Bay. His elation was tempered by the fact he couldn't see the two-masted schooner he was hoping would be waiting to deliver him back to civilization. *Please let her be there!* He forced himself to keep moving forward.

At least two hours had passed since he'd sighted his pursuers, and he was now running on memory. His lungs felt as though they were on fire and so weary was he, he'd been reduced to a slow jog.

The forest track Nathan followed ended abruptly at the top of a high cliff. If he hadn't pulled up immediately, he'd have plunged to his death onto the rocks nearly a hundred feet below.

Nathan was too exhausted even to look up. He stood there, bent over, hands on knees, gasping for air. When he did look up, he saw her: the two-masted schooner that represented his one and only chance for freedom—not to mention his survival. She was so close to shore, he could clearly make out the facial features of the crewmembers on deck. He could even read the vessel's name plate on her bow. It read: *Spirit of the Sea*.

Nathan's weariness fell away in that instant. It was replaced by a feeling of elation. *I've done it!* Then he remembered he wasn't home yet.

Some sixth sense made him look back along the cliff-top. He started when he saw two musket-bearing Makah braves running toward him. They were so close he could recognize them. One was Tatoosh. More braves appeared behind the pair. Tatoosh had already seen Nathan and was now sprinting toward him.

Nathan took off in the opposite direction along the cliff-top. He discarded his tomahawk as he ran.

The track he followed was leading him away from the *Spirit of the Sea*. Desperate to descend the cliff and swim out to the schooner, he looked frantically for a path he could follow to the water's edge.

Finally, he spotted a path. It appeared to end some twenty or thirty feet above the sea, but it would have to do. He began scrambling down it.

Musket shots boomed out behind him. His pursuers were firing as they ran. The shots were wayward, but Nathan felt the wind of one musket ball as it flew past his ear.

The crewmembers aboard the schooner thought they were under attack. They began arming themselves and taking up defensive positions on deck.

Nathan could hear his pursuers now. They were shouting to each other as they ran. He thought he recognized Tatoosh's voice, but couldn't be sure.

Descending the cliff-face required caution. One slip would mean death. Unfortunately for him, the danger of being shot outweighed the need for a cautious descent, so he was forced to throw caution to the wind and make haste while he still could.

As he'd feared, the path he followed ended a good twenty feet from the base of the cliff. Nathan judged he could just clear the rocks at the bottom if he jumped out far enough. *Here goes.* He leapt out as far as he could and safely cleared the rocks.

Underwater, he swam hard to try to distance himself from the cliff-face and his pursuers. On the surface several feet above him, he could clearly see musket balls striking the water. As the water's density slowed their progress, the spent balls sank slowly to the seabed. One was so close he could have reached out and grabbed it as it sank.

On the cliff-face, Tatoosh was the only one among the braves not firing his musket. He was waiting for the White-Eye's head to surface. Finally, he saw Nathan. He raised his musket and took aim.

Nathan was swimming frantically toward the schooner, which was some fifty yards beyond him. However, Tatoosh had him firmly in his sights. He knew at that moment it was over for his blood brother: Nathan Johnson would never make it to the schooner.

On either side of the young chief, his fellow braves were firing their muskets as fast as they could prime their weapons and shoot. The water around Nathan was being whipped up as musket balls narrowly missed their target.

Tatoosh released his breath and increased the pressure on his trigger finger. Just before he squeezed the trigger he hesitated then lowered his musket and held up his hand. "Stop!" he shouted.

The braves looked at their chief strangely.

Tatoosh avoided looking at his braves. The young chief couldn't explain to them why he'd ordered them to cease shooting. He couldn't even explain it to himself.

In the water, Nathan was now only yards from *Spirit of the Sea*. He looked up and saw several crewmembers were leaning over the near rail, their weapons trained on him.

Nathan stopped swimming and began treading water. "Don't shoot!" he shouted in English. "I'm American!" The words sounded strange to his ears. They were the first he'd spoken in his own tongue—to anyone other than himself at least—in years.

On board the schooner, the crewmen looked at each other, surprised that the brave they were looking at was in fact a white American. Reacting quickly, they threw a rope ladder over the side. Nathan grabbed it and began climbing. Half way up, he had to stop to catch his breath. He glanced behind him and saw Tatoosh and the other braves looking straight at him. Even though he was within musket range, they'd inexplicably stopped shooting.

Nathan and Tatoosh locked eyes for several long moments. They nodded respectfully to each other. The young chief then said something to his braves and they began climbing back up the cliff.

Using the last of his strength, Nathan resumed climbing. On reaching the schooner's rail, willing hands grabbed him and hauled him aboard. Nathan landed in a heap on the deck. He lay there, gasping, as he tried to recover his breath.

Gradually, the realization set in he was free. He didn't know whether to laugh or cry. In fact, he was too spent to do either.

Only now did he take note of his rescuers. They hovered around him, looking down at the strange white man who, apart from his startling blue eyes, resembled a Northwest native.

The schooner's master, a bearded New Yorker, appeared and barked orders at his men. Two sailors immediately assisted Nathan to his feet.

No-one seemed to know what to say for several drawn out moments. Finally, the captain extended his hand and said, "Captain Dean Anders, master of the Spirit of the Sea."

Nathan accepted the other's hand. He was so overcome by the touch of another European, he didn't want to let go. "Ordinary Seaman Nathan Johnson," he stammered, "crewman aboard the ill-fated vessel Intrepid."

Nathan could tell by the captain's reaction he'd heard of

Intrepid. Only later would he learn the vessel's wreckage had never been found and there'd been no other survivors. Nathan suddenly felt faint and began swaying on his feet.

"Get Mister Johnson to Doc Sanderson below deck," the captain snapped at a black crewman. "And see he gets a change of clothes and a good feed."

"Yes sir," the crewman said. He led Nathan away by the arm.

Just before disappearing below deck, Nathan took one last look back at the nearby shoreline. There was no sign of the Makah braves. It was almost as if they'd never been there.

<hr />

THAT NIGHT, LYING on a hammock a crewman had strung up for him in the schooner's storeroom, Nathan was so excited he couldn't get to sleep. *I made it!* Feelings of ecstasy, joy, relief and much more coursed through him. At the same time, he experienced feelings of regret.

Trying to make sense of his feelings, the young Philadelphian realized he was regretful that he'd never see Tatoosh again. *If only the situation had been different.* He was aware if circumstances and cultural differences hadn't come between the young chief and himself, they'd have remained friends for life. Of that he had no doubt.

There was much he admired and liked about Tatoosh, but that's where his feelings for the Makah and the other natives of the Northwest ended. His firsthand experience of the Northwest peoples — dating back to his enslavement by the Makah four years earlier — had reinforced his growing conviction that European civilization really was superior to theirs.

As the day's dramatic events caught up with him, and Nathan succumbed to sleep, his final thought was that European civilization was in fact superior to all others. It was a mantra — a belief — that would determine how he'd relate to people of other races in the years ahead.

CHAPTER 32

South Atlantic, 1848

EMERGING ON DECK, THE SEA air washed over her, providing a welcome relief from the heat and ever present stench of bilge water below deck. Looking around, Susannah was disappointed to find she was alone. *Where are you?* She wandered to the near portside rail and looked out to where she knew Angola lay somewhere behind the darkness.

Susannah took Goldie's no-show as a sign she shouldn't transgress and go against everything her father had taught her. Feeling slightly relieved, she was about to return to the stateroom when she became aware of a shadowy figure beside her. *It's him!* Her feelings of a moment earlier were replaced by feelings of yearning and lust when she realized it was Goldie. "You came," she said without thinking.

"Of course," he whispered.

Before she could resist, he drew her to him and kissed her full on the mouth. She resisted, but only for a moment. As he pressed his lean, hard body against her, she could feel all resistance melting. She wanted him like she'd wanted nothing else before.

Footsteps behind them alerted them to the presence of someone approaching from the stern.

"This way!" Goldie whispered urgently. He pulled

Susannah away from the approaching footsteps.

Together they ran, laughing softly, toward the brigantine's bow.

Goldie pulled up alongside *Minstrel's* longboat, which was chained to the starboard rail. It was covered by a canvas tarpaulin. The rigger began pulling the tarpaulin aside. "In here," he said.

Susannah was about to clamber into the longboat when something distracted her. It was a red light directly ahead of *Minstrel*. At first she thought it was a star.

"Hurry!" Goldie urged her. He needed her as much as she needed him and was anxious they hid beneath the tarpaulin before someone saw them.

Still the red light intrigued Susannah. It seemed closer now. "What's that?" she asked, pointing at the light.

Now Goldie saw it, too. "Holy mackerel!" he exclaimed.

"Is it a star?" Susannah asked.

Goldie had immediately identified the light as the warning light on the bow of an approaching ship. He estimated it was less than a hundred-and-fifty yards away and the gap was closing fast. "Ship ahoy!" he shouted at the top of his lungs. "Approaching vessel straight ahead."

Only now did Susannah recognize the danger. She could now see the other ship. Darkness prevented identification of the vessel's name or type, but her silhouette was huge and her three masts were visible. Now only thirty yards separated the two vessels and a collision seemed inevitable.

"Quick!" Goldie urged. "This way!" He dragged Susannah along the deck toward *Minstrel's* stern.

Goldie's cries of alarm had galvanized the crew into action. Within seconds, the first mate and half a dozen crewmen had appeared on deck. More followed. Even Captain Mathers made it on deck, albeit inebriated, before the two vessels collided.

At the time of impact, the mystery vessel's hull towered over *Minstrel,* blocking out the sky above, and the sound of timbers splintering was deafening. Susannah screamed and sailors shouted in fear for their lives as the other vessel tore *Minstrel's* portside rail from its hinges. *Minstrel* leaned alarmingly to starboard and then back to port and back to starboard again.

How *Minstrel* stayed afloat, Susannah couldn't begin to guess. That she and the others were still alive seemed like a miracle to her.

Goldie checked Susannah to confirm she was okay. Satisfied, he said, "I'll have to leave you now." He had to shout to make himself heard above the uproar. "I suggest you get below deck."

Susannah nodded and Goldie ran off to assist his fellow crewmembers. She prepared to return below to check on her father's wellbeing when she saw him emerge on deck with Kemp and several other alarmed passengers. "Papa!" She ran to his side.

"What on earth is happening?" a shaken Drake Senior asked.

As Susannah explained the chaotic events of the last minute or so, the other vessel had slowed and was executing a turning manoeuver with the obvious intention of returning to *Minstrel's* side.

While this was happening, first mate Fred Paxton barked orders at the crew. He made it clear their priority was to discover what damage, if any, had occurred below deck. They scampered below to inspect the damage. Meanwhile, Captain Mathers wandered the deck in a befuddled gaze, half empty rum bottle in hand.

Five minutes later, the other vessel, a barque whose nameplate read *Northern Skies,* heaved to alongside *Minstrel.* Before the barque's crewmen had even thrown ropes down to their opposites aboard *Minstrel* to secure the two vessels and keep them together, Captain Mathers had begun abusing *Northern Skies* and every man aboard her.

"A damned curse upon you all!" he shouted at the crewmen who now lined the barque's near rail. "I demand to know what flag you sail under, and who is your master?"

"I am master of Northern Skies and we sail under the flag of Mother England!" a gruff voice responded in the strongest of Devon accents. "Captain Philip Jamieson at your service." The captain, a short stocky man almost as broad as he was tall, waved down to his opposite.

Mathers eyeballed him and, using the foulest of seafaring language, proceeded to berate him uninterrupted for a good two minutes. In that time he told Captain Jamieson he was an apology for a captain and had no right being master of a floating bathtub let alone a three-masted barque.

When Mathers finally ran out of profanities and ceased his tirade, Captain Jamieson asked, "Did you not think to post a lookout aboard Minstrel, sir?"

"Of course we had a lookout posted you bloody idiot!" Mathers saw red and hurled his now empty bottle in Captain Jamieson's direction. The bottle fell short and smashed against *Northern Skies'* hull. "Yours is the bigger, faster vessel," he shouted. "The liability for the collision is yours and yours alone, sir!"

That was the last straw for Captain Jamieson who proceeded to direct profanities at Mathers.

Looking on, Susannah thought Mathers looked so angry he was about to have a heart attack. He was red with rage and appeared ready to dive over the rail and attempt to board the barque.

When Captain Jamieson had had his say, he ordered his crew to prepare to depart. The securing ropes were disconnected and quickly pulled in, and *Northern Skies* was soon on her way.

As the barque sailed off into the darkness, the two captains continued to hurl insults at each other.

Mathers, who was now standing at *Minstrel's* stern, got the last word. "You could have caused the deaths of scores, nay hundreds, of passengers and crew!" he shouted, seemingly oblivious to the exaggerated utterances that spewed from his drunken lips. "Little do you care, I now have a hundred weeping women below deck in need of comfort!"

At that, several passengers and crew aboard *Minstrel* burst out laughing. Mathers continued his tirade until only the barque's stern light was visible. Having finally run out of steam, the captain weaved his way forward and disappeared below deck.

At the same time, several crewmen emerged from below deck and reported to Paxton that, aside from superficial damage to the exterior of the hull, all was well below.

"Who was on lookout tonight?" Paxton asked.

Goldie stepped forward. "I was, Chief."

"Did you not see the barque, Mister Archibald?"

"Not until she was a hundred-and-fifty yards off the bow, Chief," Goldie replied.

"Then I would contend you were negligent in your duty," Paxton grumbled. "If this was a naval vessel, you'd be hung, drawn and quartered for that."

Goldie bowed his head in shame. Looking on, Susannah felt badly for him.

The first mate turned to the two nearest crewmen. "Escort Mister Archibald below and intern him in the store room tonight."

"Yes Chief," the crewmen said in unison.

"And he's to remain there until we reach Cape Town."

The two crewmen led a chastened Goldie below deck. As he was led away, Goldie was too ashamed to look at Susannah.

Susannah turned to Drake Senior. "I need to go below, papa." She felt ill—and not because of anything she'd eaten or because of the smell of bilgewater that wafted up from below deck.

"Of course, my dear." Drake Senior led Susannah below deck. The clergyman thought it understandable his daughter had been left shocked by the near miss. He didn't realize there was more to it than that.

As they returned to the stateroom, Susannah experienced a myriad of emotions. She felt relieved they'd survived what could have been a fatal collision, and she felt guilty that she was as much responsible for the near-catastrophic event as Goldie was. *If I hadn't tempted him so, he'd have done his duty and seen the barque in time.* The thought of what could have happened, and the lives that could have been lost, almost overwhelmed her. She stumbled as she walked.

Drake Senior reached out an arm and steadied her. "Are you alright, Susannah?"

"Yes papa," Susannah assured him.

The young Englishwoman took the night's events as a sign that she wasn't meant to give herself to Goldie, or to any man, before she was married. At that moment, she was certain God had intervened, and she promised herself she would resist any further temptations the devil put in her way.

CHAPTER 33

Pacific Ocean, 1841

SITTING IN THE CONFINES OF the tea-chest in *Besieged's* storeroom with his knees drawn up to his chest, Jack was feeling ill. He wasn't sure if it was the overpowering smell of tea or the motion of the schooner that was causing it. He guessed it was probably a combination of the two.

Unable to take it any longer, he opened the tea-chest lid and climbed out, gratefully sucking in a lung-full of sea air as he did so. Desperate to relieve himself, he hurried out of the store-room and made his way above deck. There, by the light of the moon, he urinated over the port-side rail. He had to stand legs astride to maintain his balance as the schooner ploughed through heavy Pacific swells. Fortunately, no-one else was around.

Enjoying his first pee since *Besieged* departed the Sydney Town docks a good three hours earlier, and breathing in the sea air, Jack was feeling exhilarated. Apart from the brief escapade down the river at Parramatta a year earlier, and the three weeks he'd just spent at the Todds' boarding house, this was his first taste of freedom since sentence had been passed on him in London's Central Criminal Court four years earlier. He breathed in several more lung-fulls of air. "Ah, freedom!" he sighed.

The sea air soon revived him and the feelings of nausea

passed. Not wanting to push his luck, he quickly retired below deck before someone saw him.

Back in the storeroom, he searched for some food and drinking water. He soon found fruit and fresh bread, but no water. The schooner's freshwater supplies were obviously stored elsewhere. He did find a bottle of rum, though. *This'll have to do,* he decided none too dejected.

Next, he looked for an alternative hiding place. He located an empty crate that was at least twice as big as the tea-chest he'd just vacated. Crawling inside it, he was pleasantly surprised to find there was even room to lie down.

Jack proceeded to enjoy a three-course meal of sorts. The entrée was a fresh orange, the mains fresh, doughy bread and dessert a ripe banana. Each course was washed down with generous helpings of rum, which he drank straight from the bottle. After draining half the bottle, he fell into a contented, dream-filled sleep.

In his dreams, he was cavorting naked with a buxom woman. In one dream the woman looked like Joan Todd; in another she looked like Mary O'Brien. Later, when he finally woke, he wouldn't be able to recall who the woman of his dreams was. But that wouldn't matter to him: he had equally fond memories of both.

⁂

NEXT MORNING, THE ship's Scottish quartermaster carried out what for him would be the first of many daily inspections of the storeroom. He had to concentrate to keep his balance as the schooner rolled in heavy seas.

The sound of a bottle rolling around inside a crate attracted the quartermaster's attention. He pulled the lid off the crate and was surprised to find Jack fast asleep inside. Having finished off the rum during the night, the stowaway was sleeping off the results. The now-empty bottle was still rolling around beside him.

"What have we here?" the quartermaster asked himself. He then shouted, "Stowaway!"

Other crewmen came running.

Jack woke to find himself being pulled out of the crate by several pairs of rough hands. He was hauled above deck and half-carried to the captain's quarters.

At the sight of Jack, the ship's Welsh master, Captain Jones, asked, "Who is this?

"Can't get a word out of him, sir," the quartermaster responded. "He's as pissed as a newt."

The captain could see Jack was too inebriated to respond to questioning. Turning to his first mate, Quincy Adams, he said, "Bring him back to my quarters after he's sobered up, Mister Adams."

"Aye, sir," Adams answered in a heavy Cornish accent.

The first mate escorted the stowaway topside and ordered two sailors to throw buckets of seawater over him. They performed this task with zeal.

A short time later, cold, wet and almost sober, a shivering and bedraggled Jack stood before the ship's master once more, water dripping from his sodden clothes.

"Your name?" Captain Jones asked without ceremony.

"Jack Halliday," the Cockney responded without thinking. He immediately regretted revealing his name.

"Which penal institution did you escape from, Mister Halliday?" the captain asked perceptively.

Jack feigned surprise. "I'm no convict, sir. I'm a humble citizen from Sydney Town just wanting to work me passage to Fiji."

"A humble citizen, eh?" Captain Jones glanced at his first mate. "What do you think, Mister Adams?"

"Someone wanting to work his passage doesn't stow away, sir," Adams said. With that, he suddenly reached down and pulled up Jack's trousers, exposing his ankles. The tell-tale marks left by innumerable pairs of leg-irons were highly visible. Adams looked up at his captain. "He's an escaped convict, sir. Probably from Parramatta."

"I'm a blacksmith," Jack protested.

"A blacksmith?" Captain Jones asked. "How did you come by those marks?" He glanced pointedly at the marks.

"They're caused by a rash," Jack mumbled lamely.

The disbelieving captain eyed Jack as he decided on a course of action. Without warning, the first mate ripped Jack's shirt from him, exposing the stowaway's scarred back. In the cold light of day, the marks of lashings were there for all to see.

Captain Jones studied Jack grimly. Finally, he said, "You can work your passage to Norfolk Island."

Jack wondered if he'd misheard the captain. His understanding was the vessel was Fiji-bound.

Captain Jones continued, "You won't be paid for your endeavors, and as soon as we arrive at Norfolk you'll be handed over to the penal colony commander there."

Jack didn't like the sound of that one bit. He'd heard horror stories about the infamous Norfolk Island penal colony.

As an afterthought Captain Jones added, "You'll either be interned there or, if you're lucky, you'll be shipped back to Sydney Town and returned to Parramatta, or whichever penal settlement you escaped from."

Jack prayed it would be the latter, although the prospect of being returned to Parramatta didn't fill him with joy either.

The captain turned to his first mate. "Get him a change of clothes then put him to work, Mister Adams."

"Aye, sir."

Jack opened his mouth to protest, but before he could Adams pushed him out the door. The first mate escorted Jack to stores, below deck.

As they walked, Jack asked, "I thought this ship was bound

for Fiji?"

"She is," Adams answered. "But we have supplies to drop in to the penal settlement at Norfolk Island first."

That confirmed Jack's worst fears. Norfolk Island was also a British colony. Administered by the New South Wales authorities, the penal settlement had a well deserved reputation as a hell-hole—a living nightmare for its convict population. It was common knowledge convicts interned there often committed suicide rather than serve out their sentence. Jack realized there'd be a very real chance he'd be interned on the island, and if that happened it could well be a death sentence.

Down in stores, Jack was outfitted in standard-issue working clothes then Adams escorted him back topside. There, the first mate handed him a mop and bucket, and pointed to the deck. "See that?" Adams asked.

Jack nodded.

Adams snarled, "I want you to mop the entire deck until it's so clean I can see me handsome face in it." He walked off, leaving Jack to start mopping. Looking back at the stowaway, he added, "And if you're caught slacking, there'll be no rations for you."

Jack began mopping. As he did, he rued his change of fortune. Now his future looked bleak indeed. He couldn't decide which would be worse—to be incarcerated at Norfolk Island or returned to Parramatta. The consequences of either didn't bear thinking about. He knew he had around two weeks to rewrite his future: that was how long he estimated *Besieged* would take to complete the thousand-mile voyage to Norfolk Island.

CHAPTER 34

∼◦◦◦∼

Philadelphia, United States of America, 1843

NATHAN HAD HIS HANDS FULL. He tried not to spill champagne from the near-full glass he balanced as two giggling, skimpily-clad showgirls draped over him, showering him with kisses. One, a fetching chorus girl, sat on his knee; the other, a soloist, leaned over him from behind.

It was the interval during a song and dance show at Philadelphia's popular music hall of the day, *The Merry Menagerie*, and Nathan was celebrating his twenty-first birthday with a group of boisterous friends. As was the custom at the popular nightly show, the showgirls mingled with the patrons between acts in the establishment's parlor.

Nathan's rowdy group included his blind date for the evening, three boyhood friends, their girlfriends of the moment and an assortment of hangers-on. All had had too much to drink and they'd already been asked twice by parlor employees to keep the noise down.

Nathan was almost unrecognizable as the young man who had been living amongst the Makah just one year earlier. Dressed in the finest European clothes, sporting the latest fashionable hairstyle and spending money like there was no tomorrow, he looked and acted like a spoiled beau.

As he admired the exposed cleavage of the young woman on his knee, Nathan dropped his champagne glass. Its contents splashed over the woman's breasts and the glass shattered on the wooden floor. "Anchors away!" Nathan shouted to the amusement of his companions.

Other patrons weren't so amused. Several had already complained to the management.

"More champagne for the prodigal son!" one of Nathan's male friends called out.

"I'll drink to that!" Nathan shouted, prompting more laughter among the group.

A floor manager approached the young Philadelphian and raised a forefinger to his lips, indicating he and his companions should demonstrate a little more consideration for fellow patrons. Nathan mimicked the floor manager, raising his own forefinger to his lips and making an exaggerated *shhh* sound. This prompted more laughter from his companions and drew more glares from their fellow patrons.

What no-one knew outside Nathan's little group of confidants was that the young man was determined to make up for his lost years with the Makah. Since his dramatic escape from Oregon Country, he'd indulged himself in almost every excess known to man. The past six months had been a blur of parties, gambling and women, and he had no intention of slowing down. Not yet anyway.

After evading Tatoosh and his braves at Whale Bay, and scrambling aboard the schooner that had fortuitously anchored there, Nathan had endured a six-month voyage before arriving back on America's east coast. *Endured* because he'd just wanted to get home. Unfortunately, to do that, he had to work his passage aboard *Spirit of the Sea* as she worked her way down the west coast of North and South America, and then up the east coast.

On his return to Philadelphia, incredulous friends and family couldn't believe their eyes. Nathan had long been given up for dead along with his other crewmates on the doomed *Intrepid*. He became something of an overnight celebrity when the local newspaper ran a front page article that chronicled his miraculous return. After that, there was no shortage of *friends* wanting to buy him a drink and hear about his adventures first hand.

Adjusting to civilization hadn't come easy. Even to this day, his mind and body remained in Makah mode. This manifested itself in a number of ways — not the least being he sometimes lapsed into Makah when conversing. He also shunned sleeping in a conventional bed, preferring the floor; when asleep in the arms of his latest bit of skirt, he often alarmed them by uttering Makah chants and war cries; when dining he preferred raw fish to meat; and he'd often disappear for days on end, hiking through the countryside as he'd done in Oregon Country.

Gradually, as the months went by and he adjusted back to city life, he'd cultivated some bad habits — like whoring and partying to excess — to make up for the lost years.

When the New York Times heard about Nathan, its editor offered a handsome payment for the full story on his time with the Makah. The story was serialized over four editions and occupied the center spread of each edition. The first installment was published under the heading: *Young Philadelphian returns from the dead after being enslaved by Northwest savages*. By the time the fourth installment ran, Nathan was a celebrity up and down the entire eastern seaboard.

As a result, he was a popular guest at balls and dinner parties throughout Pennsylvania and even further afield. The press loved him, too, and his handsome image was often seen in newspapers — usually with a pretty woman at his side.

Nathan's good fortune didn't end there, however. Even before the New York Times story ran, a mysterious benefactor had started anonymously depositing funds into his bank account. The funds were substantial and financed the high life he'd been leading. Furthermore, the deposits had continued, like clockwork, on the first of each month.

The ringing of a bell signaled the interval was over. Nathan's group joined the other patrons in filing back to resume their seats for the second act.

Later, as he watched the performers from the comfort of the pricey gallery seats, his mind wandered. He thought back to the reception he'd received from his sisters and their families the day he'd arrived home. Sissy and Alice had both married since he'd last seen them. Sissy was pregnant with her first child and Alice had two children. Both sisters had showered him with kisses and demanded to know every single thing that had happened to him since the shipwreck.

Nathan had learned from them that their father had contracted consumption—or tuberculosis as it would later be called—and had taken enforced early retirement as a result of that. They'd pleaded with their young brother to see Johnson Senior and make his peace with him before he died, but Nathan had refused. No amount of pleading would persuade him to reconcile with the father who had beaten him and left him with so many bad boyhood memories.

Johnson Senior, who still resided in the family home—albeit with a live-in nurse to care for him—had tried to make contact with his son on at least four occasions, but each time Nathan had ignored him.

THREE MONTHS AND countless drinks and hangovers later, Nathan was walking along downtown Philadelphia's main street. He'd just finished pleasuring a sophisticate whose husband was away on business, and he was en route to a rendezvous with friends at a local bar where, if recent experience was anything to go by, he'd drink until he couldn't remember his name.

Approaching him was an old man who shuffled along with the aid of a walking stick. It wasn't until the man was a few feet away that Nathan recognized him. *It's my father!* At first he wondered if he was mistaken. The old man was a shadow of the vibrant sea captain he remembered.

Johnson Senior resembled a skeleton. The disease that ravaged him had taken its toll and he clearly didn't have long to live.

Nathan pretended he hadn't recognized his father, but as he walked by Johnson Senior grabbed his arm.

"Son!" Johnson Senior rasped.

Nathan looked at him, vacant, as if his father was a stranger.

"It's me. Your father."

As Nathan looked into his father's blue eyes, he was taken back to the last time he'd seen him. He'd been caught in his father's out-of-bounds study, and a drunk Johnson Senior had punished him by beating him mercilessly about the head. "I'm sorry," he said to the older man, "I don't remember you." Nathan shook his father's hand from his arm and resumed walking.

Behind him, he could feel his father's eyes boring into his back. Nathan quickened his stride. He hoped that would be the last time he'd ever see his father. It was.

<hr />

ON THE ANNIVERSARY of his first year back in Philadelphia, Nathan took stock of his life. Nothing had changed yet everything had changed. On the one hand, life was still one giddy round of drinking, partying and whoring; on the other hand, he'd had an epiphany.

It happened exactly one month after he'd seen his father in the street. Johnson Senior had died at home alone. He'd been given a send-off worthy of one of Philadelphia's finest citizens. Nathan hadn't attended the funeral despite the exhortations of his sisters.

Six weeks after the funeral, Nathan and his sisters had been summonsed to the downtown office of their father's lawyer, a Mister Chumly Cummins, to hear the reading of Johnson Senior's will.

To Sissy and Alice, their father bequeathed his entire monetary fortune, which was substantial to say the least.

To Nathan, he left his trading company, *Johnson Traders*. More an empire than a company, its vast holdings included three sailing ships, vacant plots of prime land on America's east and west coasts, shares including a ten per cent shareholding in the Port of San Francisco, and many thousands of dollars worth of unsold goods procured in the course of recent trades.

In one sweep of the pen, Johnson Senior had ensured his three children would never want for anything and could see out their days in total comfort if not absolute luxury.

But that wasn't all. To each of his children, he'd also left a personalized letter. It was the contents of Johnson Senior's letter to his son that provided Nathan with the epiphany that was about to change his life.

Nathan hadn't read the letter until a week after the reading of the will. He wasn't sure he wanted to read it and had even contemplated destroying it. Finally, he read it, but only because he thought it likely it would pertain to the running of the company he'd inherited, and not for any sentimental reason.

The letter read:

Dear Nathan

It is with a heavy heart I write this to you, my only son.

I cannot take back the deeds, or misdeeds, I have done and I know I can never expect your forgiveness for the way I treated you growing up. I could blame the liquor or the pressures of business for my actions, but I know they are but hollow excuses.

I grieved for you when your ship went down and you were believed dead. How my heart soared when I learned you had survived.

I grieved for you again when you refused to see me on your return. And I grieved for myself, and cursed myself, for not being a worthy father.

If I could have my time again I would do things differently. That much I know. Believe me when I say I am proud of you, son. Your dear mother would be proud of you, too.

Despite my many faults, I ran a sound and honest business. I hereby bequeath it to you and trust you will profit handsomely from it in the years ahead.

Your father,

Benjamin Johnson

Johnson Senior's words of love and regret made not the slightest impression on Nathan, and did nothing to change his low opinion of his father. They reminded him of an old Makah saying: *Words are like clouds in the sky for even the faintest wind will blow them away.* However, Johnson Senior's reference to his business had gotten Nathan thinking.

As one of Philadelphia's wealthiest citizens, and one of the youngest members of the nouveau riche on the entire eastern seaboard, he knew the world was his oyster. He could do anything he liked. He could even retire if he wanted to and party all day, every day. Tempting though that idea was, he felt he owed it to himself to do something with his life.

If I'm ever gonna do something, it has to be now.

Despite the foolishness and immaturity he'd demonstrated since his return to Philadelphia, he was wise enough to recognize he needed to change. He vowed to change immediately.

As he folded the letter away, he noticed his father had written something on the back of it. It read:

P.S.—I am sure you will agree there is now no further need for a continuation of the monthly cash deposits into your bank account. I have discontinued those.—B.J.

231

So now Nathan knew for sure why the monthly deposits had recently ceased. He'd already guessed his father had been making the deposits as they stopped as soon as he died.

In the weeks ahead, Nathan threw himself into his father's business. It wasn't that hard. Johnson Senior had surrounded himself with good people, and Nathan retained them and made good use of them. While he had the casting vote in all company matters, he gave the company's senior managers even more autonomy than his father had given them. That didn't always work out, and he had to fire one or two, but Nathan learned fast and the business continued to prosper.

After six months as the new head of Johnson Traders, it was as if Johnson Senior had never been away. At the end of Nathan's first year at the helm, the company posted a record profit.

CHAPTER 35

South Atlantic, 1848

N EARLY TWO WEEKS LATER, BENEATH clear winter skies, *Minstrel* rounded Africa's scenic Cape of Good Hope, at the bottom of Cape Colony. Passengers and crew were treated to the sight of a rugged coastline interspersed with white sand beaches. Neat cottages nestled in the valleys reminded some of Devon.

The Drakes, along with most of the other passengers, had been on deck to view the spectacle ever since the cape had been sighted hours earlier. They were all rugged up in their warmest coats and scarves, the heat of the Tropics long forgotten.

As *Minstrel* merged with scores of other craft in Cape Town's beautiful harbor, children squealed with delight when a pod of dolphins provided an impromptu escort for the brigantine. The dolphins were almost close enough to touch. Several performed spectacular somersaults alongside *Minstrel,* prompting more squeals from the children and cheers from the adults.

The passengers' eyes were drawn to the majestic Table Mountain. Towering over Cape Town like a granite sentinel, it was impossible to miss. Atop it was a narrow blanket of cloud which ran its full length. The cloud cover was likened to a tablecloth by Miss Finch, and Susannah thought that most apt.

When Susannah thought about the mountain's name, she realized others had thought it apt also.

First impressions of *Minstrel's* latest destination were highly favorable. Even before stepping ashore, passengers and crew were unanimous in their praise of the British colony that would one day be known as South Africa.

After weeks at sea, everyone was looking forward to the stopover. For Susannah, her excitement was tempered by the fact she hadn't completely recovered from the near-catastrophic collision with the barque and the events that led up to it. The young Englishwoman now viewed those *events* as shameful, and had prayed frequently for forgiveness.

Susannah hadn't seen Goldie since that night for he'd remained incarcerated in the hold. She feared what fate awaited him in Cape Town and fervently hoped he wouldn't be punished further.

"Everything alright, my dear?" It was Drake Senior who asked. He'd noticed his daughter seemed distracted.

"Of course, papa." Susannah forced a smile.

Drake Senior wasn't fooled. He knew his daughter well enough to know when she had something on her mind. The extra time she'd set aside recently for her daily prayers and bible studies was a clue that Susannah may be wrestling with some inner torment. The clergyman smiled and placed a caring arm around her. "Well, you know I'm here for you if you need to talk to someone," he said tenderly.

"Thank you, papa." Susannah leaned her head on Drake Senior's shoulder. How she wished she could go back and undo the events leading up to *that* recent night. She'd slept poorly ever since. Her dreams had been filled with Goldie; in some she was with him, making love. The more she prayed and asked God for forgiveness, the more sexually explicit her dreams had become.

Susannah was starting to feel like she was trapped between two worlds: the strict religious world she'd been born into and the secular world—the world that allowed for more freedom of expression—that she was beginning to realize her heart desired.

The one bright spot in her life was her father was recovering well from his wounds. Since his setback after discharging himself from hospital in Bata, he was getting stronger every day and was almost back to his old self. Susannah clung to that and forced all other thoughts from her mind.

LATER THAT MORNING, as the Drakes and other passengers lined up on deck in preparation for going ashore, a now sober Captain Mathers gave them the same pep talk he delivered on arrival in every new stopover port.

"Ladies and gentlemen, I would remind you we are only here for four days," Mathers said.

Everyone was aware the original ten-day stopover had been cut because of the delays *Minstrel* had experienced in Bata.

Mathers continued, "In that time we will be reprovisioning Minstrel. As always, take care ashore, watch the children closely and never venture anywhere alone."

As the captain rambled on, several male passengers—the single men in particular—were growing impatient. They couldn't wait to hit the bars and, in some cases, the brothels in town.

"Departure is scheduled for mid-morning June twenty-ninth, and anyone not on board then will be left behind!" Mathers warned as the men finally broke ranks and strode down the gangplank onto the wharf.

As the Drakes queued to descend the gangplank, Susannah caught her first and last glimpse of Goldie. The rigger had been brought up on deck and was being addressed by the first mate Paxton. Having spent so long in the hold, he looked pale and drawn.

Susannah caught Goldie's eye when she drew level with him. She mouthed the word *Sorry* to him as she passed by. He smiled at her. The young woman felt relieved and grateful all at once. Goldie's smile had signaled to her that he didn't blame her one jot for what had happened.

Later, Susannah would learn that other than having his pay docked, Goldie had been released without further punishment.

After spending an enjoyable afternoon ashore, the Drakes dined as guests of Harry Kemp. The colonel had been invited to dine at the home of old family friends, and had assured Susannah and her father that two extra guests would be most welcome. That turned out to be true, and all three shared a wonderful evening at the home of a retired London surgeon and his charming Dutch wife.

Susannah struck up such a rapport with the Dutchwoman she accepted an invitation to stay over for a couple of days. For the young Englishwoman, those two days flew by and she regretted she had to return to *Minstrel* so soon. Before departing, she assured her generous hosts she'd remain in contact by letter.

For *Minstrel's* passengers, the first few days in Cape Town passed without incident. Then tragedy struck.

The morning before *Minstrel's* scheduled departure, one of the female passengers reported her husband had not returned from a visit ashore the previous night. Bill Compton, a God-fearing gentleman, had gone ashore to purchase medicine for the youngest of his three children.

When he hadn't returned, his wife Thelma thought he may have decided to overnight on shore for some reason. However, when he didn't show up the following morning, she knew something wasn't right.

True to form, Captain Mathers was too drunk to arrange a search party, so his first mate Paxton took over. A dozen men — passengers and crew — were quickly appointed to search for the missing man. Drake Senior had volunteered to join the search party, but Susannah had intervened, pointing out he was not yet back to full health and needed to conserve his energy. His protestations had been quelled by the timely intervention of Miss Finch, who proved a valuable ally for Susannah at such times.

⤙⤙◦◉◦⤚⤚

WHEN THE SCHEDULED day of departure dawned for *Minstrel* and her passengers, Bill Compton still hadn't been found. Thelma Compton was beside herself with worry, and Susannah took it upon herself to stay by her side to comfort her and help care for her three children.

No-one could imagine departing Cape Town minus a passenger. No-one, that is, except Captain Mathers. He'd sobered up after hearing of Compton's disappearance and was, to his credit, helping coordinate the search effort. However, he was also threatening to stick to the mid-morning departure time he'd scheduled.

Only Harry Kemp's intervention dissuaded the captain from carrying out his threat. As the man who had chartered *Minstrel,* and who ultimately paid for Mathers' services, the colonel had final say on such matters. Mathers' authority only exceeded Kemp's on matters of on-board safety and other maritime issues when at sea.

Despite every able-bodied man aboard *Minstrel* now being involved in the search, the day passed without Compton being found. One day led to another and then yet another. Thelma Compton hadn't slept in all that time and was now ill with worry.

By the dawning of the fourth extra day, Kemp had to make a decision. He consulted with Mathers and with several male passengers whose opinion he respected, but his mind was already made up. "We have to depart now," he said after some heated debate.

The others—of whom Drake Senior was one—finally agreed. As a still sober Mathers had pointed out, they could keep searching for another month for no different result.

"Someone should break the news to Missus Compton,"

Kemp said.

"I will do that," Drake Senior offered.

"I don't envy her decision," Mathers said.

Everyone knew what decision he referred to: Thelma Compton had to decide whether to relocate herself and her children ashore in the hope she'd be reunited with her husband, or continue on to New Zealand without him. It was a hellish decision for any woman to make and none of the men envied her.

"I'll inform her now," Drake Senior said, taking his leave.

The others watched him go. Each was pleased it wasn't himself who had to deliver the news.

Drake Senior found Thelma in a drawing room that adjoined the dining room. The distressed woman was being comforted, as always, by Susannah. Miss Finch was nearby, watching over the three Compton children.

Thelma took one look at Drake Senior's face and burst into tears. She knew what was coming.

The clergyman placed a caring hand on her shoulder. "I'm sorry, Missus Compton," he murmured. "We can wait no longer."

Although the announcement came as no surprise, Thelma let out a heart-rending cry of anguish.

Susannah held her tight. At the same time she looked up at Drake Senior. "Papa, surely we can delay departure another twenty-four hours?"

Drake Senior shot his daughter an angry glance that told her now was the time for a united front, not for prevarication. "I'm sorry Colonel Kemp has made his decision. We can wait no longer."

"What am I to do?" Thelma implored.

Drake Senior had been dreading that question. He'd been expecting it, but had no answer. "That's for you to decide," he said at length. "No-one else can make that decision."

CHAPTER 36

Pacific Ocean, 1841

THE TWO WEEKS IT TOOK for *Besieged* to reach Norfolk Island was uneventful enough. Jack's days were spent scrubbing decks, cleaning and emptying latrines, and attending to whatever menial task first mate Quincy Adams threw his way; his nights were spent interned in the hold.

A day out from Norfolk Island, everything changed. A fierce storm swept in from the north, preventing the schooner from approaching the island's harbor and transferring supplies from ship to shore. It also prevented Captain Jones from handing over his uninvited passenger to the penal settlement's authorities.

As one day became two and then three, Jack started to believe he may have dodged a bullet. The storm was showing no sign of easing and conditions remained far too dangerous for *Besieged* to enter the harbor. Equally, it was too dangerous for any craft to leave the safety of the harbor to approach the schooner.

Jack had overheard crewmembers saying the captain was under pressure to continue the voyage to Fiji. Apparently, whalers there were depending on *Besieged* for urgently needed supplies as the whaling season was fast approaching.

Captain Jones was torn between fulfilling his obligations to Norfolk Island's penal settlement authorities and to the anxious whalers awaiting their supplies in Fiji. It wasn't an easy decision because the penal settlement needed supplies also, and the next supply ship wasn't scheduled for another two months.

As the fourth day dawned, Jack received a big scare when the wind eased sufficiently for the island's residents to send a large, covered longboat out to try to connect with *Besieged* and transfer some of the most urgently needed supplies back to shore. The boat, which was manned by ten hardy oarsmen plus another man on the tiller, reminded the stowaway of a similar craft he'd once seen used by Marine Lifeguard personnel in a rescue mission off England's southern coast.

On the orders of Captain Jones, Jack was brought out on deck to await the longboat's arrival. First mate Adams took great delight in informing his prisoner the authorities were more likely to intern him on the island than send him back to Parramatta. To rub it in, he accepted a one guinea wager from the second mate over whether Jack would ever see New South Wales again.

The stowaway held his breath as the longboat edged closer to *Besieged's* side. Its task was made easier as the wind eased for the first time since the storm had struck. *Just me luck!* Jack cursed his misfortune.

While the wind had eased, the swell hadn't. A huge wave picked the longboat up and smashed it against the schooner's hull, snapping oars and damaging the smaller craft.

That was enough for longboat's captain. He immediately ordered his oarsmen to heave to and return to shore. As if to reinforce that he'd made the right decision, the wind chose that moment to increase and the longboat was dashed against *Besieged's* hull a second time.

Looking on, it took all Jack's will power not to cheer loudly and break out into a jig. Instead, he celebrated quietly, contenting himself with a smile. *Reprieved!*

The smile wasn't lost on Adams. "Lucky bastard!" he

cursed, realizing he'd just lost his wager with the second mate. Turning to a crewman, Adams snapped, "Get him below!"

"Yes chief," the crewman said. He grabbed Jack by the arm and marched him below deck as ordered.

AFTER FIVE DAYS of being assailed by unrelenting gale-force winds and heavy seas, Captain Jones made the difficult decision to resume the voyage to Fiji. As he explained in his log, *The whalers were afforded priority ahead of the Norfolk Island penal settlement because their entire season depended on receiving the supplies.* The captain just hoped his employers would agree with his decision. If he'd got it wrong, he knew his job could be on the line.

Jack was emptying a latrine over the schooner's side when he heard first mate Adams give the order to weigh anchor. As usually happened the wind blew the urine and crap, and other unsavory contents of the latrine, back into his face. Jack didn't mind this time. In fact, he didn't even notice. He was elated. *Fiji here we come!* His prayers had been answered.

The stowaway had been hoping against hope the storm would be his salvation. And so it had transpired. Ahead of him now was another two-week voyage — this time to Fiji.

While he'd undoubtedly bought himself some time, Jack was under no illusions that his problems were over. He'd simply replaced one set of problems with another. The voyage to Fiji would pass soon enough and then he'd be handed over to the British authorities there and transferred back to Parramatta. However, he'd had a stay of execution and, for the moment, that's all that mattered to the irrepressible Cockney.

A day out from Norfolk Island, Jack received further good news when the captain ordered that the stowaway could bunk in with the men and dine with them in the mess. Until now, he'd been confined to sleeping and eating alone in the hold. At least now he'd have some company for the remainder of the voyage.

Furthermore, Captain Jones decided to put Jack's blacksmithing skills to good use, and ordered that he assist the schooner's carpenter with general on board repairs as required. The promotion was timely as *Beseiged* had suffered damage to its timber structures in the continuing storm, so Jack was kept busy—too busy to empty the latrines. That thankless task fell to an ordinary seaman.

So began a new routine for the stowaway. By day he put his smithing skills to good use and at night he bunked in with the crewmen. He now enjoyed full rations and most of the privileges of a normal crewmember. Almost inevitably, his friendly demeanor and cheeky personality endeared him to the crew and they quickly accepted him as one of them.

While Jack appreciated his new status, the fate that awaited him was never far from his mind.

Three days out from Norfolk Island, the storm finally passed by, leaving in its place calm seas, blue skies and balmy temperatures. The temperature rose steadily as *Beseiged* ventured deeper into tropical waters.

—⚬—

TWO DAYS OUT from Fiji's outer islands, the wind died and *Beseiged* was becalmed. Captain Jones allowed the men some rare free time. Some took advantage of this by fishing for any one of the numerous tropical fish varieties found in these waters while others caught up on lost sleep or lounged around above and below deck, playing cards or reading.

Though the free time didn't officially extend to Jack, not even the first mate objected when he set his duties aside to try his luck with a spot of fishing.

Shouts alerted the men to the arrival of a school of tiger sharks off the schooner's starboard side. Several sailors threw fish bait and food scraps down to the man-eaters and a minor feeding frenzy developed. Jack and the others watched, intrigued, as a dozen fins sliced left and right through the water. The sea in the immediate vicinity became a churning mass of foam as the sharks fought for the morsels being tossed down to them. Several sharks turned on each other, fresh blood only adding to their frenzy.

The schooner's youngest crewmember, thirteen-year-old deck boy Thomas Brown, laughed gleefully as the sharks fought for a large piece of bait he'd just thrown down to them. In his excitement, Thomas leaned over the rail for a better view.

"Careful, lad!" a burly rigger called out.

The warning came too late. Thomas lost his balance and fell into the sea. He landed a short distance from the sharks and momentarily disappeared beneath the surface. Jack and other horrified crewmen rushed to the near rail.

As Thomas resurfaced he started panicking and thrashing about. It was immediately clear he couldn't swim. "Help!" he spluttered after taking in a mouthful of water.

A quick-thinking sailor tossed a rope over the side. It landed next to the lad. "Grab the rope!" the sailor shouted.

Thomas grabbed hold of the rope. He tried to climb it, but lacked the strength. Crewmen shouted their encouragement to him.

Captain Jones arrived on deck, attracted by the commotion. He became distraught when he realized who it was in the water. "For God sake, someone do something!" he screamed, distressed.

Observing him, Jack thought the captain's reaction was out of character given that he was normally very calm when faced with difficult circumstances. The Cockney wasn't to know that Captain Jones was the boy's uncle.

Until now, the sharks had been so pre-occupied fighting over the food scraps none had noticed Thomas. Suddenly, a big shark peeled off from the others. Its fin sliced through the water toward the boy. Thomas saw it coming and started screaming. He frantically tried to climb the rope, but kept falling back into the water.

Captain Jones shouted, "Loop the rope around your arm and we'll pull you up, Thomas!"

The boy froze as the big shark nosed up to him. For some reason it veered away at the last second. The reprieve motivated Thomas to renew his efforts to climb the rope. Again, he failed.

"Loop the rope around your arm!" the captain shouted again. He looked like he was about to dive over the side.

Looking on, Jack willed the boy to do as the captain ordered. He knew if Thomas could loop the rope around his arm, the sailors could haul him on board. Unfortunately, the lad was too frightened to think clearly.

The shark returned and made a second pass. Another shark joined the first. Their fins zigzagged urgently through the water, indicating they were preparing to attack.

Jack knew the boy was on borrowed time. *Help me, Lord!* Kicking off his boots, he dived over the rail and landed next to Thomas. Jack resurfaced just as the nearest shark rolled over onto its side, exposing its teeth and one eye. He eyed it fearfully. *The bastard's grinning at me!* The Cockney reached up and grabbed the rope, entwining it several times around his strong right arm. With his left arm he enveloped Thomas and held him tight against his chest. Looking up, he yelled, "Pull!"

The rope immediately tightened as a dozen sailors began pulling on the other end. Jack and Thomas were hauled from the water just as one of the sharks came in for the kill. The shark rose high out of the water as it tried to grab Jack's legs. Jack swung his legs up, narrowly avoiding the shark's jaws. In that split second, he saw all the shark's teeth. Moments later, he and Thomas were safely on deck.

Willing hands whisked Thomas below deck while other crewmen crowded around Jack to confirm he was okay. Shaken but otherwise unharmed, the Cockney was subjected to much back-slapping as crewmembers bestowed their hearty congratulations on him. His heroic actions had earned him the respect of all — in particular that of Captain Jones.

From that day on, Jack would be treated as a fully-fledged member of *Besieged's* crew, and he had a friend for life in young Thomas.

That night, Captain Jones summonsed Jack to his cabin. He greeted his nephew's savior with a warm handshake. "That was a hell of a thing you did today, Mister Halliday," he smiled.

"I did what anyone would do," Jack said.

"But anyone didn't do it," the captain pointed out. "You did it."

The conversation lapsed. Jack wondered what was coming next. He hoped it was a reprieve. *He's gonna tell me I'm a free man!* Jack held his breath, and not for the first time on this dramatic voyage.

"I'm afraid you're not going to like what I have to say next," Captain Jones said somewhat embarrassed.

Jack could tell his hopes were about to be crushed.

"Unfortunately, nothing has changed as far as you're concerned. You are still an escaped felon and I'd be neglecting my duty if I didn't turn you over to the authorities." The captain hated himself at that moment. He'd have liked nothing better than to inform the young Cockney he was a free man, but his sense of duty wouldn't allow that. He hastily added, "God knows you deserve to be free, and rest assured I'll put in a good word for you when we hand you over."

"Thanks," Jack said lamely. He was tempted to plead with the captain to reconsider his hard line, but that wasn't his style.

As Jack turned to leave, Captain Jones restrained him. "One minute, Mister Halliday." The captain went to a drinks cabinet and pulled out an unopened bottle of rum. He held it up, a twinkle in his eyes. "I understand you are partial to rum?"

Jack's eyes lit up. "I am at that, sir."

"Good," the captain said. "Because I'd like to share a drink with the man who rescued my nephew from certain death."

The two unlikely drinking companions proceeded to enjoy a glass of rum together. If either thought it strange, neither said so. Given what had transpired earlier that day, it seemed the most natural thing in the world.

CHAPTER 37

Navigator Islands, South Pacific, 1848

NATHAN SLOWLY DRAINED A GLASS of whisky as he studied transcriptions of ships' logs left to him by his father. The transcriptions recounted past trading ventures to the Pacific Islands by vessels in Johnson Traders' fleet.

The young American, now twenty-six, was in a well appointed cabin aboard *Rainmaker,* a schooner that was traveling from San Francisco to Fiji, a three-month voyage allowing for stops at various island groups along the way. She'd not long berthed at Apia, in the Navigator Islands, an island group that would one day be renamed *Samoa* and one which Nathan had never visited previously.

Rainmaker was only scheduled to stay in Apia for a couple of days—just long enough to unload supplies for English missionaries stationed there and to load goods for her next destination. She was heading for Fiji, another seven hundred miles to the west, where Nathan intended to trade muskets to the Fijians in return for their prized beche-de-mer, exotic sea slugs which he planned to ship to China where they would fetch exorbitantly high prices.

Since he'd inherited his late father's trading empire several years earlier, Nathan had experienced the good and bad side of business. Johnson Traders, under his leadership, had gone from strength to strength during his first year at the helm. In the light of what followed, his competitors and critics unkindly labeled that first year *beginner's luck.*

Everything changed in the second year when a series of financial disasters—some related, others not—hit the company.

The first disaster was an unwise partnership Nathan struck up with a San Francisco entrepreneur who offered to represent Johnson Traders' business interests on the west coast. A series of unwise moves ranging from bad property investments to doomed merges resulted in Nathan having to cash in personal investments and sell many of his east coast assets to try to cover the debts. The situation wasn't helped by Nathan's partner who helped himself to much of the company's cash reserves and disappeared into the night.

All this coincided with a temporary downturn in west coast property values. As Nathan had invested heavily in west coast property—as had his father before him—the resulting downturn saw Johnson Traders' net worth plummet. Although short-lived, the downturn proved catastrophic for the company and for Nathan personally.

After two traumatic years trying to trade his way back into profit, Nathan had been forced to sell his company to a competitor for a fraction of its original worth. That had been a year earlier.

Since then, he'd ploughed every cent he had into a new trading venture. This venture had no company behind it; it didn't even have a name. Nathan had simply set himself up, quite unofficially, as a sole operator responsible only to himself. There were no senior managers, or middle managers or any employees of any kind; he didn't even own a ship. Finances dictated that he charter vessels for his various ventures or, as he'd done on this occasion, simply secure a berth for himself and his cargo as a normal fare-paying passenger. This time, his cargo comprised several hundred brand new muskets plus shot and powder for the weapons.

Under this new modus operandi, the young man had struggled for the first six months. Then he had yet another change of fortune — for the better this time.

Two major events saw Nathan's stocks rise.

The first was the United States' annexing of Texas, which happened three years earlier, in 1845. The ranchers and other new settlers who flooded into Texas urgently needed supplies, and Nathan was happy to oblige. Using all his savings, he chartered a vessel to transport firearms, tools, furniture, non-perishable food and other supplies to the Texans. One profitable voyage followed another — and Nathan was back.

The second event was the bloody Mexican-American War, which had been raging for nearly two years now. It proved the catalyst Nathan needed to further improve his financial position. He used the same formula he'd used for the Texan settlers, chartering ships to transport supplies to the American soldiers engaged in the hostilities — the main difference being the supplies were almost exclusively firearms and other useful items for waging war.

The young American's newfound success prompted him to relocate to San Francisco. He believed America's west coast held more promise and, since relocating there six months earlier, he hadn't looked back. Nathan now had sufficient resources to employ staff and purchase his own ships, but he'd resisted that temptation. If the past four years had taught him anything, it was that he operated best alone.

In hindsight, he believed his failure running the business he'd inherited from his father was the best thing that had ever happened to him. It had taught him he was, by nature, a loner who worked best alone; more importantly, the collapse of Johnson Traders had materially and emotionally cut any final link that may have existed between him and his father. Now he could truly say he was a self-made man, and he was proud of that.

Nathan had kept no reminder for himself of Johnson Senior.

Much to the dismay of his sisters, he'd even refused to take the portrait painting of his father that had once hung on the wall of his study in the family home. They'd remained miffed to this day over their brother's refusal to make his peace with Johnson Senior before his death. Reminders that their father had beaten him, not them, had fallen on deaf ears.

The siblings' attitude to the portrait painting of their beloved mother, however, was quite different. All three had wanted it. After much arguing, they agreed to let the toss of a coin decide who would inherit the painting. Nathan's oldest sister Alice won the toss. To her credit, she commissioned a local artist to paint two copies of the original, and a month later presented these, encased in beautiful frames, to her grateful siblings. Nathan and Sissy agreed the copies were almost identical to the original.

Nathan ensured the painting accompanied him on all his travels—as was the case on this particular voyage. It currently occupied pride of place on the wall facing Nathan's bunk. Pretty Charlotte Johnson's smiling face was the last thing he saw before going to sleep and the first thing he saw when he woke up.

A reflected face in a mirror hanging next to the painting distracted him. It took Nathan a second to register it was himself he was looking at. Studying his reflection, he didn't like to admit it—not even to himself—that the resemblance between himself and his father was uncanny. His long, black hair framed a ruggedly handsome face that sported stubble which he cultivated to ensure it always appeared as though he'd last shaved the previous day.

But it was his startling blue eyes that most reminded him, and others, of his father. They were mesmerizing and world-weary at the same time. This had proven a fatal combination for members of the opposite sex. Exactly why, Nathan wasn't sure, but he'd never been short of female company and he was grateful for that. The world-weariness, he guessed, came from having filled his twenty-six years with enough living for two lifetimes, and having witnessed so much of what life had to offer — good and bad — in those years.

The similarities to Johnson Senior didn't end there. Nathan wouldn't admit it, not even to himself, but the years had hardened him. He now shared many of the same traits he'd once despised in his father. Those traits had been molded during his violent childhood then solidified during the years of enforced living with the Makah and further solidified during his tumultuous years in business. The end result was Nathan was a self-centered individual who measured a man's worth by his wealth and whose only ambition in life was to accumulate money and possessions, and to bed as many women as he could along the way.

One result of his self-centeredness was he now had no friends. Worse, he had no need for friends. *Make money, not friends.* That was his philosophy.

As for the native races of the world, he had no time for them — not since his years with the Makah. Whether it was them or the Indians of South America, the Zulus of southern Africa, the Maoris of New Zealand or the islanders of the Pacific, it was his opinion they weren't interested in embracing civilization and all it had to offer. Consequently, he believed, they'd forever remain stuck in the Stone-Age. *Where they belong,* he thought.

Nathan had stopped sharing his opinions of the native races with others long ago. Family and associates branded him a racist whenever he'd share his views. He didn't like the term *racist* — not because he wasn't one, but because he didn't want to be known as one — so had learned to keep his views to himself. As his job all too often involved trading with native peoples, he knew it wouldn't be good for business to be known as a racist.

As the years ticked by, Nathan had made a conscious effort to forget his time with the Makah and to banish any hangovers left over from that life-changing experience. He no longer shunned red meat in favor of raw fish, and he'd given up sleeping on the floor long ago; he no longer even dreamed of his Makah experiences and, if recent bedmates were to be believed, he no longer spoke aloud in the Makah tongue in his sleep.

Truth be known, he'd occasionally think of Tatoosh, his blood brother and chief of the Makah, and also the beautiful Tagaq, his former lover, but would force them from his mind just as quickly. *No profit in that,* he'd remind himself.

The sound of a bell ringing above deck announced the start of a new shift aboard *Rainmaker* for sailors on the night shift, and jolted Nathan back to the present. He debated whether to go topside, to view Apia by night, but decided it could wait until he went ashore in the morning.

Nathan thought he heard women's voices. The feminine tones of a woman's voice were rare on this voyage as the crewmembers were exclusively males and there were only two women amongst the passengers—both the wives of male passengers. To Nathan's dismay, neither was remotely pleasing on the eye. One was in her late seventies and toothless while the other was so corpulent Nathan was sure the schooner leaned to port whenever the woman left her cabin to walk to the dining room to satisfy her seemingly insatiable appetite—something she did all too frequently in his opinion.

Consequently, the young man looked forward to shore visits during which time he availed himself of local women on offer. That usually entailed paying for their services—something he wasn't averse to doing.

The women's voices grew louder. Nathan realized they were close by in the passageway outside his cabin.

There was a knock at the door. Nathan opened it to find Diamond, the ship's black purser, standing there, a huge smile on his face.

"Hello Diamond," Nathan said. It was only then he noticed

the two women standing behind the purser. They were islanders and both very easy on the eye. Nathan assessed they were in their late teens or perhaps early twenties. He knew immediately what Diamond was up to. The purser had gotten to know what the well-heeled, young American liked in a woman and hadn't been slow to exploit that during stopovers at various islands along the way. In return for his thoughtfulness and his knack for selecting attractive women, Nathan recompensed him handsomely.

"Hello, Mister Nathan," Diamond beamed. He stepped aside so Nathan could see the two Polynesian women he'd brought aboard. "I wasn't sure which one you'd prefer, so I brought both."

After a succession of late nights drinking and playing cards with the hospitable captain and crew, Nathan had been looking forward to an early night. However, looking at the two women standing before him, he had to admit Diamond had provided a tempting alternative.

Giggling and chatting to each other in their native tongue, the women were fine specimens of island womanhood. Both strong-looking and athletic, they were at the same time feminine in the seductive way the women of the islands are. Their skin gleamed golden in the flickering lamplight of the passageway, and their eyes flashed as they took in the handsome young white man in front of them.

Diamond looked hopefully at Nathan. "You like?" he asked.

Nathan knew the purser was thinking of his commission. He'd always tipped him generously for his *thoughtfulness* in the past. Nathan nodded reluctantly, indicating he was interested.

Diamond's grin broadened further.

It was the taller of the two women Nathan liked the look of. She was statuesque and beguiling all at once. He smiled at her and she immediately sidled up to him, her thigh brushing his. "What's your name?" he asked.

The Polynesian beauty looked at him uncomprehendingly, unable to speak a word of English.

Nathan looked to Diamond for assistance.

"Sally," Diamond said a little too quickly. "Her name's Sally."

The young woman didn't look like a *Sally* to Nathan, but he didn't mind that. Looking back at the purser he asked, "Can I tip you later for Sally?"

Diamond nodded without reservation. "Yes sir." Confident he'd collect the dollar Nathan owed him for the delivery, he led the other woman away to find another customer who would care to pay for her charms. There was no shortage of such customers on this vessel.

Now alone with his new companion for the evening, Nathan led her into his cabin and locked the door. When he turned back to her, she was already undressing. Nathan felt his manhood hardening at the sight of her. *What a beauty!* Unable to restrain himself any longer, he tore his clothes off and lay the woman introduced as Sally down on his bunk. He then lay on top of her and they proceeded to make vigorous and unrestrained love.

THE MORNING SUN was shining through the porthole of Nathan's cabin. It bathed the Philadelphian and his Polynesian bedmate in its warmth. Sally, or whoever she was, stirred on his chest, but remained asleep. Nathan felt blissfully satiated. He'd lost count of the number of times they'd made love during the night, but that didn't matter.

His thoughts turned to payment. Nathan's experience of the island women was they had little use for the white man's money. Rather, they lusted after the trappings of the white man. Garments were at the top of their list. Since the arrival of missionary women, the island maidens had come to love European clothing and would happily sell their bodies for the chance to own and wear a foreign lady's dress or blouse.

Cotton sheets — or better still silk or satin sheets — were even more popular than clothing amongst the island women as, with a little skillful cutting and sewing, these could easily be fashioned into garments of their choice. So that's what Nathan offered as currency for having his way with the women of the islands.

So far on this voyage he'd parted with silk sheets to the value of almost a hundred dollars, but he was more than satisfied he'd gotten his money's worth.

CHAPTER 38

Southern Ocean, 1848

ONE DAY OUT FROM CAPE Town, the mood among passengers and crew aboard *Minstrel* was as foul as the weather. The Southern Ocean was living up to its reputation: ice-cold, gale-force winds combined with rough seas made for an unpleasant voyage all round.

The conditions meant it was too cold and dangerous for passengers to venture above deck, so they were forced to hunker down below and put up with the inescapable stench of bilgewater. An outbreak of food poisoning affected half the passengers and crew, and added to their misery. The Drakes were among those struck down.

But that wasn't the worst of it. The passenger list was now four passengers short following the disappearance of Bill Compton. After much anguish, his wife Thelma had opted to part company with *Minstrel* and take her three children ashore in the hope they'd all eventually be reunited with her husband.

For the Comptons' fellow passengers, it was a difficult time. They'd grown fond of the God-fearing family and missed them dearly. Those among them who were Christians privately thanked God the same fate hadn't befallen them.

Susannah had taken the loss of the Comptons badly. She'd become close to Thelma since departing England, and even more so since her husband had disappeared.

Now, after an enforced break of several days, Susanna turned her attention to making an overdue diary entry in the privacy of the stateroom she shared with her father. Drake Senior was occupied elsewhere aboard *Minstrel*, leading a prayer meeting, so she had the room to herself for the present time.

Susannah wore several layers of winter clothing, as did all her fellow passengers, to help ward off the cold. Even that wasn't sufficient, and she shivered violently as she dipped her quill into an open ink bottle and began writing.

July 4th, 1848

Alas, it is only now I feel well enough to resume my diary obligations. Symptoms of the food poisoning I contracted in Cape Town have only just left me.

Temperatures have plummeted and I am feeling weak and miserable, but my miseries are slight compared to those of poor Thelma Compton. After her beloved husband Bill went missing in town, she made the difficult decision to take her children ashore in the hope they can all be reunited with her husband. Papa arranged for the three to board with the resident Methodist minister and his family for as long as it takes her to find Mr Compton.

The first mate confided in papa he believes some misfortune befell Mr Compton for it is completely out of character for him to disappear so. I do fear for his wife and children. They are now strangers in a foreign land, and may well have to fend for themselves for the rest of their days.

The other married women on board have been very quiet since these terrible events happened. Those who still have husbands realize it could just as easily have been their beloved who disappeared.

The weather has been just awful since departing Cape Town. This has added to my personal misery for I am not sure when exactly my food poisoning ended and my seasickness began. Dear Miss Finch has been a constant source of strength to me and I shall miss her when she leaves Minstrel at our next stopover.

To add further to my misery, the belligerent Mister Donovan has reasserted himself and focused his unwanted attention upon myself since the departure of a young crewmember who thankfully kept him in line until we reached Cape Town. As much as possible I keep to my stateroom to avoid him, but ' tis a small ship and it is inevitable our paths cross from time to time.

Susannah deliberately avoided mentioning her golden-haired rigger by name. She wanted to leave no record of her feelings for Goldie—especially not in her diary in case it fell into the wrong hands, like her father's. Drake Senior would immediately suspect the worse, and she knew that wouldn't bode well for the remainder of the voyage.

Still, that didn't stop her thinking about Goldie, or dreaming about him, as she often did. How she wished it could have worked out differently. Just thinking about him and his athletic body took her breath away.

As always happened when she thought about the young rigger, memories of the near-disaster their night-time assignation on deck had almost caused sprang to mind. They served to remind her the collision with the barque was God's way of telling her she'd sinned and needed to stay on the straight and narrow.

Susannah forced Goldie from her mind and returned her attention to completing her diary entry.

Minstrel has now entered what the first mate refers to as the "Roaring Forties." Apparently, they will hasten our arrival at our next port of call, Hobart Town, in Van Diemen's Land, at the bottom of the world.

Feeling sick again. Flying along at 9 knots.

On completion of her entry, Susannah rushed to a bucket Drake Senior had left in the adjoining bathroom for just such occasions, and she promptly brought up the breakfast she'd had earlier. The young Englishwoman had to hold onto a rail to brace herself as *Minstrel* climbed yet another wave and fell down the other side of it. The impact as the brigantine struck the trough between waves jarred Susannah's teeth, prompting her to ask herself yet again why she'd volunteered for this voyage.

First mate Paxton had warned the passengers this leg of the journey would be the hardest. He'd explained that *Minstrel* would follow the great circle route that clippers of the day followed along the parallel of forty degrees south from Cape Town to Hobart Town—or *Hobarton* as the first mate called it—in Van Diemen's Land, and then on to New Zealand. Dipping to sixty degrees south, the route was shorter than other routes, and therefore quicker. The downside was the stronger winds could be unpleasant at best and extremely hazardous at worst.

What Paxton hadn't mentioned for fear of unnecessarily alarming the passengers, was the *Roaring Forties* dipped inside the southern ice zone, and the risk of encountering icebergs was high. For that very reason he intended to remain closer to the forty degree parallel than the sixty.

⚬⚬⚬

AFTER A HELLISH voyage of nearly five weeks, it wasn't an iceberg that nearly sunk *Minstrel*. It was a whale.

The brigantine was still two days out from Hobart Town. Up in the crow's nest, young English seaman Arnold Dervish had the unenviable task of looking out for icebergs, ships and other obstacles *Minstrel* should avoid. At sixteen, Arnold was the youngest crewmember aboard. This was his first voyage, and he swore even before the brigantine had reached Cape Town it would be his last. A sailor's life, he'd decided, was not for him. Now, freezing to near-death at the top of a swaying mast, he was convinced more than ever it wasn't for him.

It wasn't Arnold's fault he didn't see the sperm whale that rammed *Minstrel's* side in time to sound the alarm. The whale surfaced just a heartbeat or two before colliding with the vessel.

In that moment, the young seaman thought he was seeing things. He'd been told icebergs were the real danger, and for the past hour he'd been looking for the tell-tale flash or glint of ice bobbing about in the ocean. To his eyes, the whale seemed as big as *Minstrel*. Possibly bigger. The warning shout he uttered coincided with the collision, and the resulting impact almost flung him from the crow's nest.

Below deck, Susannah had been reading her bible on her stateroom bunk when the collision occurred. The jolt was so savage she was thrown from her bunk. Other passengers had similar experiences, including Drake Senior who had been returning to the stateroom and was thrown to the floor in the passageway outside.

It was pandemonium above and below deck. Men were shouting, women were screaming and children crying. Many were convinced *Minstrel* had struck an iceberg and some thought they were about to die.

With Captain Mathers confined to his quarters, drunk, since departing Cape Town, the chief mate Paxton had command of the vessel. He quickly confirmed with the young lookout the culprit was a whale and immediately ordered his crewmen to check for damage below deck.

Minutes later, the second mate advised Paxton that *Minstrel's* hull had splintered on the port side, but thankfully the damage had occurred above the waterline. "Even so," the second mate said, "water is pouring into the store room."

Paxton barked orders at the crewmen. He made it clear their immediate priorities were to do whatever it took to stem the flow of water and then ensure food items, perishables and other essentials were clear of water on the store room's floor. "When that's done, take more water pumps down to the storeroom and pump the water out."

The second mate and other crewmen returned below to carry out Paxton's orders while the first mate was left to steer *Minstrel* and, at the same time, pacify a steady procession of passengers who were convinced the brigantine was about to sink. Paxton assured them that was not the case, even if he wasn't certain about that himself.

After laboring for the rest of the day, the crewmen patched up *Minstrel* sufficiently well to ensure that with a little luck she could make it to Hobart Town. Three manned water pumps working twenty-four hours a day were needed to pump the water from the hold and keep her seaworthy. Volunteers from among the male passengers were recruited to help overworked crewmembers operate the pumps.

The passengers didn't know it yet, but the damage *Minstrel* had sustained would add another two days to the voyage.

ON AUGUST 8TH, four days after colliding with the whale and just over five weeks after departing Cape Town, *Minstrel* limped in to port at Hobart Town. The wounded brigantine had been reduced to around three knots after sustaining damage, and it was the first mate's assessment she wouldn't have lasted more than a few more days in the Southern Ocean.

Christians aboard *Minstrel* swore that it was their prayers that had delivered her safely to port. Although not a God-fearing man himself, Paxton was prepared to believe that God had intervened for until the hills of Van Diemen's Land had been sighted off the bow, he hadn't been convinced they'd reach their destination.

As *Minstrel* berthed at Hobart Town's main wharf, the Drakes and other passengers emerged above deck—some for the first time in weeks—to view the new land that would one day be known as Tasmania.

Those passengers who were informed knew Van Dieman's Land was an island that was officially part of New South Wales. Several would be leaving *Minstrel* in Hobart Town to join other vessels bound for Sydney Town or Botany Bay, on the mainland, several hundred miles to the north.

For other passengers, like Miss Finch, Hobart Town would be their final destination. In Miss Finch's case, she was taking up a position as head nurse at Hobart Town's penal settlement; in other cases, a Scottish couple were starting a new life managing a boarding house while the Irish troublemaker John Donovan had decided to stop over on a whim. Few of the remaining passengers would miss him. Especially not Susannah.

For the young Englishwoman, the miseries of the last five weeks were forgotten in an instant as she took in her new surroundings.

Situated as it was in a picturesque bay, Hobart Town was already a thriving port city of some twenty thousand people. Ships of every description were in evidence for this was one of the finest deep water ports in all the Southern Hemisphere. Whaling and sealing ships were predominant, reflecting the economic importance of those activities in this part of the world.

"Look!" Susannah implored her father. She pointed to green fields of potatoes and yellow fields of corn that extended all the way to the tree-line of the hills beyond the town.

"Beautiful," Drake Senior agreed. He smiled, pleased to see his daughter so happy after weeks below deck in a tiny vessel which, he knew, could have sunk at any minute.

As Susannah surveyed the spectacular view, she decided the only blot on the landscape was the penal settlement the town had been built around. Its moss-covered stone walls and forbidding towers cast a shadow, metaphorically at least, over the town. Susannah didn't know its history, but she'd heard stories about the harsh treatment of convicts sent to such places throughout the colonies, sometimes for as little as stealing a loaf of bread. And she'd often prayed for wellbeing of those same convicts.

CHAPTER 39

Mana Island, Fiji, 1841

TWO DAYS AFTER THE SHARK incident, *Beseiged* arrived in Fijian waters. Her ultimate destination was Ovalau Island, further to the east, but first she had a scheduled call to make at Mana Island, a favored stopover in the picturesque Mamanuca Group west of the main island of Viti Levu.

Beseiged crewmembers were looking forward to shore leave, so it was with much disappointment they received the captain's announcement they would only be staying at Mana Island as long as it took to unload a small consignment of supplies for a whaler anchored there. Shore leave would have to wait until *Beseiged* berthed at Ovalau Island.

None was more disappointed than Jack. Every day he remained free—if *free* was the right word—was a day he could try to engineer an escape from his present situation. On arrival at Mana Island, he even considered diving overboard and swimming to the island. However, he dismissed that when he realized the island was far too small with too few hiding places for an escapee to remain at large for long. That plan would have to wait.

As it turned out, the whaler Captain Jones had been told would be waiting here was nowhere to be seen. In such an eventuality, the required supplies were to be left at the residence of a local chief on the island. That residence turned out to be a bure, or thatched hut. Larger than the others around it, it occupied a prime location overlooking a turquoise lagoon.

Crewmen not involved in the ferrying of supplies ashore lined the near rail to watch the activity on shore and admire the fetching Fijian maidens who could be seen wandering semi-naked along the beach and between the huts of their village. Several maidens responded with uninhibited smiles and friendly waves to the wolf-whistles being directed their way from the sex-starved seamen aboard *Besieged*. That only served to further encourage the men who began competing with each other to attract the attention of young women who had taken their fancy.

"Keep it down to a dull roar!" first mate Adams growled.

The men quietened, but only for a while.

Jack, who had been on deck since the schooner had arrived in the Mamanuca Group hours earlier, watched with interest as a tall stranger emerged from amongst the huts on shore and walked out onto the jetty. Too far away for his features to be discernible, the man was clearly European.

The stranger approached the oarsmen aboard the longboat that had been used to ferry the supplies ashore. They were about to return to *Besieged*. To Jack's surprise, the stranger boarded the longboat, which then began heading back to the schooner.

Jack had a bad feeling about the stranger. He didn't know why, but he trusted his instincts.

Minutes later, the stranger boarded *Beseiged*. Now that Jack had a close-up view of him, the bad feeling he'd had earlier intensified.

The stranger had a menacing look about him. Taller than most at close to six foot five, he had a hard, wiry frame that reminded Jack of a coiled spring. His lean, tanned face sported a day-old stubble, and his gray, gun-sight eyes were never still. They continuously surveyed everything and everyone around him, resting for a moment on Jack before moving on. The stranger traveled light, his only luggage being a leather satchel which hung from his shoulder on a strap—unless the pistol he wore tucked into his belt should be counted as luggage. And the way he carried himself signaled to one and all he wasn't a man to fool with.

In the thirty seconds that had elapsed since the stranger boarded, Jack's opinion of him had changed. *He's not menacing. He's dangerous. Bloody dangerous!* The Cockney hadn't yet determined how the stranger presented any danger, but he suspected that would be revealed in due course.

First mate Adams approached the stranger and engaged him in earnest conversation. Jack moved closer to eavesdrop, but aside from detecting an American accent heard nothing that could tell him who the stranger was or what he was doing on board before Adams escorted him away to the captain's quarters.

The young Cockney didn't have long to wait to learn who the stranger was. Less than ten minutes had elapsed before the second mate advised Jack the captain wanted to see him.

When Jack entered Captain Jones' cabin, he saw the stranger and Adams were with him. The stranger was the only one seated, his long legs stretched out before him. As he'd done earlier, he ran his eyes over Jack—only more slowly this time. Jack returned the other's stare, his mind racing. *Who the hell are you?*

"Jack, this is Frank Sparrow," the captain said. "He's a Government agent."

The Cockney instantly knew who Sparrow was. In this part of the world, *Government agent* was a euphemism for a contractor employed by the British Government to round up escaped convicts and return them to whichever penal colony they'd fled. Back at Parramatta, the convicts had referred to such contractors as *bounty hunters*. One convict who had had personal experience of such people, said bounty hunters had the authority to use force, deadly force, if necessary. *And they're not slow to use it,* he'd warned.

Looking at Sparrow, Jack had no doubt he'd use deadly force if required. His estimation was he wouldn't need much of an excuse.

Captain Jones continued, "It's Mister Sparrow's job—"

"I know what Mister Sparrow does," Jack interjected. He looked coolly at Sparrow who hadn't taken his eyes off him since he'd entered the cabin. "Mister Sparrow's a bounty hunter."

Sparrow smiled at that. He'd been called worse and it didn't faze him.

Captain Jones continued, "It's his job to return escaped convicts to where they came from." The captain took a deep breath. He clearly wasn't enjoying this. "He asked me if I had any stowaways on board, and of course I was duty bound to—"

"You had to tell him," Jack said, finishing the captain's sentence for him.

Captain Jones had the good grace to look embarrassed. Memories of Jack's actions in saving his nephew's life were still fresh in his mind. He continued, "Although I am master of this vessel, the law demands that I immediately hand you over to Mister Sparrow. He will accompany you to Ovalau Island, and there . . ." He tapered off and looked at the bounty hunter. "Perhaps you'd like to explain."

"There you'll be interned as a guest of the Government until I can arrange a berth for ya on a British vessel bound for Sydney Town," Sparrow said without preamble. His deep voice was as cold as the expression in his gray eyes, and he spoke in a monotone that was devoid of any expression.

It sent a chill down Jack's spine. The distinctive American drawl also reconfirmed the man's nationality.

Sparrow was in no doubt Jack had escaped from the

Parramatta penal settlement. Just a week earlier, he'd received an official written report drafted by a Parramatta official — delivered courtesy of another supply vessel — on the Cockney's escape. It was one of several such letters he'd received from various penal settlements in the past month.

Jack had come across many hard men in his time, but Frank Sparrow was on another level. *A stone cold killer if ever I saw one,* he told himself.

The Cockney wasn't to know Sparrow was one of three agents contracted by the government to scour the Pacific for escaped convicts. Sparrow's territory covered a triangle that spanned hundreds of thousands of square miles and extended from Fiji in the west to the Cook Islands in the east to the Navigator Islands in the north. He'd been doing the job for five years and had never failed to get his man.

It was the captain who broke the silence. Turning to Sparrow and Adams he said, "Gentlemen if you'd give me a minute alone with young Mister Halliday."

The bounty hunter and the first mate departed without a word, leaving the captain alone with Jack.

Captain Jones looked earnestly at the young man. "If there was any other way I'd have taken it, Jack. You know that, don't you?"

Jack wasn't sure he did know that, but he nodded all the same.

Relieved, the captain continued, "He identified you as an escaped convict as soon as he stepped aboard."

That surprised Jack. He'd thought he could easily pass as a crewmember.

Captain Jones noted his surprise. "He's been doing this job so long they say he can smell an escapee a mile away." The captain waited for a response. When there was none, he continued, "Anyway, you are formally under Mister Sparrow's authority now. He is insisting you serve the duration of the voyage in the hold, under lock and key."

"And you agreed to that?" Jack asked.

"I had no choice."

Jack understood, but he didn't want to make this any easier for the captain, so he said nothing.

There was nothing more to be said. Captain Jones opened the door to find the bounty hunter and first mate waiting. "He's all yours, Mister Sparrow," he said.

Jack avoided looking at Captain Jones when he joined the two men awaiting him. As he accompanied his escorts along the passageway toward the hold, he could feel the captain's eyes boring into his back.

LATER, IN THE semi-dark of the hold, Jack had plenty of time to rue his misfortune as *Besieged* sailed steadily eastward toward its destination. A sympathetic Quincy Adams had told him the estimated arrival time was two days hence; the totally unsympathetic bounty hunter Sparrow had told him any escape attempt wouldn't be tolerated. Sparrow had tapped the butt of his pistol as he'd delivered the warning to the would-be escapee.

It was only after he'd been interned in the hold that Jack had wondered what an American was doing on the British Government's payroll. He guessed he'd never figure that one out.

Jack had lost track of time when a key rattled in the hold's door, and the door opened. Able Seaman Jonty Price, a young Cornishman, entered holding a tray that contained Jack's dinner.

"You okay?" Jonty enquired.

"As well as can be expected," Jack replied as cheerfully as he could as he took the tray from his visitor.

Jonty hesitated before departing. "I have a message from some of the lads," he murmured conspiringly.

That got Jack's attention.

"Later tonight we'll be sailing close to the Coral Coast," Jonty said.

Jack had heard crewmembers talking about Viti Levu's scenic Coral Coast. It stretched west to east along Viti Levu's southern shoreline between the main settlements of Nadi and Suva. "Carry on," he whispered, his interest growing by the second.

"Our route will take us to within a mile of the coast." Jonty let the statement hang in the air for a moment.

It was evident to the Cockney that Jonty was suggesting he could swim for shore. This was confirmed when the young seaman next spoke.

"Someone will unlock the door to the hold when the time is right," Jonty added.

Footsteps alerted them to the arrival of Sparrow. The bounty hunter stuck his head through the open door. "What's the delay?" he asked Jonty.

"Nothing," Jonty said a little too quickly. He hurried to the door, but Sparrow blocked his path.

The bounty hunter stared hard at Jonty who looked as though he'd rather be anywhere else in the world but where he was. Finally, Sparrow let the young seaman past. Jonty scampered off into the darkness.

Sparrow turned his attention to Jack. In the gloom of the hold, the Cockney could only see the bounty hunter's imposing silhouette and the whites of his eyes.

"Don't try anything silly tonight," Sparrow warned. "I'll be on deck all night. And I'll be wide awake." He was aware of the route *Beseiged* followed, and he knew if Jack was going to try anything it would probably be tonight. Sparrow closed the door, locked it and then tested the handle once to ensure it was locked.

Now alone and in total darkness, Jack turned his attention

to his dinner. He quickly realized he wasn't hungry and set the tray aside.

The Cockney had much to think about before the door was next unlocked.

CHAPTER 40

Apia, Navigator Islands, 1848

THE SUN WAS HIGH IN the morning sky before Nathan emerged from below deck aboard *Rainmaker*. He'd not long sent his overnight bedmate Sally on her way, having parted with an expensive pair of silk sheets in return for her companionship. Nathan would see the Polynesian beauty once more before *Rainmaker* departed, and that would be on Apia's jetty as she and her friends waved the schooner off. Sally would be wearing a European-style dress fashioned from one of the silk sheets she'd acquired.

On deck, the young American was greeted by the sight of Apia in all its scenic glory. Located as it was on the northern coast of Opolu, the second largest island in the Navigator Islands group, Apia was a sizeable village strategically sited at the mouth of a river. The thatched huts of its residents hugged the riverbanks and lined the sandy shore of the sheltered bay that currently provided safe harbor to a mix of local and visiting craft. At a glance, Nathan counted three other sailing ships at anchor besides *Rainmaker*.

Behind the village, to the south, was the sacred Mount Vaea, and between it and the sea pandanus and breadfruit plantations stretched east and west along the narrow coastal plain—interrupted only by glades of the perfume-laden hibiscus and, of course, groves of palm trees.

For Nathan, the voyage thus far had more resembled a vacation than a trading venture. His work wouldn't begin until *Rainmaker* reached Fiji in about ten days time. Until then he was determined to take it easy.

Taking it easy was something he hadn't done since foregoing his partying and whoring lifestyle in Philadelphia after escaping the Makah. Trying to keep Johnson Traders afloat, and then reinventing himself as a sole trader, had taken their toll. The past year had been especially taxing, keeping American troops supplied with arms in the Mexican-American War, which continued to this day.

If living with the Makah had taught him one thing, it was to listen to his body and recognize the signs. In recent times, the signs had been telling him he needed to ease up or he'd end up having a breakdown, or worse. So, he'd heeded the signs and booked a leisurely passage to Fiji aboard *Rainmaker*.

Nathan was under no illusions. He knew he'd be working very hard, very soon. However, until then, he was determined to relax and enjoy himself. So far, he'd been doing just that.

"Ah, good *afternoon*, Mister Johnson."

Nathan recognized the voice even before he turned around. It belonged to Captain Jonathan Marsden, the schooner's New Orleans master and an old sea dog to boot. Despite his grizzled appearance, he was friendly and accommodating, and always up for a joke.

"I hope my men didn't wake you from your slumbers too early this fine day," Marsden enquired, a twinkle in his eye.

"Not at all, captain," Nathan responded in good humor. The young American noticed crewmen were preparing to launch the schooner's longboat in preparation for a shore excursion. "Is there room aboard the longboat for this weary traveler?" he asked.

"I'm sure there is," Marsden said. "Let me check." The captain wandered over and spoke to his second mate. The second mate nodded and Marsden waved Nathan over to join them.

Minutes later, Nathan was being rowed ashore in the company of two fellow passengers—the overweight woman and her husband—who were also intent on exploring what Apia had to offer. During the short journey from ship to shore, Nathan wasn't at all certain they'd arrive without being tipped into the sea first. The longboat leaned alarmingly to one side until one of the oarsmen politely suggested their hefty passenger move to the middle of the bench she occupied. This she did with much fuss, almost capsizing the craft in the process.

On shore, Nathan quickly went his own way, keen to distance himself from the woman who, it turned out, was as garrulous as she was corpulent. He soon found himself in the village center, some distance from the beach. Everywhere he looked, he saw villagers going about their daily business. Women weaved baskets, mats and other useful items in the shade of the numerous palm and hibiscus trees while their children ran about naked beneath the hot sun.

Those men who weren't away fishing or hunting sat in small groups beneath the shade of awnings that extended from thatched huts. They were drinking kava, the vile-looking traditional herbal drink made from the kava plant that grows so prevalently throughout the Pacific Islands. It wouldn't be until he reached Fiji that Nathan would drink kava, and then he'd learn the hard way that the ceremonial drink possessed a strong kick for the unwary.

As one of the few whites around, Nathan attracted stares from the villagers. Invariably, they waved and flashed friendly smiles his way. He returned their waves and smiles even though he wasn't feeling especially sociable.

While Nathan had no particular empathy for the islanders, or indeed for any native people, he had to admire their resourcefulness. His reading on the voyage out had revealed the forefathers of these islanders had explored and settled much of the vast Pacific since migrating to these shores almost fifteen hundred years earlier. That they'd achieved that aboard flimsy catamarans, guided only by the stars and other signs provided by Mother Nature, made their seafaring feats all the more remarkable.

As he continued through the village, Nathan came across a group of teenage boys playing a rough-and-tumble game on a grassy clearing between the huts. The youths had split into two equal teams of around twelve aside and were fighting — for want of a better word — over possession of a coconut. There appeared to be no rules and, as a consequence, the contestants had an assortment of black eyes, cuts and bruises.

From where Nathan stood, the object of the game appeared to be to get the coconut to one end of the clearing. Which end depended on which team you played for. It reminded Nathan of a game the Makah had played — except they'd used a human skull in stead of a coconut.

Comparing the islanders to the natives of Northwest America, Nathan deduced the former were a sturdier breed. In fact they were some of the biggest people he'd ever seen. At least as big as the Zulus of southern Africa. Athletic and muscular — and aggressive if the games they played were anything to go by — they would, he decided, make fearsome enemies.

The coconut suddenly ended up at Nathan's feet. It had been jolted out of the grip of a member of the losing team, and had rolled to within a foot of the white spectator. Only now had the youths noticed him. They waited for him to throw it back to them.

On an impulse, Nathan picked up the coconut, tucked it under one arm, and ran headlong at the members of the winning team. The youths of both teams welcomed his involvement with cheers and laughter, and Nathan underwent a baptism of fire as he threw himself into the game.

NATHAN WAS REGRETTING his impulsive actions as he walked slowly back to the jetty and the longboat that waited there. He'd only lasted ten minutes playing with the island youths, but that had been long enough to leave him feeling battered and bruised. Weeks of enforced inactivity aboard *Rainmaker* had left him a bit soft, and he'd just been painfully reminded of that.

At the jetty, his fellow passengers and the longboat's oarsmen greeted him with strange looks. Little wonder — his shirt was torn and bloodied, he sported a cut above one eye and he was looking most disheveled.

"So you've met the locals," one of the oarsmen observed dryly.

"Yep," Nathan responded as cheerfully as he could.

The others waited for an explanation. Nathan offered nothing more as he boarded the longboat and sat on the last free bench in the stern. No sooner had he sat down than the corpulent female passenger and her husband appeared on the jetty. They joined him in the stern of the craft. *This should be interesting.* Nathan hung on tight to the side of the longboat as it threatened to sink beneath the weight of the over-sized woman.

The return journey to *Rainmaker* proved as hazardous as the journey to shore — possibly even more so as the longboat's stern just cleared the surface of the water by an inch or so.

The rotund woman seemed as oblivious to the very real danger of sinking as she was to her great size. She passed the time gorging on what was left of a pile of pre-cut sandwiches the schooner's chef had prepared for her trip ashore.

CHAPTER 41

❦

Kororareka, New Zealand, 1848

SUSANNAH FELT DECIDEDLY NERVOUS AS she accompanied her father the short distance from the wharf to the main street of Kororareka, a thriving port settlement on the east coast of New Zealand's North Island. The town was widely recognized as *the hell-hole of the Pacific.* Looking around, Susannah could see why: it had, in her opinion, attracted the biggest collection of lowlifes, riffraff and undesirables who had ever walked the earth, and there was no sign of law enforcement of any kind.

As the only white woman in the township at that moment — and as one of the few white women to have ever visited the district — she was attracting considerable attention. The sailors, whalers, sealers and others of their kind openly leered at Susannah as she and her father walked along the dusty street. A symphony of wolf whistles followed them both. More reserved were the local Maoris who congregated in small groups on street corners and who seemed to be minding their own business. They appeared surly and resentful of the presence of pakeha, or whites, on land that was theirs not that long ago.

Shopkeepers appeared to be doing a roaring trade, but the busiest establishments by far were the brothels. Although still only early afternoon, queues of men lined up outside the seedy establishments. Some of those queuing jostled to maintain

279

their position and sporadic fighting broke out.

Susannah caught sight of several prostitutes inside one of the brothels. They were all Maori and appeared to range in age from around fifteen to fifty. The older women wore the moko, or Maori tattoo, on their chins. None of the prostitutes — young or old — seemed remotely attractive. *I guess for men who have been at sea for months on end, they look like beauties.* Susannah quickly looked the other way. It saddened her to see women selling their bodies to whoever was willing to pay.

"Not far to go now, my dear," Drake Senior murmured to reassure his daughter. He could sense her unease.

"It can't come soon enough, papa," Susannah said.

They were heading for a recommended boarding house whose hoarding could be seen some fifty yards ahead.

The Drakes had just arrived in Kororareka after a three-week voyage from Hobart Town. Drake Senior had secured berths for them aboard another brigantine, *Sea Mistress,* after they'd learned that *Minstrel* would be laid up in for three weeks in dry dock for repairs after her run-in with the whale. Rather than wait, the Drakes and several other passengers had decided to take up an offer of berths on *Sea Mistress,* which was departing for Kororareka just a few days after their arrival in Hobart Town.

Thankfully, the trans-Tasman crossing had been uneventful after the dramas of the previous leg from Cape Town to Hobart Town. The often dangerous Tasman Sea hadn't lived up to its reputation, and *Sea Mistress* completed the voyage without incident. Even so, the Drakes hadn't yet had time to find their sea legs, and the ground beneath their feet seemed to be rising and falling as they walked.

The boarding house they were heading for would be home until Drake Senior could organize a berth for them aboard a vessel leaving for Fiji. They'd been assured Fiji was on a major shipping route and they shouldn't have long to wait.

"We're here!" Drake Senior announced, stopping outside

the boarding house they'd been heading for. The hoarding above its front door read: *Jensen's Boarding House. Vacancies.*

Looking up at the sign, Susannah noticed a smaller sign beneath it. It read: *Welcome to Kororareka.* The town's name had been crossed out by some wag. In its place he'd scrawled *the hell-hole of the Pacific,* confirming what Susannah had heard earlier.

In no time, the Drakes secured adjoining rooms on the establishment's first floor.

Susannah had no sooner started to unpack when there was a knock on her door. "Come in, papa," she called. "It's not locked."

Drake Senior opened the door and looked in. "I'm heading back down to the waterfront now," he announced. "I suggest you keep the door locked while I'm away."

"Of course, papa." Susannah needed no encouragement on that score. Apart from her father and Mister Jensen, the boarding house proprietor, she hadn't seen one trustworthy looking individual since arriving in town.

Drake Senior said his goodbyes and headed off. He was returning to the waterfront to enquire about berths to Fiji.

Susannah locked her door then recovered her diary, quill and ink bottle from her travel bags. She had some writing to catch up on.

Minutes later, she commenced drafting her first diary entry in several days.

August 31st, 1848

It is with some relief I can write that we have arrived safely in New Zealand. Having survived the Roaring Forties, we were nervous about the trans-Tasman crossing for it has doomed many ships and claimed many lives. Our prayers must have been answered for the weather was kind and the seas calm for most of the voyage.

Sailing into Kororareka, on the east coast of New Zealand's northernmost island, early this afternoon was a sight I shall never forget. I swear it is the prettiest coastline I have seen. Bush-covered hills, horseshoe-shaped bays and inlets, and golden sand beaches. The harbor was filled with craft of every description, and we saw a Maori war canoe being paddled by fierce-looking, tattooed Maoris.

The township itself is something I shall never forget also. It seems a lawless place and I am grateful I am here with my father for it is no place for a single white woman.

Papa and I still miss those traveling companions we parted company with in Hobart Town. Dear Miss Finch and Colonel Kemp and the others we forged lifetime friendships with. We miss them all. I shall write to them of course, but it isn't the same.

We learned before departing Hobart Town that John Donovan, the Irishman whom we suspected was an escaped felon, drowned trying to save an Aboriginal boy who fell into the Derwent River. Fortunately, the boy survived. The boys' relatives planned to give Mister Donovan a decent burial. He deserved that much. His bravery has reminded me there is good in everyone. 'Tis a lesson I must bear in mind for the trials that surely lie ahead in Fiji.

Susannah was suddenly overwhelmed by tiredness. Lengthy voyages had that effect on her. Even though she napped whenever she could, the sea air tired her and she never seemed to be able to get enough sleep. She wasn't alone. Her father and other passengers had the same complaint.

Yawning, the young Englishwoman pulled the curtains across to block out the sunlight then stripped off and crawled between the sheets of the room's single bed.

Sleep wouldn't come immediately. As happened with increasing frequency these days, whenever she tried to sleep she thought about Goldie, the young rigger she'd been so attracted to during the voyage to Cape Town. And then when she finally drifted off to sleep, she would dream about him.

Today was no different. When she closed her eyes, Susannah could see the golden-haired rigger so clearly it was as if he was in her room. He was working bare-chested half way up *Minstrel's* mast. His lean torso glistened with sweat and gleamed in the sunlight as he climbed down the mast and joined Susannah on the deck.

At this moment, Susannah didn't know whether she was asleep and dreaming or awake and fantasizing. She didn't care. Goldie took her by the hand and led her along the deck to the same raft they'd planned to make love in before *Minstrel* had almost been sunk by the barque. They climbed into the bottom of the raft and pulled the tarpaulin cover over so they were hidden from prying eyes. Before she knew it, they were both naked. Goldie kissed her and she responded with urgency. Unable to delay the moment, she gave herself to him.

A knock at the door brought Susannah back to the present. She realized she hadn't fallen asleep and immediately felt guilty that she'd been fantasizing whilst awake.

"Are you there, Susannah?"

The voice that came from the other side of the door was her father's.

"I was just sleeping, papa," Susannah replied. "Give me five minutes will you?"

"Certainly, my dear."

Susannah listened as Drake Senior entered his own room next door. She lay where she was for a minute to two to catch her breath. The fantasy she'd just had was so vivid it was as if she really had made love. She was aware such thoughts and fantasies were sinful—the scriptures told her that—but her sexual desires seemed like an avalanche of inner lust that seemed impossible to stop no matter how often she prayed they'd go away.

Determined not to dwell on her desires, Susannah climbed out of bed, quickly dressed and joined her father in his room. She soon learned Drake Senior had had had mixed fortunes during his waterfront visit. He'd met the master of a trading schooner that was Fiji-bound, but wasn't departing Kororareka for another three weeks. Subsequent enquiries revealed other vessels were departing for Fiji earlier, but they were whalers or sealers and not suited to fare-paying passengers. So the clergyman had booked berths aboard the trading schooner for Susannah and himself for three weeks hence.

Before returning to the boarding house, he'd visited a Wesleyan mission station on the outskirts of town. It was run by George and Shelly Bristow, a missionary couple from Newcastle, in the north of England. They weren't surprised to see Drake Senior as the London Missionary Society had previously alerted them of his likely visit.

The Bristows had insisted the Drakes stay with them until their departure. Drake Senior had readily agreed to accept their hospitality, but only on condition they allow Susannah and himself to assist them with their work at the mission station. This they'd readily agreed to for they were understaffed and overworked.

So began a busy but enjoyable stay for the Drakes at the mission station. It provided a dress rehearsal of sorts for what lay ahead. More importantly, it provided them with their first contact with the native people of the Pacific—the local Maoris. An experience they would never forget.

CHAPTER 42

Coral Coast, Fiji, 1841

JACK JUMPED INVOLUNTARILY WHEN HE heard the faint sound of a key in the keyhole of the door to *Besieged's* hold. That was followed by the faint sound of footsteps as someone hurried off.

The young Cockney didn't know how much time had passed since his dinner was delivered. He guessed it was around three hours, which would make it about nine o'clock in the evening. Jack had spent all of that time deep in thought. He'd had to make one of the toughest decisions in his life: whether to risk drowning by trying to swim ashore or accept his punishment and resign himself to being shipped back to Sydney Town.

In the end he'd decided to risk it all. *Better to die trying than live like a slave,* he'd reasoned. Now that the time had come, he wasn't so sure.

Jack wasn't sure he could swim half a mile let alone a mile—especially not at night in shark-infested seas. Worse, he wasn't even sure the schooner was a mile off shore. He only had Jonty's word for that. For all he knew, *Besieged* could be ten miles from the coast. And then there was the reef to worry about. He'd been told a coral reef separated the open sea from the shore right along the length of the Coral Coast and, indeed, around much of Viti Levu. It had been the cause of many a shipwreck and he didn't fancy being hurled into it by the ocean waves.

Even if he could survive the swim, Jack knew that first he must contend with the bounty hunter. He sensed that Sparrow would be waiting for him on deck—as he'd promised he would be—and wouldn't hesitate to kill him if he had half a chance. While Jack could handle himself, he wasn't sure he could take Sparrow.

Aware that time was ticking, Jack stumbled through the darkness toward the door. His mind was made up. Fumbling for the handle, his hand closed around it. *Here goes. No turning back now.* He turned the handle and was relieved to feel the door open.

Now in semi-darkness, Jack walked as quietly as he could toward the steps that would take him topside. Already he could hear the *boom* of waves that crashed against the offshore reef. The sound filled him with dread and he tried not to think about what lay ahead.

At the first landing, the sound grew louder, like rolling thunder. Then he heard something else. *Footsteps!* The footsteps came from the deck above him. Someone was pacing up and down. He guessed it was Sparrow.

When Jack reached the open doorway leading out onto the deck, he paused and cautiously looked outside. He was just in time to catch a glimpse of a tall, shadowy figure as it moved toward the stern. *Sparrow!* There was no doubt it was him.

The steps had fortuitously delivered Jack to the portside rail. Beyond it, through the darkness, he could see the luminescent white of the waves as they broke over the reef, which appeared to be around half a mile away. Jack had always found distance over water hard to judge, so he knew his estimate could be well out. And beyond the reef he could see the flickering lights from native villages and huts along the coast.

How far the shoreline was beyond the reef was anyone's

guess. He just hoped it was closer than the reef was to the schooner.

Keen to dive into the water before Sparrow, or anyone else, caught him, he removed his boots and prepared to run at the rail and dive over. Before he could move, a sinewy arm snaked through the doorway and a strong hand grabbed him by his shirt collar. It was Sparrow.

The bounty hunter had sensed someone had arrived on deck and, when that person hadn't shown himself, had assumed it was Jack. Realizing he couldn't get to the rail in time to prevent Jack diving overboard, he'd pretended he wasn't onto him. As soon as he was out of sight, he'd doubled around to the starboard side and had snuck up on the young Cockney.

Sparrow pulled Jack through the doorway so forcefully that the younger man ended up in a heap on the deck. Before Jack could recover, the bounty hunter kicked him in the ribs, winding him.

When the would-be escaper looked up, he saw Sparrow had drawn his knife. Even in the dark Jack could identify it as a Bowie knife. Its wickedly sharp blade glinted in the moonlight.

"Well, well," Sparrow murmured. "What do we have here?"

Jack looked around desperately hoping to see a tool or something, anything, that he could use as a weapon. There was nothing handy.

The bounty hunter seemed to read his mind. He reached down, pulled Jack to his feet and threw him back hard against the bulkhead. The force knocked the wind from his lungs, winding him a second time. Before he could recover, Sparrow held the Bowie knife to his throat.

"Now why don't ya give me an excuse to slit yer throat?" Bowie murmured.

Jack could see his assailant meant it. There was murder in the bounty hunter's eyes. The young Cockney bowed his head in surrender.

"That's more like it," Sparrow smiled cruelly. He pushed Jack along the deck ahead of him. "Now we're gonna go below, and you ain't gonna give me any more problems, right?"

Jack nodded vigorously, indicating he'd comply. Sparrow chuckled and pushed his prisoner toward the same open doorway he'd not long arrived at. As they walked, the bounty hunter sheathed his knife and drew out the pistol that was tucked into his belt. Jack hadn't seen him do that. If he had, he may have thought twice about what he was planning to do next.

Just before reaching the doorway, Jack pretended to stumble. At the same time, he spun around and caught Sparrow with a thudding right hand that struck him just below the ear. The force of the blow felled the bounty hunter to his knees and sent the pistol he'd been holding flying across the deck and overboard.

Jack let fly with a kick. It was intended for Sparrow's face, but even in his stunned state the bounty hunter had the presence of mind to turn his head away and roll with the blow. Jack's foot connected, but the impact was lessened by Sparrow's evasive action.

As quick as a snake, Sparrow was on his feet. He drew his Bowie knife and brought it up savagely. Its tip was aimed at his opponent's heart. Jack managed to parry the blow, but the knife still slashed the right side of his chest open to the bone.

The young Cockney didn't feel it at first. The only sensation was a warm, sticky feeling as blood flowed from the wound. Then a searing hot pain confirmed the worst. *I've been stabbed!* He hadn't a clue how serious the wound was. All he knew was if he wanted to live, he had to act now.

Sparrow came at Jack, slashing at him with his knife. Jack had to back-peddle to avoid the flashing blade. He ended up with his back hard against the near rail and had nowhere to go.

As Sparrow prepared to finish him, the young Cockney brought his foot up between the bounty hunter's legs. Sparrow grunted in agony as his testicles compressed beneath the blow. As the bounty hunter doubled over, Jack punched him on the side of the face. Sparrow went down, and this time he stayed down.

The exertion of the past minute took so much out of Jack he had to bend over, hands on knees, for several seconds to regain his breath. His slashed chest hurt like hell and blood dripped onto the deck. He glanced at the Bowie knife, which Sparrow was still holding. Its blade was streaked with blood — *My blood!* — confirming what he already knew.

Almost without thinking, Jack prized the knife from Sparrow's fingers. His eyes flicked from the blade to Sparrow's throat. Jack knew he should kill him. *If I don't he'll come after me.* He bent down and prepared to do the deed.

Only then did Jack become aware he was being observed. He looked up and saw first mate Quincy Adams staring at him from the shadows. How long he'd been there was anyone's guess.

"Don't do it, Jack," Adams warned.

The young Cockney hesitated. A moment earlier, he'd been convinced killing the bounty hunter was the sensible thing to do. Now he wasn't so sure.

"It would be murder," Adams added, stating the obvious.

Against his better judgment, Jack decided to spare Sparrow. Now he had another decision to make — whether to risk attempting to swim ashore in his wounded state or to give himself up. *To hell with it!* Jack grinned at the first mate, turned and staggered to the portside rail. Only now did he drop the knife. He half expected Adams to try to apprehend him, but the first mate remained where he was.

Clambering painfully over the rail, Jack jumped into the sea. The cold water was a shock to his system. As he surfaced, he looked back and saw Adams staring down at him from the deck.

"God go with you!" Adams called out to him.

The young Cockney replied with a wave then started swimming toward the reef. He was quickly swallowed up by the darkness.

JACK DIDN'T KNOW how long he'd been swimming, but it felt like hours and the reef seemed no closer. In the water, he couldn't even see the reef. He could hear it though, and it was the noise that guided him to it.

The pain from his chest wound was worsening and Jack could imagine every shark in the South Pacific would soon smell his blood—if they hadn't already. This drove him to swim harder. He'd heard the reef acted as a barrier to sharks and other ocean predators. *I must get to it!* Gradually, the booming thunder of the waves crashing on the reef grew louder.

Jack knew enough about the reef to know it could kill him as easily as it could save him. He'd heard there were openings in the reef big enough for canoes and sometimes even ships to pass through. He prayed he'd find such an opening.

That proved wishful thinking. There were such openings, but they were few and far between. For the most part, the reef was one long, uninterrupted mountain of razor sharp coral whose base began on the seabed and whose summit protruded above the surface of the sea—sometimes by a matter of inches, often by several feet, depending on the tide.

As luck would have it, Jack had struck it at high tide. Even so, the sharp corals and shells that adorned the reef tore at his flesh as a wave carried him across it. The wave dumped him into a placid lagoon on the other side of the reef, leaving him cut and bruised from head to foot, and almost unconscious.

Using his last reserves of strength and endurance, he struck out for shore. He was so weak he could only dog-paddle. Thankfully, the flickering lights he'd seen from the schooner were a lot closer now. Even so, the swim seemed to take forever.

Bloodied and battered, and beyond exhausted, Jack wasn't even aware he'd reached the sandy shore that lined the lagoon. He lost consciousness soon after crawling up onto the sand.

———⊙⊙⊙———

JACK THOUGHT HE must be in heaven when he woke. Three beautiful Fijian girls were hovering over him. Their dark eyes sparkled and they beamed smiles his way when they realized their white guest had returned to the land of the living.

The girls were sisters—daughters of the chief of Koroi, the Coral Coast village whose beach Jack had been washed up on. They'd helped nurse him and care for him after a villager had found him unconscious at the water's edge. Jack didn't know it, but five days had elapsed since then. He'd been in a critical condition and had nearly died. The knife wound had done some damage, but it was the cuts he'd received after being smashed against the reef that had caused most problems. They'd become infected, as coral cuts often do, and that's what nearly killed him.

Jack recalled none of this as he struggled to focus on his new surroundings. He could see he was on the verandah of a large bure hut. It was surrounded by other smaller bures. A thatched canopy kept the tropical sun at bay, and a fresh sea breeze kept the temperature down.

Word had spread that the white stranger had regained consciousness, and villagers were appearing from everywhere to stare at him. There was much chatter and laughter, and somewhere, someone was singing. Bright-eyed children stared at Jack in awe, giggling shyly whenever he looked at them.

Fighting against the tiredness that threatened to overwhelm him, Jack tried to make sense of everything. It gradually dawned on him. *I'm free!* Not legally perhaps, but free all the same. It felt wonderful and yet strange at the same time.

Then he remembered the bounty hunter. *Are you coming for me?* He suspected he hadn't seen the last of Sparrow.

Jack felt himself drifting off to sleep again. Before he did, he became aware of a warm, soft touch against his check. It was Namosi, the oldest of the sisters caring for him. Beautiful beyond words, she smiled down at him. And then everything went black.

CHAPTER 43

Apia, Navigator Islands, 1848

NATHAN WAS UP AT DAWN to experience *Rainmaker's* departure from Apia. Two days had elapsed since he'd joined the rough-and-tumble game ashore with the island youths—*coconut bash* he'd called it—and he was still stiff and sore even if his bruises had faded. The painful after-effects reminded him not to be so impulsive in future.

Other passengers were on deck to join with Nathan in bidding farewell to Apia. All, it seemed, had enjoyed the brief stopover.

As crewmen readied *Rainmaker* for departure, a small crowd of villagers gathered on the jetty to wave her off. Nathan spotted a statuesque island woman amongst them, wearing a white silk dress. He thought she could have been Sally, but wasn't sure. Memories of his night with the young woman came flooding back. He'd considered looking for her ashore, but had decided against that after the battering he received playing *coconut bash*. He didn't think he'd be up to any more exertions for a day or two yet.

Calm seas beneath blue skies greeted *Rainmaker* as she left the harbor. Ahead was a ten-day voyage to Fiji. First, the schooner had to stop some twenty miles along the coast to collect an English missionary from Opolu's Wesleyan mission station. The missionary was also Fiji-bound. He was being transferred to boost numbers at an understaffed mission post on one of Fiji's outer islands.

As the schooner followed its westward route along Upolu's northern coastline, a cataclysmic event occurred beneath the seabed several hundred miles to the north. A mile below the ocean's surface, the earth's tectonic plates moved, causing a massive earthquake whose effects were felt throughout the Navigator Islands and beyond. In Apia and elsewhere on Opolu, huts and other structures were destroyed within seconds, though there was little loss of life. Not yet at least.

The passengers and crew aboard *Rainmaker* were as yet unaware of this event. They only learned there had been an earthquake hours later when the schooner anchored offshore, opposite the Wesleyan mission station, to pick up the missionary.

Even from a mile distant, the earthquake damage the station had sustained was very visible. One wall of the main building had collapsed and the entire structure had been left on a lean. Surrounding European-style houses had sustained similar damage while the thatched huts of the islanders had been completely destroyed. Missionaries and islanders could be seen assessing the damage and salvaging possessions.

Then a strange thing happened: the tide slowly but steadily withdrew. Where there'd been a mile of ocean a few minutes earlier, now there was only the exposed seabed. *Rainmaker* was left sitting high and dry along with hundreds of flapping, gasping tropical fish, which looked as confused as the humans who were gawking at them.

"What the hell's going on?" an incredulous Earnest Featherstone, the first mate, asked.

No-one had any idea. They'd never seen anything like it.

Finally, the tide returned and all seemed back to normal.

The small wave that passed beneath *Rainmaker* a few minutes later was so small it wasn't noticed by anyone on board. But it was traveling fast. Faster than a man, or even a horse, could run.

It wasn't until the wave reached shallow water it became noticeable. Passengers and crew stared in disbelief as the wave grew rapidly in size. It showed no sign of slowing as it reached shore.

"Tidal wave!" someone shouted.

Nathan had already identified it as a tsunami. Though he'd never seen one before, he'd heard about them. Johnson Senior had witnessed one in the Philippines. It had claimed many lives, he'd said.

By this time the wave was higher than a two-storied house. Only now did those ashore notice the approaching danger. Although they were little bigger than ants in the distance, the terror they were experiencing at that moment could be imagined. The missionaries and islanders began fleeing inland, dragging each other and their children with them.

"They're doomed!" a male passenger cried out.

The man wasn't exaggerating. Those unlucky enough to be on shore at that moment, had nowhere to run. The mission station was hemmed in by high cliffs. Even from this distance, it was obvious the cliffs were too steep to climb.

Throughout this, the sea around *Rainmaker* remained unnaturally calm. All the mayhem was happening ashore.

Those aboard the schooner could only look on helplessly as the wave swept over the people ashore and crashed against the cliffs. Before it retreated, it grew to the height of a five-storied building, perhaps higher, and seemed to be trying to reach the other side of the island. When it finally withdrew, the bodies of some of its victims could be seen being tossed about in its turbulent waters. There appeared to be no survivors.

THAT AFTERNOON, AFTER leading a search party ashore to look for survivors, a grim Captain Marsden confirmed there were none. Nor had any reports been received from up or down the coast, but the captain said he feared the worst.

Nathan thought it required little intelligence to imagine the damage and loss of life that would have occurred if the tsunami had hit Apia and other heavily populated villages along the coast.

It wouldn't be until after *Rainmaker* reached Fiji that he and the others would learn that Apia had somehow missed the worst of the tsunami. The main damage had been around the mission station and the small villages to the west of it, and loss of life had been surprisingly small.

As night fell and Opolu disappeared behind a veil of darkness astern of *Rainmaker,* Nathan wondered what adventures awaited him in Fiji. He hoped the terrifying drama of the day just gone wasn't a precursor to events to come.

CHAPTER 44

Kororareka, New Zealand, 1848

THE DRAKES' ARRIVAL AT KORORAREKA coincided with a period of tension in northern New Zealand between the whites and the warlike Nga Puhi, the predominant Maori tribe of the north. Tensions, over land ownership in particular, frequently manifested themselves in violence.

Those tensions didn't end there. Age-old disputes between tribes continued to this day. Where those disputes were traditionally settled with meres, or clubs, and other traditional weapons, these days they were settled with muskets. Understandably, the British soldiers garrisoned nearby were on continual high alert. Their twitchy mood—and that of the white settlers—wasn't helped by rumors of cannibalism, which persisted despite the recent introduction of Christianity to these shores.

Caught up in the middle of all this were the English couple George and Shelly Bristow. The Wesleyan mission station they ran on the outskirts of Kororareka was slap bang in the middle of an area of fertile soils and ideal growing conditions—an area whose ownership was currently being bitterly contested.

White settlers who were breaking in the land for farming were being constantly harassed by Maori warriors who resented the presence of the pakeha. Descendants of the great Nga Puhi rangatira, or chief, Hongi Hika, the warriors were becoming increasingly aggressive, burning down settlers' homes and occasionally killing whites.

Atrocities occurred on both sides. The settlers and soldiers were never slow to seek retribution. Against the ever-increasing numbers of whites and the superior firepower they brought with them, the Nga Puhi were never going to prevail. However, they were going to make life difficult for these pakeha intruders.

While houses burned and people died, the Bristows and the other members of the mission station were left alone. The Nga Puhi respected the mission station and the kindly people who manned it. The pakehas' god intrigued them, and several had already embraced Christianity.

And so it was into this maelstrom the Drakes arrived. Their hosts made them immediately welcome, affording them every hospitality and introducing them to the residents of the mission station. Those residents included the Bristows' growing flock whose number comprised both local Nga Puhi and members of other tribes.

Susannah was fascinated by the Maoris she came into contact with at the mission station. She found she was afraid of them and endeared to them at the same time. Her hosts assured her that her reaction was entirely understandable. Though fearsome warriors whose tattooed faces made them look even more frightening, the Maoris were naturally friendly people who were generous of spirit to those they called friends.

The young Englishwoman found this out for herself on her first night at the mission station. She and Drake Senior joined the Bristows for dinner in their modest bungalow and discovered they weren't the only guests: a new Christian convert had also been invited. He was Manu Te Whaiti, a young Nga Puhi warrior and proud descendant of the great rangatira Hongi Hika.

Manu wasn't at all like Susannah expected. He was well

educated, having attended a missionary school in his adopted hometown Auckland, and spoke excellent English. He wasn't shy either, and he kept his white audience entertained with intriguing and often humorous stories well into the night.

One tale, in particular, caught Susannah's fancy, as it did her dining companions. It began when she asked Manu whether he'd ever met Hongi Hika.

"I was too young to remember Hongi," Manu said, shaking his head. "But my father knew him well and he told me many stories about him."

"Tell her the one about Hongi's suit of armor," George Bristow said.

Manu needed no encouragement. It was one of his favorite stories. Turning back to Susannah he said, "Before I was born, Hongi traveled to England where he met King George the Fourth."

"He was a sensation there," Shelly Bristow interjected enthusiastically. She'd heard the story many times, but never tired of it.

"Yes," Manu agreed. "He became quite the socialite and was courted by high society wherever he went."

"How exciting," Susannah enthused.

Warming to his story, Manu continued, "King George was so enamored with Hongi that he presented him with a suit of armor."

"This is where it gets interesting," George Bristow advised Susannah.

Manu continued, "I'm told Hongi was so taken with his suit of armor he wore it often during the return voyage to New Zealand. Even at meal times when he had to lift the visor of his steel helmet to eat or drink."

Manu's audience laughed heartily at the thought of a Maori rangatira dining in a suit of armor.

When the laughter died down Manu said, "But that is not

all. After Hongi returned to Kororareka, he distributed muskets he had acquired to his warriors and embarked by canoe on a journey south, attacking enemy tribes along the way."

Shelly looked at Susannah. "It was horrible," she lamented. "Hundreds were killed."

"And eaten," George added.

"Eaten?" Susannah asked, aghast.

"Yes my people were cannibals," Manu said honestly. "Eating our enemies was the worst insult we could bestow upon them."

The conversation lapsed as the diners considered the grizzly news Manu had just shared with them.

"The suit of armor," George said, prompting the young warrior.

"Ah, yes," Manu said. "Hongi was so proud of his suit of armor he wore it on his raids."

"That didn't last long!" George chuckled.

Manu continued, "On one of his raids, Hongi's canoe overturned and the rangatira nearly drowned under the weight of his armor." The young warrior smiled. "Fortunately, the canoe overturned in shallow water, and he survived. But it taught him a lesson and he never wore the suit of armor again to my father's knowledge."

Listening to Manu, Susannah found it hard to reconcile the savage looking, tattooed warrior sitting opposite her with the likeable, educated young man he really was. She couldn't help thinking if there were other Maoris like him, the race had a promising future in store.

Drake Senior was thinking along similar lines. Looking at Manu, he asked, "What are your plans for your future, young man?"

"I do not know," Manu said thoughtfully. "I have given my heart to God. I know he has a plan for me, but he has not shared that plan with me yet."

"I'm sure he will soon enough," Drake Senior said.

"Amen to that," George said. "Shall we pray?"

With that, the diners held hands around the table and bowed their heads while George led them in prayer.

CHAPTER 45

⎯⎯◦◎◦⎯⎯

Coral Coast, Fiji, 1848

NAMOSI LAUGHED JOYFULLY AS SHE watched Jack frolic with their three young children in the shallows of the turquois lagoon in front of the village they called home. Five-year-old Mara, four-year-old Joni and two-year-old Luana loved the irrepressible Cockney as much as she did. Namosi considered him a wonderful friend, husband and provider, and a doting father, which was just as well as she had another baby on the way.

Jack, now thirty-two, interrupted his play with the children and waved to his Fijian princess to join them. She declined with a return wave. The baby was only a month or so away, and she was feeling tired.

Life had changed as much for Namosi as it had for Jack after he'd been found, near death, washed up on the beach here at Koroi, on the Coral Coast, seven years earlier. He'd been found close to the very spot he now frolicked with their children.

As the oldest daughter of Koroi's ratu, or chief, she'd been expected to marry a Fijian of royal bloodlines—not a lowly vulagi, or foreigner, which is what Jack was to the ratu and his extended family. Especially not one who had literally been washed ashore and had no prospects. However, that had all changed after Namosi nursed him back to health.

The attraction between the two had been mutual and instant. He'd proposed very early on in their relationship and she'd accepted.

Namosi's father, Tau, had opposed the relationship, but his opposition gradually crumbled as his people adopted the friendly Cockney as one of their own. The wedding that followed — six months to the day after Jack appeared uninvited in their midst — was one of the biggest Koroi had seen in a decade.

Jack's new status as the ratu's son-in-law proved a Godsend in the years that followed. After mastering the Fijian tongue and establishing himself as an interpreter for the sandalwood traders so prevalent in Fijian waters, he then followed his entrepreneurial instincts and purchased cutting rights to the Fijians' coastal sandalwood plantations before on-selling those rights to European traders and making handsome profits.

As profits grew, Jack purchased a large quantity of muskets, which he donated to his father-in-law. The donation had been timely as Koroi was at war with a neighboring village. Koroi's enemies backed off when they realized they were outgunned all of a sudden, further boosting Jack's popularity with the villagers and with his father-in-law in particular.

Namosi giggled as her three children tried to drown Jack in the shallows. The children shrieked with laughter when Jack emerged spluttering and spitting out seawater.

While she was content with her lot and still deeply in love with her *prince,* as she called him, Namosi was also very aware of Jack's reputation as a womanizer. He seemed irresistible to many of the women — married and single — throughout Viti Levu and indeed on many of the outer islands, and he just didn't seem to be able to help himself. As a result, run-ins with irate husbands were a fairly frequent occurrence. Unfortunately, his travels as a trader provided plenty of opportunity for him to indulge himself in his extramarital interests.

Namosi had given up complaining to Jack as he'd laughed it off, saying she was imagining things. She'd complained to her father, but that had fallen on deaf ears because he had four wives of his own and considered Jack's philandering entirely normal.

So she'd learned to accept Jack as he was. She never doubted his love for her, and she knew he'd always return home for that was where his heart was.

Namosi's thoughts were interrupted when Jack dragged the children up the beach to join her in the shade of the palm trees that fringed the edge of the lagoon. "How was that?" she asked.

"Beautiful!" Jack said. "You should have joined us." He set the children down on the sand then lay down beside Namosi and kissed her cheek tenderly.

This day was precious to the Hallidays for tomorrow Jack was heading out on a new venture that could see him away from his family for quite some time.

LATER, ALONE, JACK sat looking out to sea. Namosi had taken the children up to their nearby bure. As he often did when he was on his lonesome, the Cockney took the opportunity to look back on the last seven years and remind himself how lucky he was.

Life couldn't be better, he decided. Having survived his poverty-stricken years in London and then the hellish years as a convict in New South Wales, Fiji seemed like paradise on earth.

Looking back on his first year here on the Coral Coast, Jack recalled the specter of bounty hunter Frank Sparrow had hung over him like a hangman. He'd never mentioned Sparrow to anyone—not even to Namosi—but he'd been half expecting the bounty hunter, or one of his associates, to show up.

That all changed shortly after the first anniversary of his

arrival in Koroi when news reached him that the British Government had laid off its South Pacific contractors, or bounty hunters. The official reason was the retention of such contractors was uneconomic despite the undeniable success of Sparrow and his associates in rounding up escaped convicts. Unfortunately for the contractors—and fortunately for escapees like Jack—the economics of tracking, apprehending and returning convicts to the penal settlements they'd escaped from didn't add up.

Despite the good news, Jack had still kept an eye out for Sparrow for the next year or so—more out of habit than anything else. He needn't have worried. A few months after the South Pacific contractors were decommissioned, Sparrow was found dead, his throat slit, in a back alley in Apia, in the Navigator Islands. Rumor had it a former convict from Hobart Town, in Van Diemen's Land, had tracked the bounty hunter down and exacted retribution. Apparently Sparrow had given him a hard time after apprehending him during a failed escape bid several years earlier.

All that was in the past. Right now Jack was looking forward to his next venture. It would take him into the island's interior. But first, he had to travel to Levuka, on Ovalau Island, to the east of Viti Levu.

While Jack was content with his lot, the sandalwood trade had all but collapsed as a result of short-sighted Fijian landowners selling off the sandalwood plantations to greedy European traders without any thought being given to conservation of the precious natural resource. This had forced him to diversify and find new trading opportunities.

Jack's focus now was on securing cutting rights to the Fijian kauri forests of Viti Levu's interior. Before he headed into the interior, he'd arranged to meet with one of the island's most respected ratus who also happened to be a major landowner and who was currently—and inconveniently—visiting an ailing brother at Levuka. Rather than wait indefinitely until the ratu returned, he'd opted to go to him.

It wasn't only the thought of a new business venture that excited Jack. He was also looking forward to seeing his latest lady friend who conveniently happened to live at Levuka.

The sight of a schooner attracted Jack's attention. Sailing eastward, she was a beautiful sight with her sails flapping in the faint nor'wester. How he loved the sight of sailing ships as they passed by. He estimated this vessel was half a mile beyond the offshore reef — close to where he'd parted company with *Besieged* all those years ago. Passing ships always reminded him of that dramatic night, but he'd learned to push the memory from his mind as quickly as he could. That was another *Jack Halliday,* he always told himself. He'd long since decided there was no mileage to be gained thinking about his past life.

As he always did when he watched the passing ships, Jack wondered where this particular vessel came from, where she was heading and who sailed aboard her. He wasn't to know the schooner was none other than *Rainmaker* and she was heading for Levuka, his next destination. Nor was he to know that among the passengers on the schooner's deck at that very moment was an American by the name of Nathan Johnson.

The Cockney was distracted by an unusual cloud formation that had formed above the schooner in an otherwise cloudless sky. It resembled a seagull in flight. He took that as a good omen for his journey ahead.

On board *Rainmaker,* Nathan had been distracted by the same cloud formation. He studied it for a moment then returned his attention to the distant shoreline. If he'd had his telescope with him, he'd have seen Jack Halliday looking directly at him, but the distance was too great for the naked eye.

Nathan could see the village behind Jack, however. He idly wondered who lived there and how its residents passed their days.

CHAPTER 46

Levuka, Fiji, 1848

NATHAN COULDN'T WAIT TO GET ashore as *Rainmaker* sailed into Levuka's harbor at scenic Ovalau Island. The voyage out from Apia, in the Navigator Islands, had been the final leg in a three-month voyage from San Francisco, and it seemed to take forever. After the horrors of the tsunami, the young American had just wanted to get to Fiji and resume doing what he did best: trading and making money.

As *Rainmaker* was going into dry dock for scheduled maintenance in Levuka, Nathan needed to organize a berth aboard another vessel for the brief voyage to Momi Bay, on the western side of the main island of Viti Levu. There, he would trade his muskets to Fijians in return for their beche-de-mer. He'd heard the sought-after sea slugs were plentiful in that region, and the local tribes were warlike and hungry for the white man's musket.

It irked him that *Rainmaker* had sailed frustratingly close to Momi Bay on arrival in Fijian waters, but Captain Marsden was running behind schedule and had made it clear that any deviation was out of the question. So Nathan was resigned to having to cool his heels in Levuka until he could organize alternative transport.

SUSANNAH NEVER TIRED of looking out over Levuka from the bedroom window of the two bedroom cottage she shared with her father. The cottage was situated on a rise above the town in the well appointed grounds of the Wesley Methodist Mission Station. From her window, she could see the township, the harbor and beyond.

Fiji's capital of the day was built around a harbor that accommodated all manner of craft. The harbor and the township reminded her of Kororareka, the North Island settlement she and Drake Senior had stayed at in New Zealand. The same colorful characters wandered Levuka's streets. They included adventurers, sailors, entrepreneurs, whalers, explorers, escaped convicts and the usual assortment of social misfits. Even so, Susannah felt safer here than she had in New Zealand. Exactly why, she wasn't sure. She imagined it had something to do with the friendly Fijians whose dazzling smiles and generosity had made her feel instantly welcome.

In Levuka's township and down on the waterfront, the Europeans rubbed shoulders with the local Fijians who, to Susannah's eyes, were even more colorful than the Maoris and other native races she'd observed in her travels. Especially the men, many of whom wore large, frizzy hairstyles—some dyed all colors of the rainbow.

If Susannah had one complaint it was the weather. It reminded her of Bata, in Equatorial Guinea. The wet season was approaching and she found the heat and humidity oppressive. Although the rains hadn't arrived yet, rain clouds constantly threatened. The high humidity they brought with them ensured residents and visitors alike were continually bathed in sweat. For new arrivals like Susannah and Drake Senior, it was an ordeal just getting through the day. And the nights were even more oppressive.

The Drakes had arrived in Fiji ten days earlier after an uneventful seventeen-day voyage from New Zealand aboard *Southern Cross*. Susannah had made use of the voyage out to immerse herself in her studies of Fiji and the Fijian language.

Her studies had been aided in no small way by the presence of one Marika Serevi, a Fijian crewman aboard *Southern Cross*. Fluent in both English and Fijian, and with a good understanding of the languages spoken throughout many of the Pacific Islands, Mariki was used by *Southern Cross's* master as an interpreter during stopovers at various ports. He was also a natural teacher, and Susannah hadn't been slow to take advantage of that. By the end of the voyage, she had a much better understanding of Fiji's culture and language.

Despite her application to her studies, and her devotion to her daily prayers and bible readings, Susannah remained torn between her spiritual and sexual selves. The fantasies and dreams she'd had about Goldie—and others if truth be known—on the voyage out had if anything increased since she and her father had arrived in Fiji. And the more she'd prayed about it and asked for God's forgiveness, the more frequent and vivid her fantasies and dreams became.

Susannah hoped it was a passing phase. She was aware she needed to sort herself out—and quickly. Very soon, she and Drake Senior would be departing Levuka for Momi Bay, on the island of Viti Levu, to run the fledgling mission station there. That's what they'd journeyed from the other side of the world to do, and as the departure date drew closer, Susannah's misgivings over what she was getting herself into grew. She kept those misgivings to herself, however.

~◦◊◦~

ON ARRIVAL AT Levuka, Jack Halliday wasted no time in making contact with his consort of the moment, a fetching lady of royal bloodlines. Talei Serevi was the first wife of a respected tribal headman, and she was as taken with Jack as he was with her. A secret tryst was arranged for the following morning when her husband was scheduled to depart the island for a three-day visit to Viti Levu.

That suited Jack just fine. He was confident he could achieve what he'd come to do before then. And so it transpired: the Cockney met with the ratu and landowner whose considerable land holdings in Viti Levu's interior accommodated many of the Fijian kauri forests that he so desperately wanted to secure the cutting rights to. The ratu took a shine to Jack; he also liked the sound of the profits he could make in the transaction that was on the table. And so a deal was struck.

The next day dawned full of promise—for Jack at least. He'd arranged to meet Talei as soon as her husband had departed for Viti Levu. The venue for their rendezvous was the vacant home of a discreet friend of Talei's. They planned to spend the next two days there pleasuring each other.

Jack was so full of anticipation he arrived a full hour before the scheduled assignation. The next hour was the longest he'd experienced since receiving three hundred lashes at Parramatta. When Talei finally arrived, he felt ready to burst.

The two lovers went to it immediately and remained locked in each other's embrace, almost without a break, for the rest of the day and all that night.

Their pleasure was rudely interrupted after Talei's husband Tahu, a surly man who was as big and tough as he was belligerent, returned to Levuka prematurely. On arrival at Viti Levu, he'd discovered his meetings with other ratus had been postponed. After returning home and finding his wife was mysteriously absent, he began making enquiries. Those enquiries led him to Talei's friend whose home she and Jack were currently using. Discretion went out the window when the friend told Tahu of his wife's whereabouts in return for not being beaten to a pulp.

As luck would have it, Jack was ensconced in the outside toilet when Tahu and two equally large male friends invaded the house he and Talei were using. A noise alerted him to their arrival and he watched them through a crack in the outhouse door as they entered the house. He was about to intervene when he noticed they carried knives and, in one case, a meat cleaver. And they appeared to be more than ready to use them.

A minute later, Tahu dragged a naked Talei outside by the hair. She was kicking and screaming, but so far appeared unharmed.

Jack watched from his hiding place as Talei interrogated his wife, using a combination of cajoling, questioning and slaps to her face. To Jack's everlasting relief, whatever Talei said seemed to pacify her husband. Tahu gradually calmed down and ordered his wife to collect her possessions and accompany him home. This she did with alacrity.

Soon, the Cockney was alone on the property. Cautiously emerging from the outhouse, he breathed a sigh of relief as he realized he'd evaded a savage beating, or possibly worse. Jack vowed that from then on he'd remain faithful to his darling Namosi. But of course that was a promise he could never keep.

EPILOGUE

decorative divider

A<small>FTER NARROWLY AVOIDING BEING FOUND</small> out by the husband of his latest lady friend, Jack had wasted no time in preparing for the next stage of his venture into Viti Levu's interior. Armed with the all important signature to the contract that gave him exclusive cutting rights to some of the island's most lush Fijian kauri forests, he'd secured a berth on a sailing ship soon to depart for Nadi, the major settlement on Viti Levu's west coast. From there, he would trek inland after purchasing the necessary supplies.

While he hated the thought of being parted from Namosi and their three — soon to be four — children for any length of time, he was excited about what lay ahead. It was a gamble: there was no guarantee the traders who had lusted after Fiji's sandalwood would be similarly enamored about the timber of the giant kauri. But that only added to his excitement.

Before he could even start approaching traders, he had to map the area he'd secured cutting rights for. It covered around a hundred square miles, and Jack imagined mapping an area that large could take the best part of several months.

The ship Jack was soon to depart Levuka on wasn't just any sailing ship. *Seven Seas* was a magnificent fore and aft-rigged vessel whose overall length topped one hundred and twenty feet, and that wasn't allowing for her bowsprit and aft spar.

She was moored close to shore and, as happened wherever she dropped anchor, she commanded the attention and admiration of everyone within sight of her.

Few were more admiring of her than Jack was at that moment. He took in her beautiful lines and curves as he was rowed out to her aboard the ship's longboat.

Another who was equally taken with her was Nathan. He, too, only had eyes for *Seven Seas* as he was being rowed ashore from *Rainmaker*.

The two longboats passed within a few yards of each other. If the two men hadn't been so enamored by *Seven Seas*, they may well have acknowledged each other. They could have exchanged pleasantries without even having to raise their voices — so close were the longboats when they passed by.

Today was the day Nathan was parting company with *Rainmaker*. He was relocating to a boarding house he'd be staying in until he departed for Momi Bay. Since arriving at Levuka, the young American had been busy purchasing supplies for his forthcoming trading venture. And he'd overseen the transfer of his stockpile of muskets from *Rainmaker's* hold to a secure warehouse on shore.

Nathan had also spoken to local seamen familiar with these waters, and had learned as much as he could about the tribes domiciled on Viti Levu's western coastline — around Momi Bay in particular — and on the outer islands west of Viti Levu. He was focused on that area because it was known for its reserves of the prized beche-de-mer.

What he'd learned from the seamen he spoke to was music to his ears: the tribes to the west were warlike and they lusted after the weapons of the white man; muskets were in high demand and Nathan could expect his forthcoming trading venture would be highly profitable. That confirmed everything he'd been told back in San Francisco.

The young man had received some disquieting news from one old sea dog he'd spoken to. "This place ain't called the

Cannibal Isles for nuthin!" the old man had told him. He'd advised that cannibalism was still practiced by the natives in some of the areas Nathan was planning to visit. In particular, he warned about a tribe of outcasts—appropriately named *the outcasts*—who terrorized villagers on the western side of Viti Levu, and who took delight in eating their victims.

As the longboat ferrying Nathan and his possessions ashore berthed alongside the jetty, he noticed crowds of people— whites and natives—walking up toward the mission station on the rise overlooking Levuka. The mood was festive with much singing and laughter, and no-one seemed remotely concerned about the rain clouds that were threatening overhead.

Enquiries would reveal it was market day, a weekly event hosted by the Wesleyan missionaries, and enjoyed by residents and visitors alike. In return for hosting the event, the missionaries received a small percentage of the stallholders' profits, which helped finance their work at the mission station.

Many of the residents among the procession of people carried goods for sale. These ranged from clothing, wood carvings, tools and furniture to fresh fish, fruit, vegetables and all manner of foodstuffs. Some needed horse-drawn carts to transport their wares up the bumpy track leading to the mission station.

Nathan thought he may check out the market after he'd settled in at the boarding house. First, he decided, he needed a cold bath and a change of clothes. Despite the early hour, the high humidity had left him drenched in sweat even though he hadn't been exerting himself. He prayed for cooler temperatures.

Then, as if the weather gods had been listening, a gentle breeze blew in from the south, cooling the air and blowing the clouds away.

BEFORE THE SUN was half way across the morning sky, the mission station's grounds were almost packed to capacity. It seemed nearly everyone in the district had converged on it to enjoy the bustling market. The Drakes were also in attendance. They'd volunteered to help their missionary hosts.

Market day was something Susannah looked forward to. She'd already experienced one since she and Drake Senior had arrived in Levuka, and she'd thoroughly enjoyed it. The confluence of Europeans and native Fijian people socializing and conducting business together was like nothing she'd seen before, with the possible exception of Bata, in Equatorial Guinea. There, she'd glimpsed similar markets, but had been too busy keeping vigil over her gravely wounded father at Bata's hospital to take any notice of them or anything else for that matter.

Bucket in hand, Susannah was circulating amongst the market-goers, soliciting donations for the mission station. It was a task she enjoyed as it was for a worthy cause and it brought her into contact with many different people. Most were happy to donate, and the bucket was already a quarter full with coins.

Susannah spotted her father in the crowd. Taller than other Europeans around him, Johnson Senior was assisting at one of several mission station stalls a short distance from where she was standing. He saw Susannah and waved.

The young Englishwoman returned her father's wave. She didn't notice Nathan as he brushed past Johnson Senior in the crowd. The two men didn't notice each other either. Their attention — along with everyone else's at that moment — was on *Seven Seas* as the magnificent vessel departed the harbor and headed for the open sea.

"Thar she goes!" a man with a distinctive Cornish accent declared to one and all.

"Isn't she beautiful!" a Scottish woman exclaimed.

"A sight for sore eyes," a Welshman agreed.

Other such comments rippled through the crowd as *Seven Seas* ran before the strengthening offshore breeze, her massive sails billowing like clouds in what was now an otherwise cloudless sky.

Not twenty yards apart, Susannah and Nathan stood watching the ship, each alone with their thoughts — each thinking ahead to the next stage of their world odyssey.

Neither was aware of the other's presence and neither knew what the future held, but it excited them and filled them with some trepidation at the same time for they were soon to venture into the unknown.

The End

If you liked this book, the authors would greatly appreciate a review from you on Amazon

The adventures of Nathan, Susannah and Jack continue in
Fiji: A Novel (The World Duology, #2).

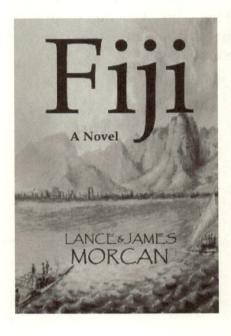

Fiji: A Novel (The World Duology, #2)

As the pharaohs of ancient Egypt build their mighty pyramids, and Chinese civilization evolves under the Shang Dynasty, adventurous seafarers from South East Asia begin to settle the far-flung islands of the South Pacific. The exotic archipelago of Fiji is one of the last island groups to be discovered and will remain hidden from the outside world for many centuries to come.

By the mid-1800's, Fiji has become a melting pot of cannibals, warring native tribes, sailors, traders, prostitutes, escaped convicts and all manner of foreign undesirables. It's in this hostile environment an innocent young Englishwoman and a worldly American adventurer find themselves.

Susannah Drake, a missionary, questions her calling to spread God's Word as she's torn between her spiritual and sexual selves. As her forbidden desires intensify, she turns to the scriptures and prayer to quash the sinful thoughts — without success.

Nathan Johnson arrives to trade muskets to the Fijians and immediately finds himself at odds with Susannah. She despises him for introducing the white man's weapons to the very people she is trying to convert and he pities her for her naivety. Despite their differences, there's an undeniable chemistry between them.

When their lives are suddenly endangered by marauding cannibals, Susannah and Nathan are forced to rely on each other for their very survival.

Fiji is published by Sterling Gate Books and available now for purchase.

Fiji: A Novel (The World Duology, #2)

Fiji is a spellbinding novel of adventure, cultural misunderstandings, religious conflict and sexual tension set in one of the most exotic and isolated places on earth.

★★★★★ "If you're a fan of adventure, history, even romance, you'll want to pick up a copy of Fiji: A Novel and brace yourself for the ride. It's an intense story that will have you turning the pages long into the night."

-Susan M. Heim, author and editor of the bestselling
'Chicken Soup for the Soul' series

★★★★★ "As a Fijian, I find the old traditions of our people fascinating and just as great as they are crude and gruesome. The novel touches on most of these now extinct practices, in mad detail and it's AWESOME! . . . Racial prejudice, religion, culture and family were the underlying messages . . . The adventure, fast-paced and nail biting . . . The romance, sizzling, exciting, forbidden . . . I give it 5 stars because that's the maximum amount of stars we're allowed to give."

-Random Writings Book Reviews (Suva, Fiji)

★★★★ "Reminiscent of the great South Pacific tales of Jack London and James Michener"

-John R. Lindermuth (historical novelist) Rambles Reviews

★★★★★ "A fabulous novel, beautiful for its blunt rawness, exotic scenery, and fascinating storyline"

-Historical Novel Review

Other books by Lance & James Morcan published by Sterling Gate Books . . .

Historical fiction:

White Spirit (A novel based on a true story)

World Odyssey (The World Duology, #1)

Fiji: A Novel (The World Duology, #2)

Thrillers:

The Ninth Orphan (The Orphan Trilogy, #1)

The Orphan Factory (The Orphan Trilogy, #2)

The Orphan Uprising (The Orphan Trilogy, #3)

Non-fiction:

DEBUNKING HOLOCAUST DENIAL THEORIES: Two Non-Jews Affirm the Historicity of the Nazi Genocide

The Orphan Conspiracies: 29 Conspiracy Theories from The Orphan Trilogy

GENIUS INTELLIGENCE: Secret Techniques and Technologies to Increase IQ (The Underground Knowledge Series, #1)

ANTIGRAVITY PROPULSION: Human or Alien Technologies? (The Underground Knowledge Series, #2)

MEDICAL INDUSTRIAL COMPLEX: The $ickness Industry, Big Pharma and Suppressed Cures (The Underground Knowledge Series, #3)

Made in United States
Troutdale, OR
08/02/2025

33366400R00194